D1572178

ALSO BY CE MURPHY

THE GUILDMASTER SAGA
SEAMASTER * STONEMASTER (FORTHCOMING)

THE AUSTEN CHRONICLES
MAGIC & MANNERS * SORCERY & SOCIETY (FORTHCOMING)

THE HEARTSTRIKE CHRONICLES
ATLANTIS FALLEN * PROMETHEUS BOUND (FORTHCOMING)

THE WALKER PAPERS
URBAN SHAMAN * WINTER MOON * THUNDERBIRD FALLS
COYOTE DREAMS * WALKING DEAD * DEMON HUNTS
SPIRIT DANCES * RAVEN CALLS * NO DOMINION
MOUNTAIN ECHOES * SHAMAN RISES

THE OLD RACES UNIVERSE
HEART OF STONE * HOUSE OF CARDS * HANDS OF FLAME
BABA YAGA'S DAUGHTER
YEAR OF MIRACLES

THE WORLDWALKER DUOLOGY
TRUTHSEEKER * WAYFINDER

THE INHERITORS' CYCLE
THE QUEEN'S BASTARD * THE PRETENDER'S CROWN

THE LOVELORN LADS
BEWITCHING BENEDICT

ROSES IN AMBER
TAKE A CHANCE
STONE'S THROE

SEAMASTER

Book One of the Guildmaster Saga

C.E. MURPHY

A Miz Kit Production

MKP

SEAMASTER
ISBN-13: 978-1-61317-142-4

Cover Art: Aleksandar Sotirovski

For Breic

CHAPTER 1

Strong hands grabbed Rasim's ankles and hauled him backward. His shirt rucked up, sticking to tar-soaked wood as he scrabbled for a grip. A splinter jabbed under his fingernail. He shouted and let go, blood welling through dirt and tar as he was yanked out from between the ship's ribs to land on its salt-damp deck.

He barely caught himself with his hands, saving his nose from the same bloody fate his fingernail had met. A big foot, bare and topped with rough toenails, caught him in the side. Rasim grunted and flipped sideways, avoiding the brunt of the kick.

Desimi stood above him, of course. Like Rasim, Desimi would be thirteen tomorrow, but he already had shoulders that promised the size of the man he would be. He had an angry man's scowl, too, burned into his face all the time and darker than ever when he laid eyes on Rasim.

Rasim wheezed, "Desi, wait—", remembering too late that with their birthdays coming up, the bigger boy no longer liked that nickname. It was too small for such a large lad, and recalling that half a moment earlier might have saved Rasim from another kick to the ribs. He coughed and used the ship's wall to push himself up, then scrambled away. "I'm not going to fight you, Desimi!"

"Coward." Desimi jumped after him.

Rasim, smaller and more lithe, caught a low-hanging beam and swung himself out of immediate danger. "Don't be stupid, Desi—*Desimi*—you'll get us both kicked out—"

Desimi grabbed for Rasim's ankle. Rasim scampered away again, slithering over beams and through narrow joists. They'd played keep-away like this as children, learning the ins and outs of the fleet's ships. It had only been recently that their friendship had soured. "Your mother was a Northern hag!" he bellowed after Rasim.

"I'm sure it was my father who was a Northern dog!" Pale Northern merchants had once been common along the Ilialio's banks and in the great city it had spawned, but there had been few indeed since the great fire that had orphaned not just Rasim and Desimi, but hundreds of other children as well. Few indeed, since the king's Northern wife had been unable to command Ilyaran magic and save the city. There was no telling which parent had been responsible for the copper tones to Rasim's skin and hair, or the green scattered through his brown eyes, but if Ilyara could blame Queen Annaken for failing to stop the fire, then Desimi could freely insult Rasim's unknown mother, and too many people would say he had the right of it. Desimi spat another curse as Rasim darted through another tight spot, then crowed triumph as Ras realized he'd wedged himself into a corner. When Desimi's fist flew, Rasim tucked himself down, arms protecting his head, and told himself again why he refused to strike back: "There's no fighting shipboard, lads, or you'll lose everything you've worked for."

A deep voice spoke the very words Rasim thought, making him lift his head in confusion. Desimi was hauled backward as unceremoniously as he'd yanked Rasim moments before, his final blow swinging wide. He kicked, twisted, saw who held him, and whined like a frightened puppy as Hassin dropped him to the deck.

Hassin, second mate on this ship, was ten years Rasim and Desimi's elder and much-admired by his younger crewmates. He was tall for a sailor, his shoulders unbowed by bending and twisting through narrow ship passages. Like all the older crew, he wore his long black hair in a tight-bound queue at his nape. Rasim curled his fingers at the base of his own neck, feeling the short-cropped hair there. Not until he became an official member of a crew could he begin to grow the long tail they wore.

And that would never happen if he was caught fighting with Desimi. Or anyone else, for that matter, but Desi seemed determined to fight whether Rasim would or not.

Even now the bigger boy got to his feet, defiant as he glared up at Hassin. "I've been stuck with this, just like we all have. We didn't work for having lost our parents, and that," he said with a thrust of his finger back toward Rasim, "is the fault of people like him!"

Hassin's long face grew longer. "The tide's washed that sand smooth, Desimi. The Ilialio saved you from the fire and brought you to the Seamasters' guild. You're barely a day from becoming crew, and you *have* worked for that, whether you'd have chosen this life or not. Don't destroy it now. Rasim," he said in nearly the same tone.

Rasim startled guiltily and pushed his knuckles against his mouth. Insisting he hadn't *been* fighting would do him no good. There would be a chance to explain, if he didn't blunder by trying to make Desimi look worse and himself look innocent.

"The captain wants to see you." Hassin looked Rasim over and sighed. "Immediately, but if you turn up in his cabin covered in tar and stick to any of his papers, he'll take them out of my own skin. Hot water, as hot as you can stand, to get that muck off you, and then to the captain's cabin as quick as you can."

"Yes, Hassin." Rasim slid from his perch and hit the

boards below with a thud that matched the nervous thump of his heart. The day before new crew members were selected was not a time anybody wanted to be called before the captain. He ran from below decks, trying to think of any recent guild transgressions he'd committed. Up the steep-pitched stairs to the upper deck, not touching the smooth banisters with his sticky hands. Across the deck with his feet smacking hollowly on good solid teak, then distance-eating strides over the ridged walkway that held ship to shore across a depth of dark blue harbor water.

Ilyara was at its best at the waterfront, where the sea was so clear that anchor chains could be seen to thirty feet. The scent of fish was heavy in the air, but no offal from the fishmongers stained the yellow stone sea walls.

That was the work of water witches. Rasim had heard that other port cities lacked enough sea witches to keep the harbor waters and sea walls clear. In Ilyara the job was done by those whose water weaving skills weren't strong enough to do shipboard duties.

Barely a day from becoming crew, Hassin had said to Desimi. Everyone knew it was true: Desimi, bully or not, could already command the brute force of waves. He would become a cabin boy tomorrow, and, in time, a captain able to steer his ship through the most dangerous waters and the worst storms.

Rasim's place was less certain. His witchery skills

were modest at best, though he loved the feeling of salt water coming to life under his fingertips, responding to the cool magic in his mind.

Not that any of it would matter if he didn't get clean and get back to the captain as quick as he could. The bathing rooms were staffed by sea and sun witches, their magic working together to turn water to steam. It softened the tar on Rasim's skin, and he scrubbed it off with rough cloth before daring to jump in a bath to rinse the last scraps away. Masira, a good-natured witch whose preference, rather than lack of skill, had settled her on land instead of a ship, grumbled at him for leaving flecks of black goo in the water. He offered his most winning smile and she laughed, scooping the tar remnants from the water with her magic while he dried and scrambled into the soft-woven linen pants and loose shirt that were his guild's usual ship-board garb.

The sun hadn't traveled a hand-span in the sky by the time he skidded back on deck. No longer sticky, he slid down the steep banisters to below-decks. A whisper of wisdom caught him, and he took a moment to rake his hands through wet hair and catch his breath before knocking politely on the captain's door.

"Aye," said the man within, and Rasim pushed it open a few inches.

"You wanted to see me, sir?"

"Aye." Captain Asindo leaned over a table

covered in maps, his broad hands holding curled corners flat. He was short, barely taller than Rasim himself, but he had to turn sideways to fit his wide shoulders through the narrow shipboard doors. A lack of height didn't mean a lack of presence, which gave Rasim some comfort. Maybe he would grow up that way, too. The captain lifted a fingertip from his maps, invitation to enter his quarters. "You were fighting Desimi again," Asindo said neutrally as the door shut.

Offense rose in Rasim's chest as he let the door close behind him. "No, sir."

Asindo's eyebrows twitched upward and a small gesture invited Rasim to speak. The captain rarely spoke when a motion would do, which made his crew watch him carefully. It made them watch *themselves* carefully, too: they were a quieter and better-behaved crew than many with more blusterous commanders. Rasim would remember that, if he ever became a captain himself.

Which he would never do if he couldn't explain the fighting. "Desimi was fighting me, sir. I was running away." He winced as he said it. Running away sounded cowardly, even if it had been smart.

To his surprise, Asindo chuckled. "So Hassin said. You'll have a reckoning with Desimi someday, Rasim, but you're wise to not let it be now. He's a lot of trouble to have on board. I'm thinking of recommending against him tomorrow, prodigious wave witchery or no."

"Don't!"

Asindo straightened from his maps and turned slowly to Rasim, incredulity straining his thick features. He looked like a man who had been in — and won — a lot of fights, and he looked like they'd all started when someone gave him an impulsive command like the one Rasim had just blurted out.

Rasim still said, "Don't," again, a little desperately. "Desi's angry at me because he doesn't have anybody else to be angry at. I've got Northern blood and everybody knows it was the Northern queen who couldn't stop the fires when they swept the city, so I'm easy to blame. He says he doesn't care about making cabin boy, but it's not true, Captain. It's the only thing he's got, just like all of us. If you turn him away he'll only be angrier, and in the end it'll make him—"

Rasim ran out of words suddenly, miserable with uncertainty. He had seen men drunk along the docks, bitter and sharp with regrets. It wasn't hard to imagine Desimi, already angry, joining those men, though it was harder to really understand the path that would lead him there. Rasim faltered in trying to explain, instead seizing on what he was certain of. "Desimi could be a good captain someday, sir. He could keep his crew and ship safe in the storms. If you take that away from him now, even for a year, it'll only make him angrier, and he'll blame me. I'm not big but I can take care of myself." His mouth twisted wryly. "At least, I can if you don't make Desi so angry he comes after me with a boat hook."

"Hnf." Asindo sounded amused. "Kind words for an enemy."

Rasim shrugged uncomfortably. "We used to be friends."

"I'll think about it, but it's not why I called you here. I—"

"Captain." The door burst open and Hassin, grim-faced, ducked in. "Captain, the fools have done it. They've lit the memorial fires early, without supervision, and they've gone too high. The city is burning."

CHAPTER 2

Asindo recoiled, a physical response that matched the cold terror knotting Rasim's stomach. But the captain rebounded, shoving past Rasim and Hassin so swiftly he was out the door before it had even finished closing behind Hassin. The second mate followed on Asindo's heels, and Rasim, uninvited, chased after Hassin. He had been so young when the last blaze ravaged Ilyara that he had no memory or fear of fire. But like everyone else, he had grown up in the flame-scarred city, seen the black stains so deep in golden stone that it had taken years of work to cleanse them. Some of those stains had been left deliberately, a reminder of the city's recent devastating past, and a warning to those who would play with fire. Not enough warning, it seemed.

Asindo stopped on the deck like a landslide crashing into a wall. Hassin, for once looking young and gangly, managed not to slam into the captain, though he pinwheeled his arms to avoid it. Rasim, smaller and more accustomed to keeping out of the way, darted to one side and climbed the first few yards of the ship's mast to better see the burning city.

Greasy dark smoke reached for the sky above the city center, grey coils grasping toward thin distant white clouds. Ilyara was built of stone, but enough wood and straw littered it to burn a fierce heat. It could be only minutes before the whole sky began to blacken with the oily smoke. "Surely," Rasim breathed. Surely there were master sun witches to watch over the firestarters; surely they could bring the flames back under control. But the memorial fires were usually lit at sunset, not mid-afternoon, and if they grew too fast, not even the Sunmasters' Guild could bring them back under control. They'd believed they could end *any* fire, thirteen years earlier, and Ilyara still bore the scars of that confidence.

It had not—quite—been their fault, thirteen years ago. A bakery oven had overheated, and the flour stores in the silo next door had exploded when the fire reached them. Burning dust had touched down everywhere, lighting straw and cloth and more grain stores, until Ilyara rocked with explosions and roared with flame. The guilds had scrambled, trying to decide how to react: their monarch was meant to be the focal point for all major witchery in Ilyara, but King Laishn had been visiting the Horse Clans far to the west and north. None of the guildmasters had either the authority or the imagination to focus the entire power of a guild through themselves. By the time they thought to try, the city was in ruins.

And since then, since Queen Annaken and her infant son had died in the fire, since King Laishn had died of grief...since then, Ilyara's political structure had been in upheaval. Taishm, the new king, had been crowned, but few people believed he had the strength to guide a guild's magic, and there were always rumors of pretenders and contenders for the crown.

People were running. Running without purpose, to Rasim's wide-eyed gaze. Some ran toward the fire, others away; some simply ran along the docks, leaping in a panic from one ship's gangway to another. Children followed some of those runners, often failing to make the long jump between one gangway and the next. Their splashes punctuated cries of alarm from adults, and begot more as parents tried to catch them.

"Bonfires," Asindo growled below their squeals of worry and delight. "What fools commemorate a fire with more fires? Come on," he urged sun witches whom he could not see and who could certainly not hear him. "Come on. Stop this before we all go up in flames again."

"They can't." Rasim barely heard himself say the words. He knew, as Asindo did, that the memorial fires weren't sanctioned, because what fool *would* commemorate fire with fire? But for thirteen years, illegal bonfires had been built within the city walls on the Great Fire's anniversary. Piles of wood appeared almost without warning as stealthy youths scurried to and fro with just one or two small pieces of wood. They added up quickly, and then someone —a sun witch if they were patient and waited until near, or after, sunset—lit one, then another, until the names of the fallen were carried on twists of wood high into the sky. It was beautiful, heartfelt, and all too potentially deadly.

Ilyara's guards tried, year in and year out, to stop them, but the ringleaders changed, new bonfire-builders inspired by years past. "Captain Asindo," Rasim said more loudly, "they *can't* put them out. We have to do it."

The captain snapped, "Shut up, boy," then glanced at him again with a scowl. "What do you mean? We're water witches, not—"

"And they're not sun witches!" Rasim scrambled a few feet higher on the mast, thrusting a finger toward the fire. "They're just *people*, Captain. The Sunmasters' guild wouldn't be there to set the fires until sunset! You *know* that's what they've agreed to, so these are just—they're just *people*. Even if they have sun witches with them, they'll be young! Young enough to be excited about doing this without being smart, and you've seen the kindling they set, the fires are huge, most young sun witches can only handle a kitchen fire, not something big—" He gave up trying to explain and bellowed, "Desimi!" instead.

Like everyone else, Desimi was on deck already, watching the fire from only a handful of paces away from Rasim's perch, though Ras hadn't seen him. He jolted forward, then glared at Rasim. "What?"

"Make a wave," Ras said desperately. "Bring the water up, Desi."

"From the *calm?*"

"You can do it." Rasim slid from the mast, all but catching Desimi by the shoulders. "I've seen you make walls of water in the baths, Desi. This is just more."

"It's a harbor! I'll beach the ships!"

Triumph splashed through Rasim. Desimi hadn't said he couldn't do it. "Bring it up between the ships and the sea wall. Captain Asindo, we need—we need —" He let Desimi go and spun helplessly. "Sky witches. We need to push the water all the way to the fires, Captain. We need the wind."

Understanding finally filled Asindo's expression before it turned to a fierce grin. "No, lad, we only need the wave. The city's better wet than burned. Desimi!"

The other boy was already at the ship's rail, looking down into clear water. The ship rocked under Rasim's feet, a more dramatic shift than usual in the calm harbor, and water surged against the sea wall. Asindo said, "Desimi," again, more softly, but the boy lifted an imperious hand, silencing the captain.

Asindo huffed, more amused than Rasim feared he might be, and silently gestured to Hassin and the other senior crew members. Together they joined Desimi at the rail.

The air thickened, became weightier, a tell-tale sign

of witchery at work. Desimi's wall-slapping wave grew taller, shaped and shielded by sparks of magic. *His* magic, Rasim thought: there was something in the wildness of the water's shape that said the boy, not yet even a journeyman, had been given control of this attempt, though Captain Asindo could easily have taken it over himself. But even the captain was following Desimi's lead, adding his own magic to the lifting of water but not wresting control from Rasim's age-mate.

A second surge rocked the ship more strongly as the combined power of the sea witches gathered water. With the third, the harbor itself dropped, enough water lifted upward to change its level. Desimi cast a panicked glance at Asindo, who put a hand on the boy's shoulder.

"You've called it up," he said. "Let me guide it into the city, lad. Just keep it coming."

Strained relief shot across Desimi's face. He clutched the rail harder, sweat beading on his forehead as he worked to call more seawater to his bidding. A sting of envy buried itself beneath the hope in Rasim's heart: he could desalinate water, a necessary talent shipboard, but that was a basic skill, not a promise of great power like Desimi showed.

But then, almost no one as young as they were had so much raw talent. What really mattered was that Desi had listened to Rasim. What mattered was that he and the others *had* the power even if Rasim didn't, and that the ships were dropping precipitously as the water wall rose.

Asindo splashed his hands, palms facing each other, fingers flaring toward the fiery city center. The massive water wall rolled forward, turning pale sea walls gold as it soaked them. A cry went up from nearby ships. Moments later a second water wall rose and rolled after the first, and then a third, as other captains and their crews followed Asindo's lead.

Under their magic's strength, water cascaded down the streets, using them like a person might instead of crashing through houses and businesses like an ordinary tidal wave. Passers-by not yet aware of the fire shrieked in astonishment as water rushed them. Captain Asindo grunted, then swore, but the wave he commanded bent upward, leaving a tall man's height between its bottom and the street.

Rasim's jaw dropped as water *flew* through Ilyara's streets. It looked alive, rolling and reshaping as it hurried forward. Its clarity magnified and shrank building corners. Fish and kelp fell to ground, splattering people and delighting dogs that ran for the unexpected bounty with glee. Enterprising children followed the dogs, snatching fish and edible seaweed from the streets.

Another captain gave a distant groan of laughter, but met Asindo's challenge: the following waves took to the air too, supported only by the will of sailors. The magic was like light on the water: bright sparks that blinded and caught different shades, green and purple and blue. The air around Rasim shivered with the weight of concentration shared by Asindo's crew. He climbed the mast again, shocked at how high the heavy air reached. It felt like the center of a storm, full of potential danger. From above, Rasim could almost see the shimmer of magic in the air, pressing up from the whole of the harbor. Because every sailor on the water was now engaged in the fire-fighting effort now, every one of them who had the power to shift the sea at all.

From his vantage on the mast, Rasim saw the first wave, Desimi and Asindo's wave, roll into Ilyara's center and crash down on a raging bonfire. Steam exploded so loudly he heard it from the distance. The oily black smoke fell apart, disrupted by billowing steam. Rasim couldn't see the aftermath, but he imagined sticks and boards scattered across the street, their hot edges blackened and hissing under the onslaught of water. Somewhere there might be a shocked and soaking children looking at the remains of their fire and — hopefully — understanding that they had been saved from being the destruction of their city.

Elsewhere other fires were crushed by falling sea water as well, until all the threatening smoke had turned to wavering steam and lingering tendrils against the deep blue sky. Desimi moved, catching Rasim's eye. He looked down to see the other boy drop to his knees in exhaustion, still hanging onto the ship's rail. Asindo put a hand on Desimi's shoulder again, silent with pride.

Then the captain turned to examine Rasim where he sat, high in the crow's nest. Rasim knotted his hands around the railing there, heart fast and sick in his chest for no reason he understood. He felt as if he was being judged somehow, weighed in the balance, and he dared not, could not, move. For a long moment they met each other's eyes, captain and apprentice. Finally Asindo nodded, just once, but it released Rasim from paralyzation. He dropped to his knees just like Desimi had done, pressing his forehead against the crow's nest railing.

Below him, visible through the nest's floor slats, sailors cheered and slapped each other on the back, shook hands and grinned, and gesticulated toward the city. Their voices carried to Rasim: they told each other what they had done, as if they hadn't all been part of it. Desimi was pulled to his feet, then lifted to shoulders, congratulations ringing in the air. Another pang of envy twisted Rasim's heart, though he smiled a little, too.

Tomorrow, Desimi would become a cabin boy on Asindo's ship for certain. Rasim, who had done nothing in the fight against the fire, was less certain of his own fate. But the flames had been drowned, the city was safe, and tomorrow was another day.

Tonight, though, there would be a *party*.

CHAPTER 3

The sun had long since set, leaving hard bright stars in a cold clear sky. That hadn't stopped Rasim — or half the Seamasters' Guild — from staggering through the streets to the city center. Well, others staggered: Rasim nursed a cup of watered wine, knowing from experience that he had no head for alcohol. Desimi had been less cautious. Instead of joining the sea witches who spilled into Ilyara to tell the tale of saving it, Desimi already lay snoring in a corner of the bath houses. Rasim smiled at the image, and half-heartedly wished a sore head on the bigger boy, come morning.

A surprising number of people touched fingertips to foreheads, a sign of respect, as the sea witches passed. Others, still sweeping water from their homes, muttered, but with little heat. Thirteen years earlier no one had thought to use sea witches against fire, and many people still remembered the destruction clearly enough to not begrudge a few inches of salt water across the floors.

Most of the bonfire wood had already been cleared away from the corners and squares. Rasim had seen children and adults alike carrying scraps of blackened kindling or nailing a length of burned plank above their doors. Warding off future disaster, perhaps, but also reminding others how quickly everything could be lost. Rasim broke away to find the crossroads where Desimi and Asindo's wave had been dropped.

It was familiar to him, only a handful of paces away from a bakery that accepted that guild apprentices would always try to barter, and sold day-old treats at a bargain, so long as everyone behaved. Every apprentice in the city knew the bakery, and a schedule had long-since been established. The Seamasters had the second morning after rest day, and on the fifth and sixth mornings it was a matter of who arrived first. Desimi had been known not to go to bed until he'd gotten a share of fifth-morning's baked goods, but Rasim had been more subtle.

The bakery door opened and a girl about Rasim's own age stepped out. She was taller than he and wore her dark hair long, sure sign she belonged to a trade and not a guild. Her clothes were finer, too: green woven pants and a belted shirt, though both were mostly hidden under the baker's apron she wore. Like many people that day, she had soot streaked across her face, a smear pushed into her hairline, as if she'd rubbed it up with her forearm while working.

There was almost no heat coming from the bakery, though. The ovens had been left to bank low after the day's excitement, and if no one built them higher, there would be no fresh bread in the morning.

Now, though, there were cold pasties and that morning's bread, unrolled from a towel beneath Keesha's arm. She sat down at the street side, pressing her spine against the stone walls, and silently offered Rasim a chunk of bread. He accepted it and sat down as well, then put his cup of watered wine between them so the mealy bread could be dipped in it. They ate silently, looking at the soot-scarred mark at the street corner. Most of the bread was gone before Keesha whispered, "It wasn't an accident, Ras."

The bread turned to a stone in Rasim's stomach. "Of course it was. How could it not be? How do you know?"

"I was right here. I got up early, half an hour before the bread went in to the ovens, because I wanted to watch them build the bonfires. They built them here when I was seven and ten, so I thought there might be one on this corner again."

Rasim blinked from her to the sooty street. "Were they there when you were four? Didn't anybody else notice they'd been here every three years?"

"Nobody listens," Keesha repeated. "I don't remember, when I was four. But I saw the heart of the fire when I got up. I thought it was just a big ball of pitch so it would burn well. It got covered fast, all the students coming by as quick as they could with a bit of wood to put on."

Both of them glanced toward the Ilyaran university, high on a hill but still blocked from their street-level view. Most of the memorialists were students, some of whom really did want to raise a flame in memory and in warning. More seemed to be interested in the pyrotechnics, and the ever-changing student body made it more difficult for the guards to lay hands on the troublemakers.

"The strange thing was when they came to light the fire," Keesha whispered. "They didn't reach into its heart to the pitch ball. They just lit the kindling around the edges and bottom. It caught, but just like an ordinary fire. It didn't go out of control. We were watching," she added with a note of severity. "We keep water for the ovens, in case one catches on fire."

"I know." Rasim helped haul buckets to the bakery several mornings a week. His small magic was good for that: he could keep water from slopping over a bucket's sides, making sure none was lost in the long walk — or mule ride — up to the bakery.

Keesha gave him an amused look. She knew as well as he that he'd started helping at the bakery because it had been a more cunning way to get extra bits of bread and pastries, but that had been a long time ago. He helped now because Keesha was his friend, and because it was interesting to do something different from his regular apprentice duties. It wasn't any harder than staying up all night like Desimi did, *and* it left Rasim awake enough to do his own work afterward.

"So I was watching," Keesha repeated. "Somebody in the family always watches when the bonfires are near us. But it didn't just go out of control, Ras. It was an ordinary fire, and then it exploded."

"Fire doesn't explode."

"I *know*." Keesha got to her feet and stepped into the street, pointing upward. Rasim twisted, trying to see, then got up to see what she wanted to show him.

Divots and scores streaked the building walls above them, as if flame had been lodged in holes and left to burn there, but there were no holes. Rasim squinted, then backed up further, trying to see the dark patches more clearly. They would be easier to see in daylight, but even under the moon's dimmer glow, they were obviously nothing normal fire would do. It didn't stick that way.

"I think it was the pitch ball." Keesha sounded defensive, as if afraid Rasim would doubt her, but he only nodded as she went on. "When it got hot enough it exploded. Baked tubers do that if you don't prick holes in them. And it happened all over the city, Ras. The fires were all set to…erupt."

"Who would do that? Why? *How?*"

"I don't know, but I've been to two of the other bon-fire sites and they both have the marks on the walls around them, like something exploded up. Look at how the streaks hit the walls, you can tell they came from below. They're wider where they hit, like they went splat! And then they thin out a bit."

"Have you told the guards?"

"My parents won't even listen," Keesha muttered. "They don't want to believe me. The Great Fire was an accident," she stressed, and for a moment Rasim could see her parents' fears in her face. "Wasn't it, Ras? It had to have been."

"Someone would know," Rasim said, more certainly than he felt. "Someone would have said if it was on purpose. But you're right, Keesh. This looks like someone meant to do it. If the Seamasters' Guild hadn't been able to put the fires out—"

"That was amazing," Keesha interrupted. "Ras, you should have seen it, the water rolling over our heads and falling like, like a, a, well, like *buckets!* It wasn't like rain at all, just sploosh! Some of the fire didn't want to go out." She frowned upward again. "Most of it went out like it does when water's thrown on it, but the sticky stuff on the walls, it didn't want to. It only sputtered out when the sand in the water stuck to it."

"There wasn't that much sand, was there?"

"More than I thought. I couldn't see it in the

water, but it was everywhere when the fires were out. I spent more time sweeping sand this afternoon than fixing water damage."

"Huh." Even at the sea wall, the harbor dropped deep enough to reach the ocean's sandy bottom rather than the shoals and rocks that shallows often boasted, but Rasim hadn't realized how much sand floated loose in the water. But then, Desimi had pulled deep when he'd lifted the wave. Maybe he'd brought sand with it. Lucky, if the fire was some magical kind that didn't extinguish with water.

A chill shook Rasim's shoulders. "Magic fire. That can't be an accident, you're right, Keesha. Someone — someone has to know. We have to tell *someone.*"

"Who? We're a Guild orphan and a baker's daughter. The guard will never listen to us. My *parents* won't even listen to me."

"Captain Asindo." Rasim seized Keesha's hand. "The captain will at least listen. But you have to come with me."

Keesha's eyes widened and she pulled back. "Traders aren't supposed to hassle the guilds!"

"You're with me, and it's not hassling." Rasim flashed a grin. "Besides, if you bring some of the pastries and fruit breads along..."

Keesha laughed and squirmed free of Rasim's grip. "My father will kill me. Hold on, I'll be right back." She ran into the bakery, making certain the door didn't close heavily, and came out again a few minutes later with a sack of baked goods. Rasim snaked a hand toward the bag, but Keesha smacked it. Rasim snatched it back, trying to look injured. Keesha said, "Hah. You've eaten your fill already."

Rasim wasn't sure that was possible, but he caught Keesha's hand and tugged her a few steps toward the docks, then broke into a run. There were revelers still on the streets, coming and going from the pubs and regaling each other with stories of the Fire That Wasn't. It would be as well-known as the Great Fire, at least for a while, and the whole of the Seamasters' Guild would enjoy a brief period of bargains and opportunities in trade and barter. Keesha slowed down more than once, trying to hear the story of what had happened at the harbor more clearly, but Rasim urged her on.

They arrived at the guild hall breathless and hot from their run. A guard at the vast, closed gates eyed their disheveled states, but recognized Rasim and waved them through the small door within the gates that most traffic used.

The common area was enormous, a massive stretch of hard-packed earth where ships were built in miniature to learn the principle, where merchants came to commission their ships, and where all the daily work of the guild was done. Beyond them stood the entrance to the guild halls themselves. Keesha dragged her feet until Rasim stopped so she could gape at the buildings rising before them.

Unlike almost every other building in the city, the Seamasters' Guild halls were wood. They had burned to the ground in the Great Fire, and the sea witches had rebuilt them of the same ancient heartwood that had graced the original halls. Everyone thought they were mad, but ship building and wood were all the Seamasters' Guild knew. Stone masonry was for the Stonemasters' Guild, and they had more than enough to do in restoring the city. The Seamasters' Halls had always been, and always would be, crafted by sea witches. The wooden halls were rebuilt.

They were reminiscent of a ship's hull, curving upward to tall prow-like points. Six halls radiated off the common area: apprentices and journeymen to the left, shipwrights and shore crew in the middle, captains and guildmasters to the right. Outsiders thought the arching halls were a waste, pointing out the seemingly dead space of each downward-pointing triangle between the tall arches, but outsiders rarely saw them from the other side. Ship-sized sleeping cubbies fit into those spaces, freeing what would otherwise be dorm rooms for more useful ends.

The vast kitchens to feed hungry crews and shipwrights lay beneath the guild's main halls. That meant sweltering summers, but in winter's cold grip, the rising heat from the kitchens was welcome throughout the hall.

Keesha whispered, "You *live* here?"

Rasim, amused, took a breath to say, "Sure," then thought of Keesha's own modest, warm three-room home above their bakery. She and her family were able to use two of their rooms for sleeping and the third as a common area, because the bakery served as their kitchen as well. Most families shared a single sleeping room, or their common room doubled as a sleeping room. By comparison, the guild halls were almost inconceivably expansive. Rasim, instead of laughing at Keesha, smiled at himself. "Yeah, but there are hundreds of us. It's not any more room to yourself than you've got."

"I'm not sure about that," Keesha said dryly, but anything else she might say was drowned beneath the sharp voice of a guildmaster:

"You, you're Rasim al Ilialio, right?"

Rasim spun. Keesha's hand wormed into his, and he wasn't sure if it was to reassure herself or him. Guildmaster Isidri, not just a guildmaster but *the* Guildmaster. The one whose storm summoning was legendary even amongst the captains and commanders. The one who apprentices whispered was over a hundred years old. She had never even looked at Rasim before, never mind given a hint she knew his name. He squeezed Keesha's hand and tried to stand up straight under the weight of Isidri's glower.

She *looked* a hundred years old. She looked *three* hundred years old, with wrinkles gobbling her eyes and her mouth a thin horizontal line through many smaller vertical ones. Her hair, like every sea witch's, was tied tight in a queue, but hers was pure white and as thick as Rasim's wrist. A band of blue was woven through it, the Guildmaster's color, and it swung impatiently as she snapped, "Where have you been, boy? Get in there. You *are* the one, aren't you? And who's this? Never mind, she can go in too, just step along, both of you. All this trouble," the Guildmaster grumbled, "all this trouble over a boy. It's past the midnight hour, boy, it's Decision Day. Your entire fate rests on the next few minutes, and you're late!"

CHAPTER 4

"But—it—what?" Rasim stumbled over his questions as much as he stumbled over his feet. Keesha kept him going in the right direction, Guildmaster Isidri's braid flicking them toward the Guildmasters' Hall. Rasim had only ever been through even the Captains' Hall arch once or twice, and had never dared the Guildmasters' Hall. He wasn't certain an apprentice could even cross the entrance way without bursting into fire or something equally horrible. They challenged each other to try sometimes, but no one was ever quite brave enough.

And this was *not* how things were done. Decision Day was a festival, a ritual. All the apprentices coming into their thirteenth year and all the journeymen coming into their eighteenth were to scrub clean, dress as well as their rank permitted, and present themselves to the masters, captains and guildmasters at the tenth bell. Their advancement to the next rank, and the masters under whom they would study, would be announced to each hopeful. The remainder of the day was spent moving from one hall to another and feasting.

Their placements were almost never a surprise. Even Rasim, who wanted desperately to be a cabin boy and sail on Asindo's ship, knew the chances were much better that he would become shore crew or a shipwright. His witchery was well-controlled but not strong, and the most adept magics were needed at sea. But even so, there was ritual to how it was done, and being shooed into the Guildmasters' Hall at a bell past midnight was not it.

He only knew of ritual being changed once, and that had been after the fire. Before then, Decision Day was held on the first of the new year. But the guilds were built from Ilyara's orphans, and after the fire there had been hundreds. Rasim had been snatched from the Ilialio itself. He and others like him, saved by the river, were clearly meant for the Seamasters. Others found buried alive beneath fallen buildings went to the Stonemasters, and those thrust into the Sunmasters' temples had become Sunmaster apprentices. The children found wandering outside the city had been taken in by the Skymasters' Guild, and all four guilds had nearly burst from the influx of orphans.

So a second Decision Day had been added. On the anniversary of the fire, apprentices and journeymen were now also promoted, because for more than a decade there had been too many to teach at once.

Rasim and Desimi were among the last of the

Ilialio's gift to the Seamasters' Guild. They had been babes in arms, lucky to float instead of drown on the day of the fire. After today, there would be no more Decision Days held on the anniversary.

Perhaps that was the reason for this change. Perhaps they were all being awakened and informed of their fate before morning. Perhaps that had *always* happened, unbeknownst to the apprentices not yet old enough to be elevated. Rasim clung to the idea as tightly as Keesha clung to his hand. Together they were ushered into a warm bright hall filled with men and women who looked not at all as if it was the middle of the night.

Rasim knew them, of course. All of them by face and name, and most to speak to. His gaze still sought Captain Asindo, whose ship he knew best, and upon whom his fate most likely rested. He was there, one of many but also one of a few: he sat at the head of a large table, as did two or three others at different tables. These were senior captains, commanders in fact if not in name. Captain Lansik—the one who had laughingly cursed Asindo that afternoon when Asindo had lifted the water wall into the air— Captain Lansik sat at the head of another table, and Captains Elissi, Midrisa and Narisa headed the others. They were all pleasantly engaged with their tables, chatting and arguing while pushing maps and cups of wine around. Their air was both jovial and business-like. Rasim, barely a step past their threshold, wondered if all captains' business was conducted with such good cheer.

Isidri pushed Rasim and Keesha forward and stepped into the hall behind them. She neither said nor did anything Rasim could see, but the hall fell quiet within seconds of her arrival. It wasn't only the apprentices who were awed by the Guildmaster. Quickly enough to seem choreographed, dozens of captains and guildmasters turned toward the door, and saw Rasim and Keesha.

Captain Asindo stood, his eyebrows quirking at Rasim's companion, but he addressed the Guildmaster behind them: "Guildmaster Isidri. I see you've found our wayward apprentice, and another besides. An unusual task for someone of your rank."

"I like to keep on my toes," Isidri said dryly. She pushed between Rasim and Keesha, striding past tables and scattered chairs to take a seat at the top of the hall. "Are we all here, then? Finally?"

"We are, Guildmaster." Asindo began to sit again, but Isidri stopped him with a wave of her hand.

"He's your crewman, Asindo. You do the talking."

Rasim's heart lurched in his chest so hard he hiccuped. Isidri wouldn't use the word *crewman* lightly. Keesha edged toward him, and this time he was certain she was offering support, rather than seeking it. He gave her a watery smile and tried to focus on Asindo.

The stout captain was looking at Keesha again. "If

you don't mind, Guildmaster..."

Isidri waved her hand again. "I'm too old for niceties, Asindo. Get on with it."

Everyone in the room chuckled except Rasim and Keesha, and their nerves made those closest to them grin even more broadly. Asindo, evidently more at home with words in the captains' hall than on board a ship, said, "I'm not sure I recall an apprentice ever crossing into this hall with a trader before. Who are you, young woman?"

"Keesha al Balian. My family owns the Crossroads Bakery."

"Ah." Asindo's face lit with recognition. "Your grandfather used to give us pastries when we were your age. I'm glad to see the fire didn't damage your family business. What are you doing here?"

"I saw something and Rasim said you would listen." Keesha eyed the other gathered captains, and muttered, "He didn't say anything about whether *they* would," loudly enough to hear. Then she kicked Rasim's ankle, making him stand at attention, and Asindo looked at him curiously.

"Keesha noticed it, not me," he started, but she kicked him again. Rasim scowled, then turned his attention back to Asindo, leaning forward a little to emphasize what he said. "The bonfires today, the way they went out of control, that wasn't an accident, Captain. Keesha saw it, and she's right. We have to listen to her." Hands clenched with intensity, he explained the peculiar scars on the walls and the magic-born fire that hadn't been extinguished by water. "Captain, she's *right*. You have to listen. You have to believe her. Someone did this on purpose. And if this was on purpose, the Great Fire might have been too." He bit his lip until it tasted red, and stared at Asindo, willing the captain to believe him.

"Rasim." Keesha put her hand on his wrist and drew his attention from Asindo, who looked serious, to the rest of the captains and guildmasters.

They were more than serious. Their mouths were held tight, expressions guarded as they glanced between themselves grimly. Unspoken concern weighed the air as heavily as magic.

Rasim's stomach dropped and his hands went clammy as he realized his and Keesha's fears were not a surprise to the guildmasters. Not just their certainty about the bonfires that day, but their suspicions about the Great Fire too. Rasim looked back at Asindo, whose gaze was locked on Guildmaster Isidri. Asindo said, "You see?" into the silence.

Isidri looked to Rasim before nodding once, deeply and slowly. As if the exchange had released the rest of them, chatter started up amongst the other captains again, lower and more worriedly than before. A few glanced at Rasim and Keesha, but their news, not their presence, was what held the guildmasters.

"Apprentice Rasim," Asindo said, cutting off the murmurs as they rose toward shouts. Surprise filtered through the guildmasters' faces, but they remembered themselves and gave Asindo their attention.

The blocky captain's face was distressingly gentle. Bad news swam with that kind of expression. Rasim sucked in his gut, waiting for the blow. "Apprentice Rasim," Asindo said again, "your witchery is of no particular regard. A decade ago, before the fire, your talent for desalinization might have been enough to win you a place on a ship, but with so many *al Ilialios,*" children of the river, or of the goddess, "with so many of us after the fire, you have no magical skill that many others can't best."

Rasim's shoulders caved, his stomach not hardened enough against the blow after all. He had known. Had suspected, at least, but hearing the words carved out an empty place in his belly. Bile filled it, making him sick, and blood rushed his ears more loudly than the tide. He barely heard Asindo continue.

"I've discussed this with Guildmaster Isidri at some length, Rasim. There is no disagreement. You should graduate to the shipwrights or the shore crew. However."

The word came as a bell across the water, a beacon through fog. Rasim lifted his gaze, blurred with tears he wouldn't let fall, to stare at Asindo and wait on hearing his own fate.

"You did something extraordinary this afternoon," Asindo said softly. "We're hidebound, Rasim, though I hadn't thought it until you broke through the bindings and made us all see something differently. Controlling fire is a sun witch's job, not a sea witch's. We didn't think to command the sea against the Great Fire. Perhaps if we had we couldn't have done it. We were too accustomed then to our greatest magics being shaped by the royal family, and without their guidance we might not have been able to lift the wave against the flame. We've grown more independent since then, but not more clever. You, with your unremarkable water weaving, were the only one to see how our stronger magics could be used to save the city.

"And then you brought this young woman, a trader, into the heart of our guild, because she saw something you believed in. Something that took cleverness to see, bravery to believe, and boldness to tell a hidebound group of old men and women — "

A choking laugh ran through the captains then, objection at being called old, though to Rasim's twelve-year-old eyes, they ranged from merely old to positively ancient. Asindo smiled, but didn't let their humor silence him. " — and we may need that kind of wit and willingness in the coming days. You'll sail with me, Rasim, and we'll sail on the morning tide."

The strength left Rasim's knees so suddenly he dipped, and only kept his feet because of Keesha's strong hand at his elbow. His heart pounded so hard the sick feeling rose in his stomach again, but this time it was fueled by joy instead of despair. His voice cracked, first promise of its change, as he gasped, "Really, sir? I'm to sail with you? *Today?*"

"A third of the fleet sails at dawn," Asindo said. "The other apprentices have already been informed of their positions. We couldn't find you," he said with mock severity, "but now I see why. Desimi will be on my ship too. I trust that will not be a problem."

"No! No, sir. Of course not." And if it was, Rasim thought rashly, he would find a way to pummel sense into Desimi without getting them both thrown to the sharks. Then the rest of Asindo's words caught up to him and he gaped at the captain. "Everyone's been told? But the festival—and by dawn? Why?"

"Because you and this girl are right. These fires, and perhaps the Great Fire, were deliberate, and if someone is seeking to attack Ilyara, she will need her fleet. The Seamasters' Guild is vulnerable, Rasim, more vulnerable than the other guilds. Our ships are wooden. A wiser enemy would have burned them rather than attack the city, but we've been given a chance. We cannot all go—the harbor needs protection, and the city needs fish for food—but if the steadiest of us slip away now, we'll have time to gather ourselves in safety and hunt our enemy down. But we must go now."

Rasim jolted forward one step. "I'm ready. What are my orders, Captain?"

Asindo smiled and the gathered guildmasters suddenly went into motion, getting to their feet and exchanging reminders of necessary duties with quick, certain command. "Be at the *Wafiya* by the third bell," Asindo ordered through the growing clamor. "We sail on the tide."

"Wait," Keesha said, voice clear and strong in the hubbub. "Wait. I'm coming too."

CHAPTER 5

Keesha might have thrown a stone into a still pond, the way surprise rippled out from where she and Rasim stood. More than one captain brayed with laughter, but Guildmaster Isidri leaned forward, elbows on her knees and fingers steepled with interest. Humor creased the sun-deepened lines on Asindo's face, but he spoke politely enough. "Are you, now. What do you know of life aboard a ship, baker's daughter?"

"Nothing," she said defiantly, "but I bet you don't know much about making hard tack or fish stew. Put me in the galley if you want to, or teach me to sail, but I'll be on board the *Wafiya* when she sails, Captain."

"She should be." Rasim returned to Keesha's side. His heart was beating too hard again, quick with the fear that supporting Keesha might lose himself a place on the ship. He wished he could tell himself it didn't matter, but it did. It mattered a *lot*. But taking the risk was right, just as asking Desimi, who loathed him, to use magic Rasim himself couldn't command, had also been right.

For an instant, he had a rueful glimmer of under-standing: doing the right thing instead of the smart thing might make being a grown-up much harder. But he wasn't grown-up yet, and that was a problem for later. For now, he said, "She's the one who saw how unnatural the fire was, Captain. She only told me, so I could tell someone who'd listen. If I'm going to be on board because I'm clever, not because I'm a great witch, then Keesha deserves to be there at least as much as I do. She made me look clever."

Far too many of the nearby guildmasters and captains were grinning openly by the time he'd finished defending Keesha. He felt color scald his face all the way to his hairline, and muttered, "Well, she did," to his feet.

Asindo's deep voice sounded like he was fighting back laughter, but he addressed Keesha politely a second time. "You're no orphan, Keesha al Balian. You have a trader's name, not a sea witch's, and you've parents to worry about you."

Keesha folded her arms and thrust her jaw out, sure signs she was nervous. "I have three brothers and a sister, too, Captain. We can't all inherit the bakery. Some of us will marry into other trades, but a guild is as fine a life as any trader's. I'll trade my name for a sea witch's, if that's what it takes. I'll be Kisia al Ilialio come dawn, and sail on the Siliarian Sea."

The laughter had stopped, and the new name Keesha had given herself rang through the hall with pride and defiance. Smiles were still everywhere, but they were touched with admiration, and after long seconds of silence, Guildmaster Isidri's slow applause cracked the air. Keesha and Rasim both jumped, then straightened themselves as Isidri stood and gave Keesha in particular an approving nod.

"All right then, girl. Kisia al Ilialio you are, if your parents will release you to the guild. If you mean to be shipboard by the third bell, we'd better hurry to ask them."

Keesha's — *Kisia's* — smile went from incredulous to thrilled inside a breath. She dropped the satchel of bread to fling herself on Rasim and hug him until he grunted, then whispered, "Don't let them sail without me!" in his ear.

Rasim nodded, setting her back on her feet. Kisia gave him a stunning smile before grabbing Guildmaster Isidri's hand as the old woman joined them. "Come on," she said to the Guildmaster, "come on, I'll show you where the bakery is!"

"I know where it is, girl. Asindo wasn't the only one who got treats from your grandparents." The amused Guildmaster let herself be hauled out of the guildhall. Within seconds the captains were in an uproar again.

Rasim stood among them, battered by their voices and by their brusque passage past him, grinning like a fool. He'd never heard of anyone challenging for a place in the guilds the way Kisia had just done. *Kisia,* so close to the *Keesha* she'd been, but with the "si" in the name that marked any sea witch as belonging to the guild. The letters were for the goddess of the sea, Siliaria, and every orphan brought into the guild was given a name to honor her. He was Rasim al Ilialio, son of the sea and river, and soon Kisia would be their daughter.

And they would sail together. *He*, Rasim al Ilialio, who was hardly a sea witch at all, would sail on the Wafiya with Captain Asindo and Hassin. And with Desimi too, Rasim thought sourly, but joy buoyed the complaint away. That trouble would be worth it. *Any* trouble would be worth it.

Rasim's smile disappeared. It was true enough: any trouble *would* be worth it, but it was easy to forget in his excitement that they sailed at dawn because real trouble, dangerous trouble, brewed in the city. This wouldn't be a training run, a first time out for the new crew to work together on a merchant run or trade route. They would slip away on the early tide, before sunrise, so they could gather elsewhere, hidden from an unknown enemy, and plan their counter-attack.

Asindo appeared in front of Rasim, stepping out of the crowd of captains and guildmasters sweeping by. He looked as serious as Rasim felt, and he put a hand on Rasim's shoulder. "Settling in, is it?"

"Yes, sir. It's not...it's not all wonderful, is it, sir?"

Asindo's expression became even more solemn. "No, lad, it's not." Then a smile broke through, becoming a grin. "But by the goddess, a lot of it is. It's your first sail as crew, boy. Enjoy it. Now up to your berth and gather your things. It's not long until the third bell."

Excitement bloomed in Rasim's chest again. He beamed at the stout captain, then ran for the berths. Ran for the apprentice's hall for the last time: he was a journeyman now, and when they came back from this journey, he would sleep in another hall.

It took almost no time to pack his belongings: two spare shirts, a second pair of trousers, shoes that would see no use on shipboard. Kerchiefs to keep his hair out of his face as it grew longer, a stone carving of the goddess Siliaria as was given to all of the Seamasters' children, and a few well-worn storybooks that he had learned to read from. Apprentices needed little and owned less, but it meant they could take their lives with them when they went to sea.

He left the apprentice hall berths with more decorum, trying to look and feel adult, like a journeyman should, rather than running around with the excitement of a childish apprentice. That lasted until he got to the gates and the same guard who had let him in an hour earlier offered a wink and a nod along with a solemn, "Strong winds and safe sailing, Journeyman Rasim."

A grin split Rasim's face, so wide it felt like it reached down inside him and lifted him off the ground. Unable to contain himself, he broke into a run again, tearing headlong down to the docks.

They had never been so busy in the small hours of the morning as they were now. Rasim slowed, astonished at the bustle of traffic. It seemed everyone from the guild was there, loading ships, preparing them to sail, finding room for newly promoted journeymen and for young masters now elevated to mates and boatswains.

It was all done in surprising silence. Normally the docks were a riot of sound and color, but under the moonlight and with the need for discretion, the noise level was barely above a murmur. Everything was blue and black, shadows deep and wavering under the two moons, but sure-footed sea witches and sailors leaped from ship to bridge to shore as if it was full daylight without a shadow to be seen.

No one was bleary with sleep, though as he came closer Rasim heard the undercurrent of confusion in the shoreside gossip. Only the captains and guildmasters knew why they were preparing to sail in the middle of the night, and a day earlier than they might have expected to.

Only the captains, guildmasters, and Rasim. His stomach dropped, and his hands went cold around the bundle of belongings he carried. No doubt the others would come to know soon enough, but it was a heavy burden for a journeyman to carry on his own.

Not quite on his own, not if Keesha's parents let her join the guild. Rasim thought they would, mostly because he couldn't imagine anyone defying Guildmaster Isidri. And if they agreed, the Guildmaster would make certain Keesha — *Kisia* — got to the docks before the *Wafiya* sailed. Boosted by the thought, Rasim tossed his bundle over the *Wafiya*'s rail and ran light-footed across the bridge.

Desimi climbed up from below just as Rasim jumped to the ship from the bridge. The other boy looked bigger in the moons' light, the blue-yellow shadows spilled from the two full orbs aging him. He would have a mean look about him when he was grown unless he made an effort to scowl less than he was doing right now. Rasim skidded back a step, unwilling to have another confrontation. His ribs, which hadn't bothered him in all the excitement, suddenly twinged a reminder that they'd been kicked, hard, only that morning. Desimi stared at him, anger as palpable as magic in the air, but then he shouldered past Rasim, barely acknowledging his presence.

Rasim's breath left him in a rush. Maybe being crewmates instead of just apprentices together would be enough to keep Desimi's temper in line. It was enough for tonight, at any rate, so Rasim grabbed his belongings and hurried into the hold to find a berth.

The only hammocks left empty were the ones below and beside Desimi's, of course. Rasim knew it was Desimi's from the other boy's goddess symbol, stuck neatly into a cubby some other journeyman had carved out just for that purpose. They were the worst of the berths, too, nearest the prow where the ship's rise and fall would be felt the most strongly. But that was the way of it for new crew members: as they rose in rank they would have the chance at better berths. That this one was on a ship at all was enough for Rasim. He threw his bag into the hammock, then darted back to the deck.

Apprentices served on ships as much as in the shipyards, learning all the most basic duties of a sea witch and sailor. Rasim fell to what he could do: shifting supplies into the hold, scampering up the mast to tie off dangling ropes, snatching up a bucket of pitch to finish sealing inner boards. The moons slipped across the sky arm in arm, pulling the tide higher and the night later. The third bell rang, and for the first time since he'd reached the ship, Rasim's stomach clenched with worry. Keesha wasn't there yet, and the *Wafiya* would cast off at the next bell. Maybe her parents had said no after all. Heart tight, he bent to his work, trying not to think. Time passed quickly, too quickly for a boy trying not to worry about whether his friend had come. The fourth bell rang just as the tide changed, and a familiar shout rang out: "Journeymen!"

There were a dozen on board, but the call was meant for the newest two. It was their duty and honor to be among those who took in the ropes that bound ship to shore and broke them from their old lives forever. Rasim ran for the rail.

And then Keesha — *Kisia*, given to the sea and river, then Kisia al Ilialio was there behind him, her long hair cropped apprentice-short and her grin as wide and fierce as the sea itself. Rasim shouted from the bottom of his heart, a huge sound of delight, and grabbed Kisia around the middle to spin her around until they both staggered when he put her down. And there was Guildmaster Isidri on the shore, her white braid a blaze over her shoulder. She nodded to both of them, and to Desimi, too, as he stepped up to the next rope over and stared between Rasim, Kisia and the Guildmaster.

"Cast off, mates!" Asindo's command rolled across the ship as a soft echo of what other captains were shouting. Rasim gave his rope a practiced flick, loosening it from the broad post on shore. Beside him, Desimi did the same, while at Rasim's elbow Kisia watched intently, repeating the motion so she might learn it. Within seconds, the ropes were coiled and set aside within the ship. Asindo nodded approvingly, then beckoned to the three newest members of his crew. Heart in his throat, a smile cracking his face, Rasim sprang up the short set of stairs that led to the captain's wheel.

Asindo spun the wheel as wind sprang up, gift from the handful of sky witches on board, and the

Wafiya turned as sharply as any ship its size could. Twinned moonlight splashed a pathway across the water. The captain, with a smile, touched Rasim's shoulder and nodded to the wheel.

Rasim whispered, "C'mon," to Kisia and Desimi. They both startled, Kisia eagerly and Desimi suspiciously, but neither wasted more time than that in laying their hands on the wheel at the same time Rasim did. It meant nothing: the ship was set on its course already.

And it meant everything, a promise of sailing, no matter what else might happen, into a new life.

CHAPTER 6

A life, Rasim admitted privately a week later, of drudgery, exhaustion and boredom. He had never worked so hard. Blisters already turned to calluses on his hands, attesting to that. Even Desimi's size and strength weren't enough to fend off weariness. He'd given Rasim no trouble since they'd set sail, too willing to collapse into sleep the moment opportunity presented itself.

Kisia was in the worst shape, having spent a lifetime punching bread dough, not hauling rough ropes or scrubbing wood planks. Moreover, she had no witchery training at all, and spent what free time she had studying magic with Hassin. She was a quick study with a natural talent that made the masters scowl at her with curious interest. At the end of her work shifts she staggered to her berth and slept, unmoving, until the whistle blare that woke her for the next shift. Rasim had not heard her offer even a breath of complaint.

They had sailed north, leaving Ilyara behind, then turned due east to sail through the narrow straits at the mouth of the Siliarian Sea. It was an outrageous distance to escape an unknown enemy. After they turned north and the waters began to grow colder, Rasim forced himself awake before the whistle and crawled on deck to seek out Asindo.

The captain never seemed to sleep. The crew rotated, three shifts a day. After a week, Rasim had worked every shift, and Asindo had always been on deck for at least an hour or two during each of them. He stood in the captain's nest now, watching the sky color with dawn. More than one crewman eyed Rasim uncertainly, but Asindo himself nodded a greeting when Rasim crept up to stand beside him.

"We're going to the Northlands, aren't we," Rasim whispered. "Because it's where the queen was from, and if it the Great Fire was set on purpose..." He fell silent, hoping Asindo would say it, but when the captain didn't, Rasim finished, "...then she was...she was murdered, wasn't she?"

Asindo said nothing, but the glance he gave Rasim confirmed the possibility.

Cold made a fist in Rasim's belly. "It wouldn't have been the Northmen who did it, would it? We're not going into a—a trap?"

"I don't think so." Asindo frowned at the horizon, then snapped fingers at a third mate lingering nearby. Trying to overhear, Rasim thought, but Asindo kept his voice discreetly soft. "The fire was more likely set by a faction within Ilyara, someone or some group who disapproved of the king marrying outside the local bloodlines. It's more likely that we go to seek allies against an enemy within, than sail into trouble."

"Captain." Rasim's voice broke again and he cleared his throat. "Captain, *no one* thought the king should marry outside the city. I know that, even if I was only born just before the fire. Everyone knows it. There are some who say the fire was his punishment for diluting the royal blood."

"All the more likely, then, that it was an Ilyaran plot, wouldn't you say? Who, Rasim? Who would you catch with your net, if you were fishing for the culprit?"

"Not the Sunmasters," Rasim said without thinking. Hassin emerged from the prow, glanced at his captain and the cabin boy, and waved a greeting as he went on with duties. Rasim smiled, pleased to be noticed, then considered what he'd said. "They might be fire witches, but they would have been prepared if they'd started it. They'd have been ready to make themselves look good by saving the city. It would take a really sneaky Guildmaster to choose to make them look bad by failing." He shot Asindo a glance, wondering if the captain knew the Sunmasters' Guild leader.

Asindo smiled. "Guildmaster Akkiro is wise, but not cunning. His life is dedicated to the god and the upkeep of the temples. I think if he had begun the fires, none of the temples would have fallen. Their ruin nearly destroyed his spirit. Who else?"

"Not us, or we wouldn't be going to the Northlands to look for help." Rasim made a face. "At least, probably not. I bet Guildmaster Isidri *is* that sneaky."

Asindo laughed, unexpectedly loud across the quiet morning. Crew members paused to look their way, then went back to work. If any of them begrudged Rasim a talk with Asindo, they didn't show it, even when Asindo leaned closer to confide, "Yes, she is, but she's also afraid of fire. If you tell anyone I told you that, you'll spend the next five years chewing barnacles off the hull with your teeth."

Rasim clapped his hands over his mouth to hide a grin, and nodded a wide-eyed agreement from behind his palms. Then he parted his fingers to say, "The Stonemasters, maybe. Kisia said the sticky fire looked like chunks of rock. Maybe they found a way to make rock burn. I don't know why, though." He fell silent, then shook his head. "I don't know why anyone would burn the city, Captain. What's the point in ruling a city that's been destroyed? And if you were even going to try, you'd need the guard to support you..."

Asindo was watching him. Rasim trailed off, then swallowed. "It could be someone in the guard, though, couldn't it? Or a noble rich enough to buy the guard, or someone powerful enough that the guard might choose to follow them anyway." Shivers ran over his arms. He was an apprentice — a journey-man now, he reminded himself — and far removed from Ilyaran politics. But like everyone, he knew a few important names.

The king's cousin Taishm, had been the highest-ranking royal in the city when it burned. Taishm had never been expected to focus the Sun Guild's magic, though, and couldn't guide it the way the king might have done. There were those—the ones who didn't blame Queen Annaken—who said Ilyara had burned because of Taishm's lack. He had been crowned after King Laishn's death, but even now he was a reclusive king, generally thought to be ridden by guilt, and unpopular with the people. But maybe he'd chosen to fail with the fire, counting the gain of a crown higher than the love of its people.

Or Yalonta, commander of the guard. She was as well-loved as Taishm was disliked, and no one doubted her ambitions. Rasim had heard rumors she'd once been considered to marry into the royal family, but Laishn had chosen his Northern bride instead. Yalonta might have motivation, and more, the guards' inability to rein in the annual memorial bonfires might be traceable to a commander who didn't want to. The thought horrified Rasim.

There were others: Nidikto, a wealthy merchant who had married royalty. He strode through Ilyara as if the royal blood was his own, and not his wife Alaisha's. He *still* spoke out against the dead queen, and no one doubted he imagined himself on the throne. Faisha, another royal cousin who wanted

Taishm to marry — ideally her — and provide an heir, thus ending the on-going maneuvering for the crown. And those were only the ones gossip mentioned often enough for an apprentice like Rasim to remember the names. Many of them lacked the witchery necessary to rule the city, but there were no doubt dozens more with motivation, means and the magic to wreak havoc in Ilyaran streets.

"The Northmen might lend us an army," Rasim said in despair, "but how do we know who to fight? We need a spy, not a soldier."

"The Northmen," Asindo said, "will have spies in Ilyara. We're going to ask who they are, far more than ask for an army."

Rasim straightened, eyeing his captain. "You're going to ask very strongly, with a fleet at your back."

"I wish to be taken seriously."

Rasim stared at him. "What if they say no? You can't fight them. We have thirty ships with a hundred sailors on each of them, and no reserves to call on."

Asindo's mouth quirked. "You're bold, lad, I'll give you that. But you're not quite thinking it through. We have thirty ships, aye, but those sailors are also witches, and the North has no magic of its own."

Rasim opened his mouth and shut it again, then turned to look across the sea at the ships of the Ilyaran fleet. Thirty ships carried hundreds of sea witches. He, the least of them, could stop water from slopping out of a bucket—or cause it to leap out and splash to the ground instead. Only a week ago he'd seen an unusual way to use water witchery to help people. He hadn't considered it as a weapon.

A few ships from Asindo's fleet could hold the mouth of any harbor. The witches on board could raise waves the way they'd done yesterday, only smash them into town walls rather than splash down on fire from above. They could turn fresh water salty with a touch, poisoning a city's supply. With the sky witches who traveled with them, they could create storms to pound the coast, and ride those storms out in relative safety. Thirty ships of Ilyaran witches could stop trade in and out of every major Northern city, could stop the fishermen who fed those cities, could stop almost anything, while keeping themselves safe and fed from the very same fish stocks they forbade to the locals. Even reinforcements brought by land or sea would be at a disadvantage to Ilyaran magic: land would be too far away to strike from, and on the sea, no one matched the Seamasters' Guild.

A boring life of exhaustion and hard work suddenly sounded wonderful. Rasim, cold with shock, whispered, "We're going to war?"

"I think not," Asindo replied. "I think the Northmen will want to see our investigation through. But the *Wafiya* could have set sail alone to ask that. I need the fleet to make a statement." He scowled. "And it's true what I said at the hall. We're vulnerable in a way the other guilds aren't. It's best to have the ships away from the city in case of another fire. Rebuilding again would end us. We've left enough of the guild behind to help fight any smaller fires that break out, and Guildmaster Isidri will get the most from them."

That broke the chill holding Rasim in place. Guildmaster Isidri would get the most from anyone, even water from a stone, if she had to. He leaned forward, wrapping his hands around the rail of the captain's nest. "I think you should take the *Wafiya* in alone first, sir. Leave the fleet off shore, out of sight."

"Do you," Asindo said dryly.

Rasim shrugged off the captain's tone, stubborn certainty rising within him. "I do. Were you small like me when you were an apprentice, Captain?" He thought Asindo probably had been: the captain was broad now, but still not tall.

Surprised, Asindo nodded. Rasim plunged on. "Then I bet you had somebody like Desimi, somebody who bullied you, or bullied other people just because he was bigger." At Asindo's second nod, Rasim blurted, "Captain, taking the whole fleet in is just like that. You're bigger and you have more magic and you know it. What did having somebody bully you make you want to do?"

A slow, wry smile crept across Asindo's face. "It made me want to fight back, lad. It made me want to prove myself."

"So do you *really* want to sail into the Northern capital like a bully who's going to make them want to fight back and prove themselves instead of listen? If we sail in by ourselves we're being reasonable. If they don't want to help, *then* you can bring in the fleet to make your point. But it's just dumb to go in like you're looking for a fight, Captain." Rasim sighed. "I've run away from Desimi enough times to know *that*."

Asindo stared at Rasim a long moment, then snorted. "When we get back to Ilyara, I'm sending you to study with the Sunmasters, lad. You've the wily mind of a diplomat and the Sun priests are the ones to develop that, not a sea witch who's been on a ship most of his life."

"You're not sending me anywhere until we find out who set those fires," Rasim said fiercely, and his captain grinned.

"I suppose I'm not. But after that, lad. After that, we'll see what's to be seen." The fifth bell rang and on its heels the whistle finally blasted, signaling the hour Rasim should be getting out of his berth. The same sound echoed across the sea from other ships, shrill notes that raised hairs on Rasim's arms despite their familiarity. The on-deck crew groaned and stretched, taking a moment's respite. They would work another hour while the day shift woke, ate, and came on duty. Only then could they bring their weary bodies to the galley for food before dropping into dreamless sleep.

The echo of the first whistle had barely faded when it blasted again, startling not only Rasim, but Asindo. Hassin appeared from near the ship's stern, frowning. "What was that for?"

By the third blast everyone in the crew was on deck, disheveled with sleep and confusion. Kisia came up scratching her fingers through newly-short hair, as if she still hadn't become accustomed to its length, and Desimi looked like a young bear roused from slumber. Rasim squinted at the crow's nest, where the sailor whose job it was to sound the whistle held it in both hands, staring at it in bewilderment. "Captain, I don't think that whistle came from the ships..."

A serpent erupted from the sea.

CHAPTER 7

It was massive, the length of three ships or more. Scales the size of Rasim's fist glittered deep blue along its back, fading toward smoother-looking white skin on its belly. A spiny fin crested its spine from a yard or two behind its head all the way to the tip of its tail. It had no other fins at all, but its slim hook-jawed mouth opened to show long glittering teeth as it blasted another call frighteningly like the wake-up whistle.

It dove over the ship closest to the *Wafiya*, wrapped around it, and snapped the ship in two with a single sharp contraction.

Screams broke out, sailors suddenly rushing to action. For a moment Rasim still couldn't move, paralyzed by awe and horror. Then he too jolted, leaping from the captain's nest to join others at the rail. None of them had remained frozen for more than a handful of seconds: that was how quickly the serpent moved, how fast it had destroyed one of the fleet. It was gone now, deep in the water, invisible while it feasted on the other ship's crew. Survivors in the water brought their magic to fore, creating tiny storm systems to protect themselves, but Rasim knew the elemental fight was useless. The serpent was too big, too wild. It would barely notice a storm built by the entire fleet, when it lived in waters where a typhoon could rage for days.

It burst out of the water again beside another ship, diving and crushing it as quickly as the first one. Spears and harpoons flew from the ships closest, bouncing harmlessly off the serpent's small thick scales. Rasim said, "The eyes," and heard the words spread through the sailors beside him.

Kisia squirmed between him and the man beside him, her own eyes wide with terror but her mouth set in a grim determined line. "But how do we get to the eyes?"

"I don't know." Rasim reached for the water with his magic, feeling it slap and brush against the *Wafiya*'s planks. There were no schools of fish below the surface: they could usually be felt, disturbing the flow of water even when they moved with it. They had fled the serpent, just as the fleet would if it could. The creature itself was too far away for Rasim's magic to sense it, but his head snapped up. "Captain! Can *you* feel it down there?"

"I've got it," Hassin said less than a breath later. His face was pale already, a long night's shift no friend to a need for working strong magic. "I can feel it, but I can't—I can't—"

The serpent flew from the water again, bringing down a third ship with its coiled strength. Screams were a constant now, like gulls at the harbor: almost unheard, because to pay attention would be to go mad. Sea witches still on ships, the ones nearest to those in the sea, were lifting their guildmates up, funnels of water whipping around to dump them safely on deck. Half a dozen rescued sailors and gallons of water were splashed across the *Wafiya*'s deck, some of them clutching small wounds and all of them sallow with shock. Rasim turned to look at them, hardly breathing as he tried to think.

"I can't stop it," Hassin said through his teeth. "I can't even slow it down. It's not like changing currents to bring fish to nets. It can swim against any current I can make."

"Take it out of the water." Rasim barely heard himself whisper, his gaze still locked on the half-drowned sailors and his thoughts not yet coherent. Then he seized Hassin's arm, disrupting his concentration, but certainly earning his attention. "Take it out of the water like they've done the crew! If we can see it we can fight it!"

Hassin said, "I can't," dumbly, though he turned back to the sea as he spoke. "Desimi. Misin." He named others of the witches able to raise storm waves, then snapped, "Rasim, make yourself useful, signal the other ships what we're doing. We can't do it alone, the beast weighs too much. A skin of water," he shouted at the crew gathering around him. "Contain it with a skin of water, enough that we can hold it but too little for it to breathe long! Rasim! *Hurry!*"

The sea boiled, magic and monster creating a froth as they crashed together. Rasim scrambled up the mast and grabbed signal flags from the crow's nest. *Storm wave surrounds* – There was no signal for *serpent.* Rasim spelled out *eel,* but from the nest's high vantage he could see that no one had time to watch for signals from another ship. The serpent had all their attention, diving and surfacing again as it burst through the magic Asindo's crew worked. The air turned heavy again, storm warning in a clear morning: if other ships noticed *that*, they might recognize that magic was being made, and lend their strength to it. Otherwise, no, they'd never see it, and given the ease with which the serpent broke through Hassin's weaving, that meant the fleet was doomed.

Down below, Kisia grabbed Hassin's arm the same way Rasim had only a minute earlier. He was angrier this time, but Kisia shoved forward, demanding he listen as she pointed at Rasim, then gestured sharply from their ship to the next, floating beyond the wreckage of the one they'd lost. Hassin followed her argument, though the words were lost to Rasim thanks to height and the sounds of battle. Then he nodded and twisted his hands, a whirlpool of sea water rising at his command.

Kisia threw herself from the deck without hesitation, splashing madly into Hassin's water devil. It spun across the water, throwing wreckage aside. Seconds later Kisia flung herself out of the whirlpool onto the deck of the next ship. She grabbed another sailor, pointed toward Rasim, then ran for the ship's far side. The whirlpool caught her again and she was gone, rushing for the next ship, and the next.

Rasim howled, a soundless cheer beneath the shrieking serpent and noise of fighting, and began his signals again. A moment later the next ship's sea witches came in line with Asindo's, all of them save Hassin bent to the same goal. *He* still swept Kisia from one deck to another, until distance made her small and Rasim could no longer easily count the ships she'd visited. She landed on yet another deck and caught yet another sailor's attention. She pointed back the way she'd come, visibly triumphant even from so far away. With hardly a missed beat, the sailors saw what was happening and began to come together, working their magic to support Hassin's.

The serpent soared from the water and crushed Kisia's ship.

Screams ripped through the fleet, Rasim's among them. Kisia was a trader, not a born sailor. She couldn't swim, nor did she have the water witchery skill to keep her alive in the water. It was *hard* to drown a sea witch, but much less so a baker's daughter. And she was here because of him, even if the choice had been entirely her own. He stretched his hands out, almost able to feel Kisia's weight in them, almost feel her fear pounding through the waves as she struggled to stay above water, to stay free of the serpent's hooked jaws. He was so far away, and not much of a witch at all, but desperation made him push from within, like he could somehow shove her to safety.

Energy rushed out of him. Rasim dropped to his knees. He couldn't even pretend he might rescue his friend without exhausting himself. Fingers wrapped around the crow's nest railing, he stared outward bleakly, trying to make sense of the chaos on the sea.

The serpent's leap out of the water had given the witches the chance they needed. For that moment, they'd been able to see it, and what they could see, they could capture. The creature was airborne, thrashing wildly in an element not its own. Water splashed and broke away in bucketsful, and more rose up from the sea so the witches could maintain their hold on the beast. Even emotionally wrung out as he was, Rasim felt the magic they worked, and the strain of working it over so much distance.

More than once the serpent managed to dive again, narrowly missing ships as it fell and was dragged back into the air. Taken from the water, it seemed even larger, a thing out of nightmares. It was beautiful, too, in a terrible way.

And they would never be able to drown it in air. Too much new water came up from the sea, holding the serpent aloft. The witches would tire long before it did: their magic was meant to survive a storm, not reshape one. Rasim slid back down the mast, defeated in spirit before his crewmates were defeated in body. Kisia was likely dead, and the rest of the fleet would soon be as well, all because of the wretched whistle.

The whistle. Rasim thumped to a stop at the base of the mast, looking to where the whistle usually hung. It was gone now, probably never replaced in the moments between waking the crew and the serpent's attack. Exhaustion and defeat forgotten, Rasim whipped around, searching for the crewman whose job it was to blast it.

She was at the rail with everyone else, brass whistle still clenched in one hand as she did her part against the serpent. Rasim ran for her, lurching as the sea rocked the ship. He pried the whistle free of her grip and snatched a long knife from another sailor's belt. Neither of them even looked around, all their concentration on the sky-swimming serpent.

Knife in his teeth, Rasim swarmed the mast again. The serpent *was* swimming through the air, changing directions and making forward motion, though not with the grace or speed it would have in the water.

Still, it could go where it wanted.

Or where *Rasim* wanted it to go. He slammed the knife's point in to the crow's nest railing and brought the whistle to his lips as he leaped into the crow's nest himself.

The blast was dismayingly quiet beneath the sounds of fighting. Determined, Rasim filled his lungs like they were a sun witch's forge bellows and tried again. It was stronger, but still not enough.

The third blast took his air away. His vision blackened, spots dancing in his eyes. He grabbed the rail to keep from falling down again. When his vision cleared, the serpent had turned his way.

Rasim, grinning viciously, loosened the knife from the rail and waited for the moment to wreak vengeance for his friend.

Awkward in the air or not, the serpent was still fast. It seemed to use the very magic that supported it as the resistance it needed to swim. Between one whistle blast and the next it closed the distance to the *Wafiya* by half, screaming its own whistle-like howl as it approached.

Panicked voices rose up from below, Asindo and Hassin demanding to know what Rasim was doing. He glanced down, but only briefly, seeing their grip on the magic faltered as their concentration broke. Desimi, of all people, grabbed Hassin's shoulder and snapped a commanding finger toward the serpent as it slid back into the water. Hassin's face contorted with anger, but he focused on the gathered power again. Asindo brought his own attention back to the serpent, but kept a scowling eye on Rasim too.

In the breath it had taken to look down, the serpent was nearly upon the *Wafiya*. Rasim sprang onto the crow's nest railing, abandoning the whistle to catch a cross-beam for support. He coiled, waiting. Water sprayed and scattered across him as the serpent came closer, close enough that he could smell it. It smelled cold, fresh, like the sea, not like a killing monster, but Kisia's memory was fresh in Rasim's mind.

The serpent dove at him, howling, and the ship plunged to the side, sea witches turning their magic to avoid the behemoth's blow.

Rasim sprang, using the ship falling away and the serpent's oncoming speed to cross more free air than he might have imagined possible. He splashed into the watery barrier that held the serpent above the sea, and only barely remembered to bring air with him: that much, at least, his magic could manage. It was harder than he expected, his witchery trembling and weak. Desimi would tease him about that, if Rasim survived to admit it.

The serpent twisted, losing sight of Rasim as he crashed against it. He didn't even need to touch the beast: the water surrounding it was deeper than he was tall, and a touch of magic pushed him through it even as the monster thrashed. He swam in the water, in the air, just as the serpent did, and for an instant it was glorious. No one had ever swum alongside one of the legendary sea monsters, much less done it in the air, in full view of a fleet of ships. A grin pulled at Rasim's lips.

Then Asindo and Hassin, struggling to save their ship, lost control of the fleet's magic, and of the serpent.

It dived, taking Rasim into the depths.

CHAPTER 8

It was *cold* beneath the surface. The water shone a deep, quiet blue that turned black the deeper they went. Rasim forgot everything but maintaining the air he'd brought with him. He thrust himself closer to the serpent, folding one hand around a sharp-edged scale. He couldn't let the knife go, not if he wanted to kill the thing, but he couldn't hold on or pull himself forward with the blade in one hand, either.

A memory of how the knife had stuck in the crow's nest railing, vibrating with energy, struck him. Rasim slammed the blade into the serpent's side, giving himself purchase to edge forward with.

The beast didn't even shudder, only swam more deeply. A pin-prick, that's what the knife's cut was. Maybe not even that, although a thin stream of blood trailed out when Rasim pulled the knife free so he could drive it in again, a little farther ahead, pulling himself toward the serpent's head. If the beast didn't even feel the blade as he climbed its body, he wasn't sure he could strike deeply enough to kill it, but he would try. In Kisia's memory, he would try.

The pressure around him grew more intense, making moving harder. He breathed as normally as he could, afraid his heart would burst from pressure if he held his breath. The air he carried with him would last because it had to. Length by length, he hauled himself closer to the serpent's head. It began to glow as they went deeper, a faint blue light of its own that came from beneath its scales and ran the length of its sinuous body. Beautiful, Rasim thought again. It was beautiful, and he was going to kill it so it didn't kill him.

It noticed him when he reached its head. Their downward journey stopped, the serpent twisting round and round itself as it tried to scrape him off. Any faster and he would be dizzy, and this was hard enough with his air running out. Its eye glowed too, deep blue around a black pupil. A target, he thought gratefully, and struck.

The serpent's scream was much worse beneath the surface. It vibrated the water, making wobbles like a stone hitting a pond. It came from just in front of Rasim, not quite from the creature's mouth, but from nose-like slits that a gilled creature couldn't possibly breathe with. He was grateful to be behind them: he would have been blasted free if the full force of the scream hit him.

But he had only caused the thing pain, not killed it, or the scream would have died already. He squirmed forward, jamming the knife deeper into its eye, then deeper still, until his wrist, his elbow, the whole of his arm, was buried in the gelatinous ruin that had been the serpent's eye. He gritted his teeth, holding back a shriek of his own. He couldn't afford to use the air, and he was afraid he wouldn't hear himself beneath the serpent's cry. He would lose his nerve if he couldn't hear his own voice.

Finally something scraped at the knife's end. Rasim swirled it around, stirring the beast's brain into goo. Its scream faltered, then failed. It flung itself wildly through the water, no longer diving, no longer fighting, just dying. Relief sapped Rasim's strength. He relaxed, weariness gathering him close. Water rushed by as the serpent began to sink. Rasim felt the current coming closer to his face, and shocked awake again. His air was nearly gone, if he could feel the water so closely.

Blood flooded the water as Rasim pulled his arm free of the serpent's eye. He closed his own eyes against it, then panicked and opened them again to watch the dying serpent begin to sink. If it went *that* way, then air, breath, a chance to live, was the *other* way. Rasim flung himself away from the serpent, using his whole body like a flipper and undulating toward the surface. When that became too much for his weakening lungs, he kicked with his legs alone, praying that the air would last. It had to last.

He pushed against the water with his magic, propelling himself upward as best he could. Desimi would be at the surface already, drinking in gulps of clean air, but Rasim's power was too slight for that. His ears blocked as he kicked up, an ache that ran all the way to his throat before they cleared in a burst of squealing discomfort. The water around him was purple with blood, swirls of it catching in the currents. There would be sharks soon, if there weren't already. The fleet had to still be nearby, or he would be dead even if he reached the surface.

He popped through with a surge of energy he didn't know he had, then collapsed into the water on his back, heaving for air. The sun made a soft gold ball on the horizon, still barely awakened for the day, though he felt he'd been working for hours.

Clever, Captain Asindo had said. Rasim was clever. Not clever enough to let the serpent go when it dived, though. Not clever enough to forget vengeance and save himself. He closed his eyes and let himself sink a few inches into the pool of salty blood that surrounded him. Not clever by half, but terribly lucky. It should be him sinking toward the ocean's bottom, or, more likely, lining the serpent's stomach. He was much warmer now, the rising sun and the surface temperature enough to take the chill of the depths away. Either that or the cold had confused his mind, in which case he was far closer to death than he had hoped after such a narrow escape.

In a moment. In a moment he would straighten himself in the water and search for the fleet. It had to be visible: the serpent had taken him into the depths, not out into the sea, hadn't it? Yes. It had, because no other option was bearable. To survive the beast only to drown or be eaten by sharks would be unforgivable, so in a moment Rasim would right himself, and wave to the fleet.

The sea closed over his head, and he sank.

A hook fished Rasim from the water. He banged against the side of a ship as he was lifted upward, no finesse or skill in the rescue. Water poured from his lungs, coughs wracking his body as he was swung over a rail and dropped unceremoniously to a deck.

Not one of the fleet's decks. The wood was the wrong color and not smooth enough: Rasim had time to notice that before he vomited water again. He curled up, hands clenched over his head, forehead against the deck, and coughed until tears ran from his eyes. He convulsed with shivers, cold all the way to his bones. Deeper than his bones, even. He might never warm up, the way the sea had crept into him, the way the serpent's blood still tasted sour and cool in his mouth. He wasn't sure he was alive, not really. Siliaria, goddess of the sea, might have taken him directly into her arms, though he would think a Siliarian death ship would be made of finer wood. On the other hand, he probably had to be dead, because the fleet had been alone on the water that morning, and this was not an Ilyaran ship.

"Turn 'im over," someone said. "Let's see what we fished out."

A kick like the ones Desimi delivered hit Rasim's ribs. More water spewed out, some of it falling back into his throat as he flipped over. He sat up, blind with tears, and leaned forward to cough until the pain in his ribs was from inside, not from the kick.

Through tears, he saw bare feet, ragged knee pants: the usual garb of a sailor. Tanned skin, though, not Ilyaran brown: where the pants ended, the color faded quickly, so as the people around him moved he caught glimpses of paler knees. Northerners were that color, and turned bright red under the Ilyaran sun. Rasim wiped his eyes and lifted them to see who had rescued him. Lifted them not to the sailors surrounding him, but to the flag they flew high above the crow's nest.

For a moment it made no sense. Not Ilyaran blue, but Rasim hadn't expected that. Not any of the other local sailing nations, either, not even one of the far distant trade nations like the Northerners. It was a black flag, a plague flag intended to warn others off, only marked with a grinning skull and crossed swords. Plunderers used that mark, plunderers and —

— and pirates.

Rasim fell back, shock wiping away whatever strength he'd had left. His head hit the deck hard enough to make him see stars, and he coughed again as unfamiliar faces bent to examine him. They were curious, not cruel. Perhaps even pirates couldn't be murderous all the time. And they'd taken him from the water, which was something. A big man with a beard shoved a couple of the others away to frown at Rasim, his face upside-down to Rasim's. "Where the devil did you come from?" He spoke the trader's tongue, the common language every sailor and merchant had at least some familiarity with. Rasim had studied it well, hoping fluency would help to make up for his stunted magic.

The question was a good one. His focus went past the bearded man to the sky. Light blue with morning, no longer sunrise-colored, but also nowhere near night, so he might have some sense of how far he'd come off track by the stars. He wet his lips, tasting salt and dried blood, and tried to find an answer. The truth was preposterous.

There was no lie any less unlikely, though. Rasim tried to speak and coughed instead. The bearded man waited, then lifted his eyebrows—it looked strange, upside-down—and Rasim tried again. "A sea serpent dragged me here."

A smile twitched the man's mouth. "Did it now. From where?"

Rasim waved a hand weakly, judging the direction from the sun's position: from the east. Closer to land than they probably were now.

"And what happened to the serpent?" the man asked genially.

"I killed it."

Guffaws roared up around him. Rasim closed his eyes, waiting for them to fade. Closing his eyes was almost all he could manage anyway. His entire body still trembled with cold and exhaustion. His stomach was sour with sea water and serpent blood, but he could feel hunger prodding at its edges. He hoped his rescuers would feed him, since they'd bothered to save him.

"Try again, Ilyaran," the bearded man said eventually. "Give us a tale to top that one."

Rasim opened his eyes again. The man was not a captain, he thought. First mate, maybe, because there was something of command in his crude joviality, but he lacked the presence Asindo had. He even lacked the presence that Hassin, who would be a captain someday, had. There was intelligence in his light-colored eyes, and although he laughed there was a flatness to it, warning Rasim that the man was dangerous. He reminded Rasim of Desimi, just a little.

Desimi wouldn't much care what Rasim said next. He would have decided already if he was going to beat him up or not, and Rasim's response would only determine how badly. Feeling confident he was in trouble one way or another, Rasim shrugged and spoke as clearly as he could. "Can you think of a more likely reason for one boy to be floating in a pool of blood ten miles from shore, with no other ships to be seen?"

"Mermaids," somebody suggested with a grin.

Rasim squinted at the speaker, a young woman grimy with shipboard work and too little bathing, and tried to think of what Hassin might say. "If it was mermaids, I'm glad they threw me back, because none of them was as pretty as you."

He stumbled at the end of it, his tongue thick with embarrassment at even trying to say such a thing, but the woman turned pink under her tan and everyone else shouted with laughter. Applause scattered through the group looking down at Rasim, and the crewmen to either side of the woman gave her good-natured, teasing shoves that made her blush all the more.

The big man laughed too, then glanced up as someone else on board called, "The gulls, Markus. Are we going that way or not? We could use a net of fish."

The bearded man — Markus, definitely not the captain if they called him by name instead of rank — twirled a finger and pointed south, command clear in the action. The crew fell into action, wrenching the ship against the wind and sailing it south more through luck than skill, Rasim thought. Even the Northmen with their big square single sails were better at guiding their ships. Markus caught Rasim's arm and hauled him to his feet, then thrust him toward the rail. "Pretty words to Carley won't keep you alive, Ilyaran. Give us a better story."

Rasim's knees gave out, not from fear, but weariness. The crushing pressure of the sea had been more debilitating than he could have imagined, and the cold still sat deep in his bones. He watched the sails buckle with wind, then turned a tired gaze toward a vast cloud of gulls, not far away from where he'd been taken from the water. He looked back the way they'd come, at the puddle of blood still staining the ocean, and shrugged again. "It's the best story I have. Give me a better one yourself."

"There's sharks," Carley reported. "Lots of sharks, Markus. We're going to fight for our supper if we want it."

"It's not fish." Rasim sank down beside the rail, not caring that Markus tried to haul him up again. He wanted to sleep. He wanted to eat, too, and he wanted to not be thrown overboard to drown again. But mostly he wanted to sleep, and his fear of a pirate ship and its first mate was nothing in the face of such weariness.

Markus grunted curiously. Rasim shrugged again. "It's not fish. It's the serpent. A deep current must have carried it back to the surface. That's why there are so many sharks, for the carrion. If you're going to throw me to them, at least hit me on the head first."

The bearded man gave him a peculiar look, then ignored him as the ship slid into the outer edge of the screaming, circling gulls. Eager birds dove at the ship and wheeled away again, disappointed with the pickings. No one spoke beneath their shrieks, only maneuvered the ship deeper into their circle. The water turned darker, purpling with blood. Rasim shuddered and dragged in a breath deep enough to make him cough again, just to be certain he could still breathe. He could, but the scent of blood rose even over the smell of salt and fish, and stuck in the back of his throat. He slouched further, folded his elbow over his mouth, and tried not to breathe.

He still knew when Markus saw he'd been telling the truth. Knew the moment the serpent's remains became obvious, because the big man finally spoke, his voice deep and very serious: "Get the captain."

CHAPTER 9

The captain was as old as Kisia's mother, weather-worn, sun-bleached, and far, far prettier than any woman Rasim had ever met before. She glanced at Rasim like she was assessing his worth, then stepped over him to lean on the ship's rail and look into the sea. After a minute she reached down and grabbed Rasim's ear, hauling him to his feet.

The serpent drifted on the surface in ugly thick coils, all its grace and beauty gone. It rolled in the low surf, turning one side of its head up, then the other.

One side had clearly been picked over by gulls, sharks, and other meat-eating sea creatures. It was torn apart, bitten, shredded, messy as anything being made a meal of might be. Its eye was eaten out, easy tender flesh there already gone.

The other side was worse. Gulls dove into the destroyed flesh, rooting around in the already-exposed eye socket. Rasim shuddered yet again at the memory of the eyeball sucking at his arm, at the coldness of a living creature so large it seemed like it should have been warm. His own small warmth had been nothing compared to its vast chill, but he had survived and it hadn't. He stared at the dead serpent, wondering why he didn't feel triumphant. Instead he thought there was nothing about the day that hadn't been awful, and that wasn't even including the terrible conversation that had started it.

"You did that," the captain said. Rasim nodded. "You're Ilyaran," she said. "A witch."

He said, "Not much of one," before realizing that imagined power might help keep him alive. But it was too late then, and the captain curled a disbelieving lip anyway.

"Enough of one, if you did that. Feed him," she told Markus. "Dry him. We'll keep him alive tonight, and probably kill him in the morning."

Markus shrugged assent and dragged Rasim across the ship as the captain gave orders to turn with the wind and sail away from the serpent's corpse. The relieved crew hurried to do so and Rasim stumbled down the hold stairs, keeping upright only with Markus's help.

It was warmer in the hold, though not much. Markus threw a broadcloth and a change of clothes at Rasim and went to fetch a steaming mug of — something — while Rasim dried himself. The mug contained stew, mild but well-seasoned, with some kind of white fish Rasim didn't recognize as the hearty meat. He hunched onto a hammock, slurping the stew eagerly and becoming more tired with every swallow and inch of regained warmth.

"Don't fall asleep," Markus warned. "The captain will want to talk to you."

Rasim nodded, then toppled sideways as he drained the lasts gulp of stew. The captain didn't mean to kill him until morning. Well, she could talk to him then, and save killing him for the afternoon.

He woke to half-familiar sights and sounds. The voices were wrong, the colors were wrong, but the smells and the rock of the ship were right. Bleary, hungry again, and filled with a terrible need for the necessary, he lurched from his hammock toward the hold stairs.

"Good of you to join us," a woman said drolly from another hammock. Rasim yelped and spun toward her, then doubled and edged toward the stairs again.

The captain's grin was as droll as her voice. "Full bladder, eh? Go on, Ilyaran. There isn't anywhere for you to run, after all."

Too hurried to be embarrassed, Rasim sprang up the stairs and rushed to the side of the ship to do his business before collapsing against the rail with a relieved sigh. The captain sauntered up beside him a minute later, leaning on the rail with her hands folded together. Rasim stole a glimpse at her. She reminded him of Guildmaster Isidri, except two generations younger and far more beautiful. Her hair was white blonde from sunshine and her eyes bleached pale green, startling in her sun-browned face. Her bones were delicate, but there was nothing delicate about her posture or voice. "How old are you, Ilyaran?"

"Thirteen."

Her eyebrows flicked upward. "You're small." She didn't sound surprised, though: an Ilyaran youth, small or not, would either be a passenger on shipboard or into his journeyman years, and Rasim hadn't been dressed like a passenger. "Tell me what happened with the serpent."

"Our ship was attacked," Rasim said carefully. There was no sense in letting pirates know how much of the Ilyaran fleet had set sail. "A friend of mine was swept overboard by the serpent." His throat closed, sorrow seizing its first opportunity to overtake him. Rasim rolled his jaw and looked away from the pirate ship's captain. "I wanted to avenge her."

"Avenge," the captain said. "Not rescue?"

Disdain rose to replace sorrow, a welcome distraction. Rasim gave the captain a hard look. "You saw the serpent's body. Would you think she needed rescuing or avenging?"

"Mmm." She nodded, then rolled a hand, telling him to continue. Rasim shrugged and told his story as quickly as he could, though in the end the captain looked unconvinced. "And you say you're not much of a witch?"

"I'm not. I can freshen water, keep it from slopping over buckets, not much more." The captain handed him her water canteen, eyes challenging. He opened it, tasted it, and made a face. It tasted of leather, salt and the chemicals non-Ilyaran ships used to make sea water almost drinkable. A touch of magic cleaned it and he handed it back for the captain to try as he finished the litany of his skills. "I can keep water away from my head beneath the surface so I can breathe, but that's the same as keeping it from splashing out of buckets, just backwards."

The captain tasted the water, her eyebrows shooting up in surprise. She drank all of it before saying, "And slay sea serpents, too."

"That wasn't witchery. It was just stupid."

The captain's mouth twitched. "Maybe, but romantic too. You'll woo a lot of women with that story."

Rasim's jaw clenched. He didn't want to woo anybody, much less using Kisia's death as the tool. Reckless with sudden anger, he said, "I thought you were going to kill me."

Her expressive eyebrows rose. "Do you want me to?"

"No!"

"Good. Someone who can make our gods-awful water drinkable will be useful. What else can you teach my crew?"

"It doesn't—" Rasim broke off sharply, thinking of Kisia. In the week she'd been on the *Wafiya*, she'd mastered freshening water and other minor magics like driving water from wet clothes. Like Rasim, she could keep water *in* a bucket, though she hadn't yet learned to reverse the trick and push water away from herself. But it went against guild tradition that she'd learned at all. it was commonly held amongst all the guilds that a witch had to begin learning magic before the age of seven to show any skill at all. Kisia was twice that age, and already nearly as broadly talented as Rasim, who had begun studying magic in infancy.

So perhaps the common belief was wrong. Perhaps he *could* teach these pirates, adults though they were, to work some minor water witchery. Or perhaps *someone* could. Rasim doubted his skills were up to the task. Even if they were, it was a terrible idea. Ilyara held its position in the world largely due to its preponderance of witches. Other cities in the region had some, but not nearly as many as Ilyara, and the farther from Ilyara they went, the fewer they were. Northern pirates had no magic-users Rasim was aware of, and it would do no one any good if they learned. He finally finished, "It doesn't work that way," but the captain shook her head.

"You hesitated."

Goddess, she noticed everything. Well, so did Asindo, but Rasim had never needed to hide anything from Asindo. "I was trying to think of a way I could do it," he lied. Sort of lied, at least; he had been thinking *something* like that. "In Ilyara we start studying witchery when we're children. I've never heard of adults learning, even if I knew how to teach."

"You know how you were taught," the captain said. "Start there. Take the youngest of the crew, if you think that matters, but teach them how to freshen water. Earn your keep, Ilyaran, or I'll throw you back overboard." She frowned at him, then jerked a thumb toward the galley. "Go eat something first, though. You look like you're fit to pass out."

Torn between gratitude and fear, Rasim ran to get food.

Before he'd finished eating, Carley, the young woman he'd likened to a mermaid, arrived in the galley with suspicious hope in her eyes. Pale eyes like the captain, but blue, not green. Rasim stared at her longer than he'd dared look at the captain. Eyes that were anything but brown were unusual in Ilyara. His own had garnered a lot of looks over the years, and they were only speckled with green.

Carley scowled and shoved her thumbs into the waist of her pants. "You're staring, Ilyaran."

Rasim startled, then ducked his head to pay more attention to his bread and stew. "Sorry. Your eyes are so bright. I'm not used to it."

"Yours aren't as dark as most Ilyarans'." She sat across from him, eyeing the cheese by his bread.

"I've got Northern blood. You want some?" He broke off a piece of the cheese and offered it to her, betting that usually the best of it went to upper crew members.

She gnawed it hungrily, then stole a sip from his water cup before sitting up straight, grabbing the cup with both hands and draining it. "That's *good.* Not brackish. Where'd you get fresh water?"

"I made it."

"You—" Her eyes widened. "Is that why the captain sent me to you? So you could teach me?"

"I'm supposed to try. How old are you?"

"Seventeen."

Far older than Kisia, even. Rasim tried not to look dismayed, but his stomach plunged with uncertainty. He got two more cups of water from the barrel, setting them both on the table between himself and Carley. "Taste one. Hold the water in your mouth. Think about its flavor, how it feels against your tongue."

Carley did as she was told, pulling a face with the first sip. She swallowed when Rasim told her to and immediately said, "It's awful. After the fresh water, it's awful."

"That's important. Tell me exactly how it was awful. What was wrong with it?"

"It felt...heavy. There was metal in it, and the salt wasn't all gone. Nowhere near all gone. And it has that flat taste from boiling, like all its personality got boiled away."

Rasim smiled. "You understand the water well. That'll help." He touched a fingertip to the cup she'd sipped from. It wasn't necessary to touch it to make the magic work, but it was easier at first. Desalinating water was so easy, such old habit, that thinking how to do it was more difficult than doing it. Salt hung suspended in the water, so fine it was impossible to see, but the magic could separate one from the other. Rasim closed his eyes, letting himself become aware of nothing but his fingertip touching the water's surface, and of how the water spoke to him.

It had no opinion, no feelings as to whether it should be salt or fresh. Only Rasim cared, and by caring, imposed his will on the element. Desimi crushed the water with his magic, forcing salt out, but Rasim lacked the raw power for that. He coaxed it instead, drawing it out until the water sparkled true and clear.

He could do it in an instant, but this time he lingered, calling the water up his finger and down again. It left salt gathering in his hand until there was none in the water, and a tiny amount glittering on his palm. Then he lifted his gaze to Carley's astonished eyes. "Ilyarans really *are* witches. I—felt that. The air changed when the water moved, like there was a storm system coming in."

Triumph and dismay shot through Rasim. "That's the magic. The stronger it is, the more weight it has. If you can feel it, that's good. All right. The water is fresh now. Taste it again. Now hold it in your mouth, hold the idea of it in your mind, how much lighter it is, how much sweeter. How all the flatness is gone, and how it doesn't taste like the wooden barrel anymore. Touch the water in both cups. Feel how the fresher water feels different? Less — greasy, less slippery. Try to make the brackish water feel the same way. Imagine reaching in and scooping the salt out. The water doesn't care if it's salty or not, but you do. Use that caring to separate the salt from the water."

Carley bit her lip, forehead furled in concentration. For long moments nothing happened, and Rasim could see her confidence faltering. "Sea witches learn this when they're three," he murmured. "Long before we're old enough to get frustrated or lose confidence in our ability to do it. It's a game, that's all. The older you get, the more your own mind gets in the way, but for Siliaria's sake, Carley, if a three year old can do it, you can too."

Water exploded out of both cups.

CHAPTER 10

Carley fell back with a shriek. Water dripped everywhere: from Rasim, from Carley, from the table, even from the low galley ceiling. Rasim wiped his face, grinning. "It responded to you. That's something. We'll start again."

By the end of the day, Carley had exploded half a barrel of brackish water over the galley without purifying any of it. Blue, bruised-looking circles lay under her blue eyes, exhaustion leaving its mark. She dragged herself up to deck, Rasim in her wake, and presented herself to the captain with a hangdog expression. "I can't do it, Captain."

The captain looked to Rasim, who shrugged. "I wouldn't have thought she'd be able to move the water at all, Captain. It answers to her. It's just going to take time to get the trick of it down."

"Time during which we'll keep you alive, eating our food and drinking our water."

"Giving you fresh water and finding you schools of

fish to hunt in, if you want," Rasim countered. He was surprised to be unafraid, but the serpent had taken most of his fear from him, at least for the moment. He was lost from his fleet, and the best he could do under this captain's command was survive until he could escape. He didn't even know the captain's name yet, nor had anyone asked him his. It would be easier to kill him that way, maybe, but he would take his chances with the sea or strange shores before he would submit to Markus's knife.

"He's blunt," the captain said to Carley. "He'd make a good pirate. Tomorrow you'll swab decks, Ilyaran, and show us what use your magic is there. In the afternoon, work with Carley again. We need that witchery."

Rasim ducked his head obediently, but snuck a glance at Carley. Her face was pale, her expression resolute, and Rasim went to bed feeling thoughtful. Sea witchery and fresh water were important to any ship, but the captain had sounded strained.

He woke before dawn, climbing on deck to study the position of the stars and the glow of the rising sun. He was a degree and more off course from where the fleet had been: too far to swim, even if the fleet had lingered in serpent-infested waters. There were no hints of land in sight, but Rasim imagined a pirate ship would want to stay near to easy pickings. There was no profit in the open sea: chance encounters with other ships were rare unless following an established trade route. With a year or two's experience, Rasim might recognize a route just by the angle of the stars above, but he had only sailed the Ilialio and the Siliarian Sea, not into the great oceans beyond. He simply didn't know where he was.

He *did* know where his fleet was, or where it would be. That had to be useful somehow, though in the pre-dawn chill, it didn't *seem* very useful. Rasim shivered and tucked his arms around himself. They'd sailed north during the night, and the air was noticeably colder than it had been the day before. Swabbing the deck was no fun, but at least the work would warm him up. He went to the rail, sent a bucket down to collect sea water to wash with, and plied it with magic to keep it from slopping out before it reached him on the way back up.

By sunrise he had cleaned yards of deck and sealed dozens of tiny cracks with a bucket of pitch he'd found below. Captain Asindo would never let a deck get so badly cracked. Rasim wanted to scold the pirate captain. Also unlike Asindo, she only came on deck occasionally, letting the first mate run the ship more often than not. It wasn't how Ilyaran ship were run.

He shied away from that thought. Anything was better than remembering about the fleet and the serpent and, most especially, Kisia. Her parents would still think of her as Keesha. If nothing else, Rasim owed it to them to escape his captors and inform Kisia's parents of their loss. Or at least visit and share their sorrow, since Asindo or Isidri would be more likely to bear the bad news long before Rasim returned to Ilyara.

Drops of hot water fell to the deck and were scrubbed away almost before he acknowledged them. Kisia, Hassin, Asindo, even Desimi, all seemed very far away, and Rasim very alone with no real prospect of escape. Not that the pirate captain had done much to restrain or threaten him, but on a ship at sea there was little need to. He wasn't large enough to be a physical danger, and there was nowhere to go. More tears, angrier tears, slid down his nose and he wiped them away savagely, then bent to scrubbing the deck even harder.

Sometime after sunrise others joined him, mumbling irritation at the hard-working Ilyaran making the rest of them look bad. They had some pride, then, which was something. Just not enough, Rasim thought. Not enough to make them honest traders or merchants. Instead they flew the black flag and preyed on the weak, including himself. Fire began to heat his belly, burning away the last tears. The nameless captain might have him at a disadvantage now, might be able to oblige him to do as she wished, but he was an Ilyaran and a sailor and a sea witch. He *would* find a way to reunite with his fleet, and with their strength do his best to scare these pirates out of the water for good.

The anger warmed him, and he'd just abandoned his

shirt for the feel of the warm sun on his back when Markus spoke above the general chatter on board: "Island colors flying starboard. Get the captain."

Like everyone else, Rasim came to his feet, looking to their right. A ship was on the near horizon, red and green flag bright from its mast. Momentary hope thrilled through Rasim. Another ship might offer him a chance to escape the pirates. But the men and women around him reached for weaponry, anticipating the captain's orders, and Rasim's stomach clenched in outrage. Carley was nearby. He caught her arm, hissing, "Stop this! What are you doing?"

"Getting food and water," Carley snapped. "Maybe some gold or new clothes, too. Taking what ought to be ours but isn't. Now get off me." She shook his hand free, and Rasim, astonished, laughed.

"What ought to be yours? Why should it be? Have you worked for it? Did it belong to you?"

Carley whipped face him, her mouth contorted in a snarl. She kept her voice low, though. "Captain Donnin was our mistress, you stupid boy. We were farmers on her land, most of us. Markus was a blacksmith. His son was the farrier, before he got killed in the raid that burned the captain's house. Most of our families are dead. All of the captain's is, except maybe her daughter. We took what we could carry when the soldiers came, and we took the ship they came in, and we ran. We ran, because all we'd done was not pay taxes we couldn't afford so the earl could build another palace and keep another mistress. My sister *died* for that, Ilyaran, and all we have left is each other and a prayer to save the captain's daughter. We can't do it without weapons, food or water, so we fly the black flag and take what we can. Now *shut up and get out of my way."*

Rasim's breath left him like he'd taken a blow. Pirates were troublemakers; that was a given, among the fleet. He had never imagined that trouble might have first come to them. Uncertain of what to do, he retreated to the stern, where he could see all the business on the ship. Captain Donnin strode on deck, borrowed Markus's spy glass, and nodded. The crew fell to tasks it clearly knew well: preparing hooks to snag the other ship with, tucking long knives into belts, arming themselves with slingshots because bows wouldn't work in the damp salt air. At least, not on any ship but an Ilyaran one.

The other ship was alone, as far from home as Donnin's ship, and sailed against the wind, oblivious to Donnin's approach until it was too late. By the time the other crew realized their danger, Donnin's ship was atop them, hooks flying through the air to catch their railing and haul them close. Screams of anger and anticipation filled the air, much different than the fear that had overtaken Ilyara's fleet when the serpent attacked. Within seconds, Donnin's crew was aboard the other ship.

The other sailors were trained fighters, better with

their weaponry than Donnin's crew. But the pirates were desperate and unleashing the helplessness they'd felt as their lands were taken away. Passion made the battle more closely matched than it should have been, the other ship's soldiers falling as often as Donnin's crew did. The fight thinned out as crew on both sides dragged their injured comrades to safety, and then suddenly Donnin's crew had the upper hand. They wasted no time in stealing supplies. Rasim watched, helpless with horror. Desimi or Hassin might have lifted waves until the fight was too wet to continue, but he could get no response from the sea, no matter how hard he tried.

Not until Donnin's crew began rolling the other ship's water barrels toward their own did he shake his paralysis off. "Stop! *Stop!* Don't take their water, Captain Donnin. They can make it to land without food, but they'll die without water. They need it more than you do."

"You know nothing."

"I know I'm not going to let you kill those people through thirst!" His outrage made his ears burn, but he meant what he said no matter how badly he blushed.

Donnin took her attention from the fight to stare at Rasim in astonishment. "How," she finally said, "how do you expect to stop me, Ilyaran? We need water. They have it."

"You have water!" Rasim bellowed. He looked

around, then snatched up a nearby bucket, throwing it over the edge to fill it. He dragged it up, tossed an errant fish back into the sea, and bent his magic to the water, turning it fresh. He dipped his hands in, making a cup of them, and drank deeply, all the while watching Captain Donnin.

He saw the gag reflex work in her throat, natural response to the idea of drinking salt water. Her eyes widened as he drank, then narrowed again. She splashed her hands into the bucket too, taking a fast sip before flinging the palmful of water aside. "You can turn *sea water* fresh?"

"*I told you that!*" Only he hadn't, now that he thought about it. He'd demonstrated, but that had only been the stale water in her canteen, not sea water.

Donnin's color was as high as Rasim's own, though more visible on her paler skin. She looked as though lightning had struck her: like Rasim had provided an answer she hadn't had a question for. More than that, though, there was a madness in her eyes, a hunger that for the first time made Rasim's gut clench with fear. But she looked away, and for an instant Rasim thought the argument was over, that he'd convinced her.

Then Donnin spoke in a terribly normal voice: "Kill them all."

CHAPTER 11

A howl of glee rose from Donnin's crew. Half of them were back on her ship already, bringing supplies from the island ship, but those who were left fell upon the other ship's crew. No longer outnumbered, and now in fear for their lives, the soldiers there fought back, screams and blood filling the air again. Rasim's voice sounded hollow through the noise, like he shouted into a drum: "*You don't have to do that!*"

They didn't have to, but they clearly wanted to. Vengeance for their fallen, just as he'd wanted vengeance for Kisia. But it was one thing to slay a sea monster destroying a fleet, and something else to put men to the sword when they only wore the same uniform as the ones who had done wrong. Rasim shouted another protest.

Donnin cuffed him across the cheek almost casually, proving to have startling strength in her delicately-boned body. Rasim's vision went white, anger so pure it bleached everything around him. He reached out helplessly, like he could stop the fight with his will alone.

A whitecap burst out of the sea between the ships, water gysering toward the sky. A third of Donnin's crew, caught moving between one ship and another, were launched upward by the sea's sudden antics. The ropes and hooks holding one ship to another were torn free and flew wildly, some splashing into the water, others, more dangerously, bashing down on both ships' decks. The pirates' delight turned to terror as water crashed across the island ship's deck, sweeping soldiers and pirates alike into the ocean. Less washed onto Donnin's deck, but enough did. Rasim kept his feet with magic's help, using it to lessen the force of the oncoming waves. Donnin herself was washed to the far rail. She caught herself there with a curse audible above the water's rumble.

A second wave slammed upward, finishing any hope of a battle between the two crews. Supplies, water barrels, clothing, weaponry all scattered under the water's onslaught, the heavier material sinking the moment it hit the ocean's surface. Then as suddenly as it had begun, the water subsided.

Rasim dropped to his knees, as drained of energy as he'd been in the moments after Kisia's ship had gone down. All around him, Donnin's crew rushed back and forth, throwing ropes to their waterlogged companions and trying to salvage the supplies that now floated in the placid sea. Donnin regained her feet and stalked to the near side of the ship, fury blazing off her.

The island ship was in worse condition than Donnin's, having taken the brunt of the waves. But fewer of their men were in the water, perhaps because they'd already been down low when the waves began to hit. Everyone was soaked, confused and afraid. Some were injured from the battle, but no one appeared to be dead. Rasim put his forehead to the deck, heart lurching with relief, then rolled out of the way as the shadow of Donnin's foot came at him. The kick missed and he rolled to his feet warily. "What was that for?"

She thrust an angry finger toward the ocean. "What do you think?"

Rasim gaped at her, then found it in himself to laugh. "You think *I* did that?"

"Water doesn't do that naturally, Ilyaran, and you're the only witch on board."

"I don't have that kind of power." Exhaustion swept Rasim, forcing him to lean against the ship's rail. If Donnin came after him with another blow, he wouldn't be able to escape it, but he couldn't bring himself to care. The three days since the serpent's attack had taken every ounce of his energy, and once more his ability to worry had faded with it.

"You have enough power."

Rasim couldn't tell whether Donnin was arguing

or making a statement about the magic he did command. Either way, she didn't seem about to hit him again, so he turned his attention to the flailing pirates in the water. Most of them clung to ropes or floating barrels now, not in any real danger, but for the space of a breath he considered the possibility that Donnin was right. That he had, in fact, commanded the sea to rise up and end the fight. If he had done it once, he might do it again, and lift the crew from the water.

Half-consciously mimicking the motions he'd seen Asindo and Hassin do, Rasim lifted both hands, swirling them around one another to shape a whirlpool. He extended his magic, reaching for the sea, encouraging it to swell.

And felt not even as much power within him as it took to purify water. He laughed again, a sharper and more bitter sound, and let his hands drop to the rail. "It was a rogue wave, Captain. Water caught between the two ships. That's all."

"It doesn't matter. You'll teach Carley to purify our water, and then—"

Rasim looked at Donnin, waiting on the pronunciation of his fate. But she only shook her head, dismissing whatever she'd been going to say, and for an instant he caught the glitter of greed in her gaze again. His stomach went cold. Without being told, he put himself to work helping to haul crew and goods from the ocean. If he made himself useful, maybe Donnin would reconsider whatever she had in mind for him.

Carley was one of the pirates he pulled from the sea. She gave him a hard look and went below to find dry clothes. Rasim let his own dry on his body, though he could have—maybe—pushed water from them with his witchery. Donnin didn't need to know that, though. Knowledge suddenly seemed precious, and he wanted to hoard it in case it was needed later as a bargaining tool.

The pirates were better off after the raid than before, though: food and clothes were rescued from the sea, and Rasim was finally able to gather enough power to desalinate enough water for everyone to drink their fill. Carley's humor improved, and with her approval, others treated Rasim more warmly. Donnin watched them all, though, and Rasim remembered too clearly how coolly she'd given the order to kill the soldiers on the other ship. He had no doubt the friendly overtures would evaporate if she gave the same order to finish him. He had no friends on the pirate ship, nor any likelihood of making them.

They'd drifted south during the fight and the clean-up. Rasim expected them to adjust course, but no one moved to. He was sent below to work with Carley again, and this time she turned a cup of brackish water almost palatable. "Maybe your swim did you some good," Rasim suggested.

She scowled. "I almost drowned."

"But now you know the water better."

"Do you have any idea how crazy you sound?"

"No," Rasim said thoughtfully. "Not really. Knowing your element is an important part of witchery. I grew up with people saying things like that. It doesn't seem crazy to me at all. And besides." He gestured at the water she'd altered. "Something changed. I'm sorry," he added after another moment. "Sorry about what happened to your sister."

Carley's face tightened, then softened a little. "Thanks. So you see why we do this."

"No. I'd understand if you were fighting the men who killed them, or if you went after the — what did you call him? An earl?" It wasn't a word Rasim knew in the common tongue, but it obviously connotated rank. "But these soldiers didn't do anything to you. Leaving them to die without water, or killing them outright, only makes things worse."

The older girl's scowl reappeared. "You're a very strange boy." She stomped out of the galley, leaving Rasim to say, "No," slowly, to her departing back. "I'm just used to being the one who gets picked on. It makes you think differently, that's all." He followed her, not to talk, but to climb the mast and sit in the crow's nest, where he could watch the emerging stars and judge the ship's place on the sea.

It took hours before he was certain, but by midnight he *was* certain: they were sailing in circles. Either they lacked the skill to sail in a straight line, or Donnin had no intention of returning to land. That would explain her need for fresh water, though it made no sense to Rasim if she was looking for vengeance. "Unless it's a fight she can't win," he said aloud.

Markus spoke from below him: "I wouldn't let her hear me say that, if I was you."

A thrill of cold rushed down Rasim's arms and made his hands icy. "I shouldn't have let anybody hear me say it."

"No," Markus agreed, "but especially the captain. Did you really not lift the waves to save that ship of soldiers?"

Rasim frowned. "I really didn't. I probably would have, if I had the power, but..." He trailed off with a shrug. "Why?"

"Because men like them killed my son, and I'd throw you to a serpent myself if I thought you'd helped them. You're too honest, Ilyaran. You should have just said *no.* How can we trust you if you admit you'd have saved them?"

"It's safer for you to trust me than the other way around. It's your ship."

"True enough." Markus swung up to the crow's nest, showing more grace than Rasim would have expected from a man Markus's size. "Carley told you about the baron, eh?"

Baron. Another word Rasim didn't know, but it must mean the same thing as *earl.* He nodded, and so did Markus. "He's got Donnin's girl, Adele. Donnin's bent on rescuing her."

"From soldiers in a fortress?"

Markus waved his hand. "A walled estate, at any rate."

It was close enough to make no difference. "So it really is a fight she can't win. She's safer sailing in circles and letting the crew think they're...what? On their way to find help?"

"Mmm. But it'll only last so long. They'll expect to make landfall, and to avenge their dead. She needs an army of her own, and coin to pay for it."

Rasim shuddered, fear creeping through him to latch chilly fingers at the back of his neck. "Why are you telling me this?"

Markus gave a heavy shrug. "I'll fight for her, and I'll kill for her, but I don't hold with selling one living soul to another, and that's what she has in mind for you, water witch. She might even just sell you to the Baron in exchange for her daughter. A witch who can turn salt water fresh is worth more than a pretty girl, to a soldier king."

It seemed to Rasim that cold had taken up a permanent place in his chest, a lump that would never quite go away. He belonged to the Seamasters' Guild. That meant he'd never feared being indentured or enslaved, though he knew outside of Ilyara orphans often suffered such a fate. And he was outside Ilyara now, and alone. It had never occurred to him what an Ilyaran witch might be worth to a people who had no magic of their own. He clenched his hands together to keep them from shaking, and wished he hadn't eaten anything earlier. It wanted to come back up now, a ball of sickness rising in his belly. Very quietly, he asked, "Will you help me escape?"

"If I can. Might be all I can do is warn you."

The sickness punched inside Rasim, producing a laugh that wasn't funny. "Thank you." He meant it, though he wasn't certain he was happier with the warning. Ignorance might have been more comfortable. More dangerous, too, though: if he suspected he might be sold, he could at least watch for the moment and be prepared to risk the sea instead of the slavers. He said, "Thank you," again, and didn't move when Markus climbed down to find a berth and sleep.

Rasim's life had been quite simple a fortnight earlier. He had hoped for a place on Asindo's ship that would someday allow him to become a captain. He'd expected a life as a shipwright or shore crew. It would have been bearable. Maybe not what he dreamed of, but he would have been with friends and worked hard at a craft he loved. He hadn't imagined a second fire, or uncovering the possibility that Ilyara's foreign queen and newborn heir might have been murdered. He certainly hadn't imagined the loss of his best friend, or a future in chains.

Terror rose in him again, a bleak empty space inside

that felt like he could fall into it forever. Rasim ducked his head against his knees, trying to push fear away, trying not to think about it, as if ignoring it would make it disappear. He didn't see how he could go on, his heart throbbing with worry, if he didn't push it away. There had to be something, some way to make it leave him alone, or he would just collapse of terror and be unable to save himself.

Eventually it proved there was something: sleep. He didn't know when he fell asleep, only that the golden dawn on the horizon awakened him, and that in the night his panic had passed into a sense of calm.

Serene, confident, and knowing being scared to death was only half a breath away, Rasim climbed down from the crow's nest to find Captain Donnin. She glanced at him dismissively, but did a double-take of interest when he spoke in a clear, certain voice: "What if I could give you an army?"

CHAPTER 12

Donnin hustled Rasim below deck before he said another word. She all but threw him into her cabin, slammed the door, and snarled, "What do you know?"

Good sense told him he should be afraid now, but he didn't dare give into it. The slavers or the sea: those were his obvious choices, so he had to force another one, one that he was more likely to survive. The thought hadn't even come to him consciously. He'd just awakened with it in his mind, and acted before he lost confidence in the idea.

Now he straightened to his full height, not tall enough to look Donnin in the eye, but straight-backed and proud, making himself feel better. "I know your people were killed in a raid by a nobleman. I know you want revenge and that your crew is mostly farmers and horsemen. You're surviving against other ships because they don't expect you, but you're going to get slaughtered if you try to get your daughter back. I can help you survive. I can help make sure *she* survives."

Donnin's nostrils flared. "I'm listening."

"I lied," Rasim said forthrightly. "My ship wasn't destroyed. I was thrown from it when I went after the serpent."

Donnin sneered. "So you think a single ship is going to turn the tide for me?"

"A ship full of sea witches? Yes, probably," Rasim said, "but my ship was only one of many. A third of the Ilyaran fleet is sailing north right now, Captain Donnin. If you want to save your daughter, all you have to do is catch up, and I'll ask them to help you." Rasim drew a deep breath and steeled himself. "But you have to do something for me, too."

Donnin barked incredulous laughter. "I hold all the cards here, Ilyaran. You're on my ship, in the middle of the ocean. What kind of bargaining position do you think you're in?"

The horrible coolness of the serpent's eye surrounding his arm, mashing against his face, rushed through Rasim's memory viscerally. He shoved the dread away and focused on remembering that he, a water witch of no particular skill, had slain a sea serpent single-handedly. It gave him the confidence to say, "I'm in a better bargaining position than you are, Captain. Without me you've got a day's worth of water left. Carley can barely make it palatable. You know it'll make your crew sick to drink what she purifies, and if they get sick you're that much weaker when you go to war. And I fought a sea serpent to death *under* the sea. Do you really think I can't make it to land if I have to? I'd rather not," he said judiciously, "but do you think I *can't*?"

Truthfully, he didn't think he could, but he didn't have to convince himself, only the captain. The greed had gone from her pale eyes, leaving suspicious hope. That was good: that meant he'd made her at least consider that he might have more value to her as a tool rather than a sale. "What do you want from me," she finally asked, grudgingly.

"This—earl? The one who's stolen your daughter. You don't just want to get her back, do you? You want to defeat him. To take his place as the leader of people."

Donnin's eyebrows shot upward. "Do I?"

"You must. Because just getting your daughter back isn't enough. If you rescue her and leave, that leaves him free to come after you. You have to destroy what he's got and take his place. So when we're done, *you're* going to have an army. And I might need it someday." He spoke quickly, his thoughts skipping ahead of his tongue like lightning dancing across the sea. He was so certain of himself it came as a shock when Donnin laughed.

"Gods, but you've got far-seeing eyes, haven't you, Ilyaran? Are you sure you're only thirteen?"

"I'm thirteen," Rasim muttered, "and clever." There was less pride in the last words than there once might have been. He hadn't been clever enough to save Kisia, and it remained to be seen if he was clever enough to save himself. He could see the things Donnin might need clearly enough, but she might not be willing to see them herself.

She exhaled sharply, almost a laugh. "Clever. I wonder who warned you that you'd need to be." Then she brushed it off, though Rasim doubted the question was laid to rest. "I was mistress of a fair estate," she went on. "Not an earldom, not a kingdom, but enough to be called a fiefdom, perhaps. We had lived in peace a long time, with a guard of twenty or so to keep our borders safe from brigands and highwaymen. The land wasn't lush enough to be coveted, and too far from any rivers to be a port stop. And too far north, for that matter, to interest other lords or ladies. Our winters are cold. Roscord had no real desire for the land, only for what he'd heard about me, until he realized I was too old to bear children."

Rasim eyed her. She looked to be Kisia's mother's age, and there were plenty of women in Ilyara that age who had a babe at breast. Donnin snorted at his expression. "I've fifty years on me, Ilyaran. They've been kind ones, that's all. Hah! Pull your jaw up, water witch, or you'll catch a fish in it. I was beautiful in my youth—"

Rasim blurted, "You still are," and for the first time Donnin's eyes gentled a little, though she also looked amused.

"Thank you, Ilyaran. I wasn't to Roscord's eyes, but my daughter was, and young besides. He took her instead of me, and my point," she said, drawing a breath, "was that yes, I have some knowledge of running an estate, and yes, you're right. I can't afford to leave him alive, nor to let someone else rise in his place. His lands and his people will be mine or I'll die trying."

"And if you don't die trying, you'll lend me an army when the fleet has helped you win your new lands."

"Half an army," Donnin said. "I'll need to protect myself, too. What does a cabin boy need an army for, anyway?"

Half an army would do. Rasim nodded, spat in his hand, and offered it to Donnin. Her nose wrinkled, but she did the same, and they shook hands before he said, "I might not need one at all, but it's always good to have resources." The corner of his mouth turned up. "Pull your jaw up, Captain, or you'll catch a fish in it."

Donnin snapped her mouth shut, though it sounded like she'd already swallowed a fishbone from the coughing and hacking behind sealed lips. "Why," she said when she'd finished choking on surprise, "why do you think you *might* need an army, Ilyaran?"

"There might be trouble at home," Rasim said quietly.

The captain's gaze sharpened again, but she must have sensed he had no intention of saying more, because after a moment she nodded and moved on. "How do we catch your fleet? No one in the world sails as fast as the Ilyaran ships, and they've two days' head start."

Rasim shrugged. "We catch them in the Northern capital, if we don't catch them before."

Carley could turn salt water fresh before they reached the north, to no one's surprise more than Rasim's. None of the others had been able to learn the magic, despite days of trying, but by all Guild dogma, not even Carley should have managed. The crew had drunk their fill in the days before she'd learned thanks to Rasim's efforts, but the morning she tended to the water barrels the ship drifted half a league off course while her friends celebrated. Rasim's mouth pinched as he watched them cavort, though he knew he was being absurd. These were not born sailors. It was amazing they'd gotten the ship out of port, never mind their fumbling ability to attack others or set a long-distance course. Still, it wasn't how an Ilyaran ship would be run. Rasim felt like a sour old captain watching cabin boys drunk on too much wine, not a cabin boy himself, surrounded by men and women ready to kill him if it meant their ends would be achieved.

Besides, he knew he'd already taught them too much. Not just in showing Carley how to purify water, but more worryingly, the crew had paid a great deal of attention when Rasim, frustrated by their ineptitude, had fallen into giving orders. He'd shown them how to best set sails to catch the wind, how to place the rudder to keep the ship from buckling too badly in high waves, and a dozen other small tricks to make the voyage quicker and safer. The pirates were far better sailors than they'd been when they took him on board a week earlier, and that knowledge could be to Ilyara's detriment.

On the other hand, he could have *swum* to the north more rapidly than they'd been making head-way under their earnest but unskilled attempts, so it had been teach them or lose all chance of reuniting with his fleet. They sailed through grey waters now, the sunlight slanting more obliquely and coloring the sea a greyer blue. Rasim had noticed the signs of land a time or two, but between the fish they caught and his — and Carley's — water witchery, he'd seen no need to point them out to Donnin. Like every sailor on the *Wafiya*, he knew the stars and sun's alignment that would bring them close to the Northern capital. If Siliaria was kind, they would see the Ilyaran fleet on the high seas, and Rasim would have the chance to plead his case before Captain Asindo.

He spent most of his time in the crow's nest, watching for the high masts that would mark the fleet. He had been on Donnin's ship two days before he suggested they sail north, and the pirates, despite his lessons, could not sail a ship as quickly as Ilyarans could. It had taken them a week to cover the distance the fleet would cover in four days, putting them five full days behind Asindo. In the worst scenario, the captain would have already convinced the Northerners of the Ilyaran cause and would have set sail south again, traveling more directly than the pirates and causing Rasim to miss his people entirely.

It didn't bear thinking about. If that was the case, Rasim *would* entrust himself to the water, and to the Northmen whose blood he shared, rather than to Donnin's need for coin to raise an army. He had begun to understand over the past week just how many uses a foreigner might have for a water witch. They were the same uses any merchant or trader might, of course: divining water along trade routes, making certain soldiers weren't sickened by bad water, washing infection away. In Ilyara those were such ordinary skills Rasim hadn't appreciated how much someone might be willing to pay to own them. It had come as a revelation, and for the first time he'd also realized why Ilyara's army and guard were so strong: the city and its people were far more valuable to the outside world than Rasim could have imagined.

It made the chances of the fires being deliberate, and the queen's death being murder, seem all the higher. There was clearly vast profit in conquering Ilyara.

"What I don't understand," he had said to Carley after drinking her first cup of sea water turned fresh, "is why only we have such strong magic. We're taught it's because the power is given to the Ilialio's children, to the orphans that each guild takes in. That gift is what makes us useful in our society. But you can learn it, and you're old —"

"I am *not* old!"

"You are for learning water witchery," Rasim said placidly. "So if islanders *can* learn it, why haven't you?"

"The lords don't like magic," Carley said with a shrug. "They say it's dangerous. That nobody right would practice it. And mostly we don't quite believe you can do it, either. Nobody turns salt water fresh."

"Every city on the Siliarian Sea has water witches," Rasim disagreed. "Ilyara has a lot more than most, but enough Northmen and islanders trade with us that they must know the magic is real."

"If you were a trader, would you come home and tell your liege there was magic down south and you hadn't been able to bring any back? Or would you keep your mouth shut about the strange things you saw, which were probably just tricks and slight of hand anyway? It's mostly traders and merchants who travel, not rich men, and you Ilyarans had better be glad of that."

She was right, he reflected now, his gaze still fixed on the horizon. It had changed, subtle shadows turning blue there, but he could only think of Carley's grim arguments. Some rich men *did* travel, and surely sailors told tales even when they shouldn't. Goddess knew Ilyaran ones did, at least. But he knew from Ilyara's history that it was rarely attacked, much less besieged. Maybe the strength of its army was as legendary as its magic was not, but a niggling itch inside Rasim's mind said there was more to it than that. He had never suspected there might be secrets about his home, but they seemed to be unfurling now, teasing at the corners of his mind. He wanted to understand those secrets, no matter what it took.

He startled, thoughts finally recognizing what his eyes had been watching for several minutes. Rasim jumped to his feet, caught the railing, and bellowed to the crew down below: "*Land ho!*"

CHAPTER 13

There was no fleet lingering between the pirate ship and the horizon. Rasim's nails dug into the railing wood, leaving gouges in the rail and splinters in his fingers. If the fleet was not still at sea, then perhaps they'd been invited into port. Five days. The pirates were only five days behind. Surely they hadn't missed the Ilyaran fleet entirely. Rasim tasted blood and winced, discovering he'd bitten his lip.

Carley swung up to the crow's nest for a better view, her gaze bright and excited on the horizon. "I've never met Northmen. I've heard they're all ten feet tall with huge beards and clawed feet like bears."

Rasim, distracted, gawked at her. "My father was a Northman. Do I look like he was ten feet tall or had bear feet?"

She gave him a dismissive glance. "No, but you're half Ilyaran." Then she looked again, more seriously. "You don't look happy."

"I'm fine." Not even he believed that, but Carley

shrugged and turned her attention back to the horizon. So did Rasim, searching for any signs of the tall ships his fleet sailed. Marks of the Northern capital were visible, smudges of smoke that blurred the air and a slight change in landscape that suggested a city buried in the depths of a long, narrow harbor. The Ilyaran ships should be obvious, but even as they came closer Rasim saw nothing of them. His heart sank, confidence seeping away. Without his fleet he had nothing to offer Donnin.

At least they were within sight of land, now. Cold as the water might be, with his witchery he could make it to safety. Nothing else mattered, though the idea of Donnin's daughter being left in the hands of her captor bothered him.

The coast became clearer. Sharp mountains capped with white rose straight out of grey water. Rasim peered at the mountaintops as Carley whistled. "Snow already. Winter comes early to the North."

"What's snow?"

Carley laughed, did a double-take, and laughed again when she saw he was serious. "I thought a water witch would know everything about snow. It's frozen water that falls from the sky."

"Like ice?" Rasim had heard that Guildmaster Isidri could make ice or boil water just by looking at it. Not many water witches could do that, and fewer still were willing to offer the service to the nobility. For a moment that, too, struck Rasim as strange: the guilds had so many talents that strangers would pay to access, and yet almost no one left the guilds to test those waters. Not that *Rasim* wanted to; the Guild was his life. Maybe others felt the same way.

"Sort of," Carley was saying drolly, "but softer, and prettier. I can't believe you don't know what snow is. It doesn't come until winter, but winter's not for another six weeks at home. It's cold here."

"We don't have winter at all, just floods." Rasim studied the approaching horizon again. They had to be in the right place: vast stone carvings rose at the harbor's mouth, a fish-tailed god with a sword on one side and a fierce trident-bearing goddess on the other. The warning was plain enough: a city that would protect itself lay beyond those statues. The water turned crystal blue past that gateway, shallower but still plenty deep for a harbor. Narrower and calmer, too; Rasim could see how waves lost their force as they slid through the gates. A minute or two later so did the pirate ship, and Rasim caught his breath.

The mountains truly did soar straight up from the water, no beach to break their rise. Thin trees with spiny leaves ran halfway up the mountains, then faded to bare rock before the snow-stuff blanketed the tops. The harbor was wide enough here, but continued to narrow as it bent around a sharp curve. Rasim glanced up to see thin rope bridges stretching from one side of the harbor's tall mountainous walls to the other. That was clever: Northmen could cross without the need of a boat, which was no doubt useful from time to time. He turned his attention back to the upcoming curve, where the outermost docks were visible. Buildings carved right into the mountain faces also came clear, just a few at the curve, but promising many more beyond it.

"You know," Rasim said slowly, "we probably should have taken the flag down before we passed through the gates..."

Three dozen Northmen fell from the rope bridges above, and took the ship.

They cascaded past Carley and Rasim, either not seeing them or not caring, and landed on the deck below with the casual confidence of people who had done this hundreds of times. Chaos broke out below, Donnin's crew panicking, racing for weapons, for ropes, even throwing themselves overboard. The Northmen, armed with short swords and clawed ropes, caught all but a few of the crew before they'd even gone a few steps. Markus threw one mighty punch that felled a Northman. The fallen man's nearest companion gave a belly laugh before clobbering Markus on the back of the head with a sword hilt.

Carley swallowed a shriek, both hands clapped over her mouth. Rasim gaped upward. He had looked at the ropes up there only seconds before. There had been no Northerners visible, not even any bowing to the ropes to hint at their weight. Now there were dangling chunks of metal on the ropes, things that looked like perhaps the Northerners had slid rapidly along the ropes from the cliffs on either side of them. More were coming, in fact, doing just that. Rasim could hear the zip of metal against rope as they swung toward Donnin's ship.

Rasim seized Carley's hand, hissing, "Can you swim?"

"What? No!"

"Siliaria's fins!" Rasim scrambled onto the crow's nest railing, suddenly dizzy with a horrible familiarity. He hauled Carley up with him, trying to shake off the memory of the last time he'd done this. "Push with your legs when you jump so you clear the sails and the side of the ship."

"*What?* I'm not ju —"

"I'll get you to shore. Your other choice is *them.*" He pointed toward the Northmen, two of whom were scaling the rigging already. "Carley, we've got to find my fleet, if we don't none of this is ever going to get explained, now *jump!*" At the last moment he released her arm, unwilling to be held back by Carley's weight if she didn't jump as well.

Diving into the cold Northern harbor was far less frightening than leaping onto a sea serpent. Rasim hit the water smoothly, hands above his head to break the surface. Cold shocked his breath away, but he laughed into the water, magic pressing it away to create a bubble of air so he could breathe.

Carley, to his astonishment, hit the water a few feet away. She landed like a stone, all splash and no finesse, then began thrashing and screaming. Rasim dove deeper, grabbed her ankle, and hauled her beneath the surface into his circle of water. She screamed again. Rasim clapped his hand over her mouth and brought his face closer to hers. "Quiet. *Quiet.* You're safe, but if you keep screaming you're going to use up all our air. If you don't fight me I can swim us to safety."

Carley's nostrils flared like a horse's, her breathing sharp and punctuated with panic. She nodded, though, and Rasim slowly released her mouth. She seized his shirt. "You're *talking under water.*"

"We're talking in an air bubble I brought with us. Now relax so I can pull you with me." He flipped her around so her back was against his chest, and slid an arm over one of her shoulders, securing his fist her other armpit. "Just relax," he said again. "I'm a strong enough swimmer to get us out of here if you don't struggle."

Carley wrapped her hands around his forearm, but nodded, the motion restricted by his arm crossing nearly under her chin. Rasim took one more deep breath himself, though he knew the air wasn't going to run out, and dove deeper. A current caught them almost immediately, throwing them the wrong direction. Rasim let it sweep them along, not fighting it, until he caught the sense of a counter-current running beneath them. He kicked, encouraging the water above them to press down a little more, and within seconds they rode the second current, moving swiftly toward the sharp bend in the harbor's layout.

The sea swept by that bend at enormous speed, flinging them forward. Rocky outcrops were sharp and dangerous, not yet smoothed by endless waves. This was a relatively new harbor, then, only cut away by the sea recently. A long time in man's terms, maybe — long enough to build a great city here — but very little compared to the patience of the ocean. Within moments the current brought them into quieter waters, though Rasim could feel the water crash against the stone sea walls ahead. Ships were above them now, big bellies a reassuring shape in the water. Rasim dove deeper, finding an anchor dug into the sand, and latched onto it. If the current couldn't move it, it wouldn't move them, either. "Carley, wrap one arm around the chain. Good. Hold on tight."

His nose was an inch or two away from hers, and they crossed eyes trying to look at one another. Rasim grinned. "And don't let go of me either. Are you all right?"

"I'm at the bottom of a Northern harbor, holding onto a North ship's anchor and a crazy Ilyaran. What do *you* think?"

"I think you're not dead or captured."

Carley hesitated, then shrugged agreement. "Now

what?"

Rasim sighed. "I see ladders built into the sea wall, but those will just bring us up on the docks, which will get us caught. I have to find Asindo, and none of these ships are ours."

Carley peered dubiously where he pointed. "You do? I can't see anything. How can you tell who built a ship from below?"

"The water feels different where it hits metal instead of stone," Rasim said absently. "Maybe 'see' isn't quite the right word, but I know it's there. And it's easy to tell, if you've ever built a ship. They all have keels, but the Northern ships have really heavy keels and a narrow hull. Ours are lighter and broader. And that one over there is Donnin's ship, the one coming into the harbor now."

"If you say so."

"It is," Rasim said with confidence. "See the joinings at the kee—" Carley gave him a look and he broke off with a shrug. "Well, it is. Anyway, we need to find a way in that isn't right off the docks, and the only thing I can think of is the sewers."

Carley reared back, disgusted. Rasim barely snagged her before she broke out of their air bubble. "Be careful! I know it's nasty, but we'll freeze if we stay in the water until nightfall. Well, we'd drown first, I don't have nearly that much air for us, but if we didn't drown we'd freeze, because I can't keep us warm."

"You're so calm." Carley sounded bemused. "Sitting

underwater talking about swimming through sewers and maybe drowning or freezing and you just sound like it's an ordinary day."

Rasim gave a low laugh. "I've had a rough couple of weeks."

"Does it have to be the sewers?"

"I think so. Just try to remember the air we're breathing is clean, and hold on."

Carley muttered something Rasim was just as glad not to understand, and wrapped her arms around Rasim's neck. He swung her around again into the carrying position, then pushed off the anchor, swimming against the current to where he felt water pouring into the harbor from underwater pipes.

Surprisingly *clean* water, when he reached the outpour. Ilyaran sewerage was fresh, the offal separated out and buried, and the rest purified by water witches. This Northern sewer pipe poured water nearly that clean out, too. Rasim hung in the sea a moment, feeling fresh water crash against salt, and wondered if the Northerners had magic, too. If they did, someone should have told the Ilyaran people thirteen years ago. They might have embraced their Northern queen more willingly, then.

It didn't matter now. Rasim went against the tide of sewer water. Darkness enveloped them within a few feet, daylight unable to penetrate the upward angle of the sewer tunnel. The water wouldn't respond to his urging, continuing to rush downward while he kicked hard to swim upstream. He was not yet out of air, but the memory of fighting the serpent, of air fading, began to build worry in his gut. He would have to decide soon whether to keep struggling upward or whether to let the water take them back to the harbor, where at least he could get them to the surface before they drowned.

All at once he went above sea level and his head broke through tumbling water. It *smelled* like a sewer, anyway. Rasim coughed and Carley gagged, both of them fumbling to get a grip on the tunnel's sides, which were aggravatingly smooth. Water had no doubt polished them, but they had never been natural: man or magic had almost certainly made these smooth round slides leading to the harbor. Rasim gasped with the effort of trying to drag himself up against the downward spill of water.

Carley, considerably taller than Rasim, flung herself an extra few inches forward and gave a yelp of triumph. "Here, I found a crack, there's a —" She offered him one hand and hauled him up, past the crack she'd found. Rasim dug his fingertips against the stone, finding another crack, like the stone had seams. He took a breath, then, grunting, pulled Carley up and past him, the way she'd done for him. She seized another crack, and they slowly launched each other upward against the rushing water, a very long distance indeed. Rasim's arms trembled with effort until every time he dragged Carley up he thought he couldn't do it again. He kept the thought quiet, though, telling himself he could do it just one more time, until Carley landed with a *splat* that sounded unlike their previous efforts.

She crowed, "It's flat!", before the sound of her own hand slapping over her mouth echoed down the tunnel. "Sorry," she whispered. "I didn't think that would be so loud. Hang on." She pulled him up onto a much flatter surface beside her.

Water still ran around them at high speed, but they'd clearly reached a gathering place. Rasim could hear it falling from pipes all around, then splashing down into the area they'd discovered. A dim glow became obvious well above their heads, and after a minute of heaving for breath, Rasim got to his feet. The water came to his knees. "Do you see that?"

"I'm trying not to because I don't think we can reach it." Despite her dour comment, Carley stood up as well. "Maybe if you stood on my shoulders?"

"I should have gotten rope from the ship before we jumped."

"You could always go back and get some."

Rasim laughed. "Can you boost me? I'll try to get into one of those runoff tunnels and see if I can reach from there. I should be able to keep the water from pushing me out of the tunnel, anyway."

"You want me to stand under one of those runoffs?"

Even in the dark, her expression was obvious. Rasim smiled apologetically and reached for her hand. They edged across the pool floor cautiously, Rasim glancing up and trying to judge if any particular runoff tunnel was closer to the dim light above. They didn't seem to be, so when water from the first one hit him, he shuddered and said, "Here. We'll try here."

Carley made a stirrup of her hands. Rasim stepped into it, cold wet feet in cold wet fingers. They both made sounds of disgust, and Carley gave a short hard laugh before flinging Rasim upward with all her strength.

He went higher than he expected, nearly touching the ceiling before they both overbalanced and crashed back to the floor in a series of shouts, groans and splashes. Rasim sat up shaking his head like a wet dog, and Carley moaned as she dragged herself back out of the water. "That didn't work."

"No," Rasim said eagerly, "But I got really close to whatever's up there. Try again. Just don't throw me so hard. Let me get a foot into the runoff tunnel, and then try to step back onto your shoulders. I might be able to reach the ceiling. You just have to hold me there long enough to see if I can move the door."

"It's a door now?"

"It's round and light's seeping through," Rasim said almost grimly. "It has to be a door. Ready?"

Carley grunted assent. She didn't lift so violently this time, and Rasim scrambled into the runoff tunnel, fingers pinched against its top to keep himself from falling. "I'm in! I'm looking for your shoulder with my foot now!" He waved his foot in the air until Carley grabbed it and guided it to her shoulder. "Are you ready?" Rasim asked.

"No. How much do you weigh?"

"Less than a water barrel?"

"I can't hold a water barrel!"

"Good thing I weigh less than one, then!"

"Fine, just...be careful!"

"Believe me, I will be." Rasim inched his toes forward until he had his arch centered on Carley's shoulder muscle, then swallowed hard. "Can you reach my other ankle? All right, when I put weight on you, try to get my foot to your shoulder right away. One, two, thrEEEEEEE!"

Rasim clenched his stomach, trying to maintain balance as Carley staggered beneath him. She staggered the right direction, though: toward the center of the room, as he flailed and tried to stay upright. Carley bellowed, "Push, push, open it!" and he scraped his fingernails along the door's underside.

"I'm not tall enough!"

"Curse it!" Carley roared and somehow surged up, shoving Rasim higher. He flattened his palms against the door and pushed with all his strength.

It lifted aside with surprising ease. Carley howled a warning and collapsed beneath him.

A strong pair of hands seized Rasim's wrists and hauled him upward.

CHAPTER 14

For one wild instant Rasim thought somehow Desimi had found him. No one else had ever dragged him out of tight spaces before, though normally Desimi did it to *cause* trouble, and this time Rasim was the one *making* trouble. But the man holding him bore no resemblance to Desimi at all, save for his general largeness. His hair was yellow, his eyes blue, and the pale skin of his face was faintly pink from the effort of dangling a boy in mid-air.

Rasim couldn't tell which of them, himself or the giant man, was more astonished. The big man said something incomprehensible. His tone was amused, a lilt at the end of his phrase, but Rasim shook his head. "I don't understand. Do you speak the common tongue?"

The man had eyebrows like sea urchins, the hairs thick, long, and prickly. They rose up, causing trench-deep lines to appear in the man's forehead. He said "Nei," which was clearly enough *no* that Rasim nodded in understanding. The man, without changing expression, threw Rasim over his shoulder and left the open sewerage hole behind.

"Wait!" Rasim thumped on the giant's back, then kicked his feet, trying to squirm around to get the man's attention. "Wait, my friend is back there! Someone else is in the hole! Carley! *Carley!* Say something!"

"Something like 'GET ME OUT OF HERE!'?" Carley called back.

The giant stopped, held Rasim out again in even greater astonishment, and spoke a second time. Rasim, guessing what he said, slumped in his grip. "Yes, there are two of us. And she'll get sick of cold if she's down there much longer, so please get her out."

With the same lilting cadence, the man said something involving gods — Rasim picked that word out, at least — and stomped back to the hole to look in. Rasim twisted to look, too. Carley stood directly below, arms folded across her chest in challenge. The giant repeated himself, then set Rasim aside with a warning waggle of one thick finger. Rasim lifted his hands, muttering, "I'm not going anywhere, I promise."

This was not how he'd expected his daring sneak into the city to end. He pressed water from his clothes with a touch of magic, shocked at how wearying even that tiny use of power was. The room they'd broken into was a simple one, round and build of stone. Not magically round, either: mortar held the bricks in place, ordinary workmanship, if well-done. He'd been placed in a large wooden chair next to an even larger wooden table. Wood carvings, a book, and maps were spread over the table, as well as a mug of fruity-smelling alcohol and a plate of bread, meat and cheese.

The giant fetched a rope from beneath the table, made a loop of it, and sent it down to haul Carley up. He wore a leather breastplate and greaves over a woven shirt and pants, and a huge sword at his side. Not a casual passer-by, then: he had been placed there to watch the manhole.

What kind of people, Rasim wondered, bothered to set a guard on a sewerage room?

The kind of people who caught enterprising trespassers, if nothing else. Carley scraped over the edge of the hole, flopped on her back, and said a fervent, "*Thank* you," to the giant. Rasim glowered at her and she scowled back. "I don't care if we got caught, it's better than being knee-deep in a stinking sewer. You're *dry,*" she accused.

Rasim looked guiltily at the puddle of mostly-clear water around him. The giant, alerted by Carley's tone, glanced Rasim's way, took in his dry clothes and the damp on the floor, and went momentarily still. It was a very large stillness, taking up more than its fair share of space in the room. Then the giant shook it off, picked Carley up, put her on her feet, and pointed imperiously at Rasim.

Rasim was nothing like fool enough to refuse him. The only way out was back into the sewers, and that would leave him where they'd been an hour earlier: at the bottom of a harbor with nowhere else to go.

He got up and followed the giant, who herded Carley in front of him and still managed to keep an eye on Rasim trailing behind. More than once he bodily turned Carley the direction he wanted her to go. More than once she threw his hand off with a curse, but neither of them seemed genuinely bothered by the other's behavior. It was as if they both agreed that was how captor and captive should behave. It made Rasim wonder what Donnin would have done if he'd been more obstreperous.

Probably throw him overboard before she discovered his skills were of use to her. Which would mean he wouldn't be here to try to get her and her crew out of trouble with the Northmen, never mind that they wouldn't be anywhere near the Northerners if he hadn't suggested they sail this direction. The circular thought made Rasim's head hurt. He hoped fervently that the giant was bringing them to someone who would know Captain Asindo. The captain would listen, and they would get everything sorted out.

The building became more elaborately decorated and warmer as the guard ushered them through halls. Bare stone walls had small tapestries, then large ones, then enormous ones, depicting great battles with sea serpents and other legendary creatures. Rasim tripped over his own feet trying to study one, but their captor clucked his tongue and scooted him along. Narrow windows became larger, giving Rasim glimpses of a city carved from the mountain, and of glittering blue water in the harbor. The sky was pale, laced with thin clouds, and from inside warm walls, it looked cold out there. But inside even the floor was warm, as if they strode over the kitchens, though not even a palace this size could have kitchens that spread its entire length. Rasim didn't care. It warmed his feet, which was all that mattered.

Carley was leaving fat water droplets as she marched along. Rasim thought about squeezing past the guard to dry her clothes, but stopped himself. The giant already knew Rasim was no longer wet, and maybe recognized the magic that had dried him. It wouldn't be smart to *prove* he had magic, not until he got to Asindo and had someone on his side.

Ahead of them, a set of double doors was thrown open to let them in. Rasim's shoulders loosened from a hunch he hadn't even known he was holding. That was a friendly gesture, the opening of the doors. Beyond them would lie the chance at explanation.

The giant guard booted them into a tremendously large room, slammed the door behind him, and spoke rapidly in his upward-lilting language. Rasim, unable to understand a word, edged closer to Carley as they both gaped around themselves.

The floor was white marble, polished until it reflected the room. A long dark wood table sat toward the room's far side, emphasizing how large the room itself was: more than a dozen people sat at the table, comfortably spread out, and it still looked small within the room's size.

White columns of rough-cut, sparkling stone soared upward, holding a domed ceiling as airy and light as anything Rasim had ever seen in Ilyara. But this one was painted brilliantly with scenes of battle. Not just sea serpents, but dragons and minotaurs and innumerable other creatures Rasim had no name for. Pale-skinned men and women fought them: either the gods or their children, from their beauty and evident strength. Some of the paintings spilled down the walls, partially blocked by the glittering columns. Rasim had the impression the images were unfinished, that new feats and deeds were added as the children of the gods continued their fight against monsters of the deep.

He shivered at the thought and took his eyes from the ceiling to see who their captor was talking to.

A woman stood up from table. She was dressed in red with a white kirtle and belt decorated with the same glittering stone that made up the walls. Her hair was paler yellow than the guard's, and worn in the thickest, longest braid Rasim had ever seen. Even Guildmaster Isidri's braid was narrower, and Isidri's was as wide as Rasim's wrist. A red ribbon, like Isidri's blue one, was woven through the woman's braid. She was a guildmaster, then, or something like one.

She was also amazingly tall. As she came closer, Carley backed up until she ran into the guard, then went stiff as a mouse hoping an eagle wouldn't notice it. There was something aquiline about the woman, in fact, though it was maybe only the sharp clarity of her blue eyes. It certainly wasn't her features, which were broad and square, not sharp in any way. She stopped in front of Rasim, and to his utter shock, spoke flawless Ilyaran: "A Seamasters' Guild journeyman would *typically* come in through the front door, young man. Whatever possessed you to use the sewers?" Her clear blue gaze snapped to Carley, then back again. "Presumably your companion persuaded you to a more unusual means of entrance."

Rasim blurted, "No," then swallowed. "I mean, she didn't talk me into it, but she's from—"

He stopped sharply and the woman said, "The islands," so dryly Rasim thought she might be teasing him. He nodded, though he'd been going to say *the pirate ship*, not *the islands*. The woman also nodded, clearly understanding what he hadn't said. "There are other islanders here," she said, still dryly. "Perhaps you know them?"

"Are there other *Ilyarans* here?" Rasim asked desperately. He would defend the pirates—explain them, at least—but he badly wanted to do it with Asindo and Hassin standing beside him. Clever or not, he was barely a journeyman, and he was trying to propose alliances that would be hard-won by master negotiators.

The woman's eyebrows furled. "A few, as there are usually a few Northmen in Ilyaran cities. Why?"

Hope drained from Rasim, leaving his face long with dismay. "Only a few? The fleet hasn't come?"

"The Ilyaran fleet? *Here?* No, lad, nor would I want them to. My people would imagine an invasion, and your pirate ship's greeting would be gentle in comparison." The tall woman studied Rasim's expression, then let go a long, quiet sigh. "I can see this is as bad news for you as a fleet on my doorstep would be for me. You're pale. When did you eat last? Never mind. Gontur," she said to the giant guard still behind Rasim and Carley, then changed languages, speaking in the North's uplifting lilt. He grunted assent, and the woman flicked her fingertips at Rasim and Carley. "Go with him, children," she said in the common tongue. "He'll bring you to a bath and get you new clothes and food. Myself or Lorens will be along shortly."

Having dismissed them, she turned away as if they'd never been there, and returned to her business at the long table. Rasim lingered a few seconds, peering over Gontur's arm to see where the woman sat. At one end of the table: a man, perhaps Lorens, sat at the other, but Rasim had no sense of either being at its foot or head. It was more evenly divided than that, somehow, equal power balancing the seating arrangements. She was at least as important as a Guildmaster, then, maybe more so.

As Gontur herded them out, Carley whispered the question Rasim was wondering: "Why's the Northern *queen* bothering with *us?*"

CHAPTER 15

Whether the sewerage water was relatively fresh or not, whether Rasim was able to dry himself through magic or not, clean dry clothes after a bath were profoundly welcome. The food was even more so, even though it was strange. Fish, but different, oilier fish than Rasim was accustomed to, and meat from something Gontur called a *rain deer* when Rasim pointed at it curiously. A rain deer sounded like an animal that water witches might have use for, or that anyone in a desert might want to breed. It was gamey but tasty, and a welcome change after the fare on Donnin's ship.

He and Carley sat close together, with a solidarity born from worry. They had thought they might be reunited with Donnin's crew, but they'd been brought to a room of their own. It was far less impressive than the council room they'd visited, but warmer due to its smaller size, and much more comfortable. A wood table, gleaming with oil, was surrounded by cushioned chairs. The table and chairs were placed an equal distance from a low-banked fire as a large bed was, balancing the room's warmth nicely.

Rasim's whole body trembled with tiredness when he looked at the bed, so he'd chosen a chair with its back to the bed, and Carley had taken the chair beside him. Even knowing Gontur didn't speak the common tongue, they hunched together quietly, reluctant to even speculate about why the Northern queen had bothered with them herself.

They both startled when a knock came at the door, Carley sloshing her mead onto the table. Chagrined, she mopped it up as the door swung open. Rasim stood, nervousness churning his belly.

A bearded man not quite as tall or yellow-haired as the woman came in, glanced at them and the table, and helped himself to a mug that he filled with mead before flinging himself into a chair opposite them. The chair scooted back several inches and tipped onto two legs. The man swore, threw his weight back the other direction, and slurped mead off his hand as the chair settled down. Only then did he say, in the common language, "I'm Prince Lorens. You can call me Lorens. You spoke with my sister Inga earlier. Who are you?"

Rasim said, "I'm Rasim," at the same time Carley said, "Carley sona Donnin," and the Northern prince waved a hand in exasperation, nearly spilling his mead again. Rasim thought he was young, though his yellow beard helped to hide it. Younger than Inga, anyway, and she hadn't been old. The beard also helped to hide the fact that Lorens was more finely-featured than his sister: without the beard, he might have been almost pretty. Like Hassin, except with the color bleached out. Rasim wondered if women liked Lorens as much as they liked Hassin, but the prince interrupted his thoughts with another question. "Not your names, though yes, it's splendid to meet you, Rasim. Carley."

The smile he gave Carley — and the one he got in return — suggested he *was* as good with girls as Rasim's shipmate. Rasim grinned and Carley blushed, glaring at Rasim like he'd done something wrong. Surprised and a little offended, Rasim folded his arms over his chest and scowled at the table. The prince shifted, making Rasim look at him again. Lorens's expression was curious, almost apologetic. "Who *are* you? Why, of all the men and women flying under that flag, did you sneak off the ship? You're one Ilyaran," he said to Rasim. "You don't belong on an islander ship at all, much less one flying a pirate flag."

"I got lost from my fleet," Rasim said stiffly. "A sea serpent dragged me away. Captain Donnin rescued me. Sort of."

Carley hissed, "*Sort* of? We rescued you entirely!"

"It's not much of a rescue if you're going to be sold into slavery the minute the chance arises," Rasim snapped back.

Clarity flowed across Lorens's face as swiftly as

shock rushed over Carley's. The prince only said, "Go on," though, and Rasim, defiant with anger, said, "I'm a Seamasters' Guild journeyman. Captain Donnin thought I'd be worth enough to slavers that she could hire an army with the coin, so her crew could avenge their dead and try to rescue her daughter, who was kidnapped by a nobleman. I told her I'd talk my fleet into helping her if she'd just catch up to them, so we came north to find them."

"That," Lorens said after a moment, "is not *quite* the same story Donnin gave us."

Rasim, still angry, said, "I imagine not."

Carley finally rallied, her spine straight and eyes bright with indignation. "Captain Donnin would *never*—"

"Ask Markus," Rasim said flatly. "He's the one who warned me about the slavers. Do you really think she wouldn't have? You were already out there stealing water and lives. What's one more, if it rescues her daughter? I was afraid I wouldn't have a chance to tell what had happened if I was taken with the pirates," he said to Lorens. "I jumped overboard and brought Carley with me."

"As a hostage?"

Carley burst out laughing, outrage turning to surprised humor. "No. I didn't want to be caught either. A hostage? Really? I'm five inches taller than he is and weigh more. And I know more about using a sword than he does too."

Lorens shrugged. "And he's a witch. We might have listened, Rasim. You're the only Ilyaran on board, and your people aren't known for working for others."

It was as much opportunity as he might be granted. Rasim blurted, "But sometimes we ask for help. Please, where's Captain Asindo? Where's my *fleet*? We lost at least four to the serpent, but we can't have lost them all, we—"

It was as if Lorens hadn't heard his first comment about the serpent. The prince stiffened now, coming out of his casual position to sit straight in the chair. "You meant it, about the sea serpent?"

"We saw its body," Carley confessed. "Rasim said he killed it."

Lorens's face went long with surprise. "Did you, now. How?"

"I let it take me underwater and stabbed it through the eye," Rasim said shortly.

The prince stared at him wordlessly a few long moments, then made a brief expression of acknowledgment. "We'll have to add you to the mural. Lad, do you know they swim in pods? Where there's one there are usually three, sometimes five. We think they swim as families, with the young eventually leaving its parents to start a new pod. Lucky for sailors they seem to breed slowly, or the sea would be overrun and no ship would be safe."

Rasim's knees went weak as jelly. He fumbled for his chair, couldn't find it, and leaned on the table.

His arms trembled with the effort of holding himself, but he couldn't even feel his legs, wouldn't believe they were still there if he didn't see his feet on the floor. He hadn't imagined more serpents. One had destroyed four or five ships in seconds. Three more could have wiped the fleet out while Rasim still fought the first.

Bad enough to have lost Kisia. The thought of having lost practically everyone he'd ever known overwhelmed Rasim. His arms gave way, too, and he sat down hard. Into his chair, which scraped across the floor unexpectedly and caught him behind the knees. He caught a glimpse of Carley's concerned face as he sat and thought she must have pushed the chair under him, but the rush of blood was like a riptide in his ears, and his vision filmed until he saw nothing but white water. He put his head down, trying to catch his breath, and distantly felt Carley pat his back in concern, then awkwardly withdraw.

His thoughts felt thick and slow, devastated by the idea of the fleet being gone. It took forever to manage a few raw words: "I...can I stay here? Until you send a ship south? I can work to earn my keep..."

"You are welcome to asylum in the Northlands as long as you need it," Lorens said gently. "Winter is coming and the harbors become ice-bound. If my mother allows it, we'll send a ship south immediately, to bring you home, but you may have to wait the winter out."

Rasim, blankly, said, "Your mother?"

"The queen. It will take a few days to get word to her. We share the royal duties between our two largest cities, and travel back and forth twice a year, but she went north again weeks ago. At least you'll be sailing from here, instead of there. They'll be frozen over soon, but we should have a little more time before the ice comes."

"He's a water witch," Carley muttered. "A little ice shouldn't stop him from sailing."

For once Rasim had no heart to argue about his lack of skills. He only nodded and drew his feet up, making himself as small on the chair as possible. Forehead against his knees, voice muffled, he said, "I made Donnin a promise. If the fleet is lost, the only people I can ask to keep it are your own, Prince Lorens. Would you even consider it?"

Carley made a sound of astonishment. Rasim lifted a dull gaze to watch her clap her mouth shut, but she then whispered, "Why would you even ask, if she was going to sell you?"

Sudden strong anger made Rasim's stomach twist with sickness. "Because I'm better than she is. Maybe I'm not brave enough to sail back with her, even if I promised her sea witches. Not alone, not when she wanted to sell me, but I can at least ask for help. Besides," he added more bitterly, "maybe if she gets home safely someone can put her on trial for acts of piracy. How many soldiers did your crew kill, out there on the sea?"

Carley looked away and Rasim's gut twisted again, loss souring any thought of apology. "Still, losing her lands, her people, her daughter, that wasn't her fault," he said in a low voice, to the Northern prince. "I know you have no reason to help her, but at the least her daughter doesn't deserve to have been taken, and she's done nothing wrong. A ship of Northmen would make a lot of recruited soldiers think twice about fighting."

"Your plea is noted," Lorens murmured. "You surprise me, Rasim. You'd be well within your rights to be more bloody-minded."

"Everyone I know is probably dead. How much more bloody do I need to get? Please, can I just be left alone for a while? I don't feel good."

Lorens stood, sympathy aging his youthful features. "No, I don't imagine you do. Carley, I'll bring you to your captain, if you wish, and myself or my sister will come to visit you again soon, Rasim."

Rasim nodded, and didn't watch as the others walked away.

CHAPTER 16

Wrung out with sorrow, Rasim slept until sunset, only wakening when bells rang a late afternoon hour. He stumbled to the window, confused by the early Northern darkness, and watched as stars broke above the horizon. The constellations were placed differently in the sky than at home. He'd known that, of course. He'd watched them shift as they sailed north, but it was different to see it from land, and to watch them peek over nearby mountains instead of the sea's distant curve.

Someone had come in while he napped, leaving a platter of food and a jug of watered ale. The food, eaten from his curled-up spot in the window seat, helped a little, though mostly he was still too tired to feel very much.

The idea of remaining in the North over the winter was tempting. It would be time to get used to the idea of the fleet being lost, and it would be time to see a part of the world he might never again visit. *Would* never again visit, if Ilyara had to rebuild its fleet for the second time in twenty years, and this time without the expertise of half its older and wiser heads.

But a question remained in Ilyara, too. The question of what had happened to Annaken: the question of whether the fires had been set deliberately and she had been murdered. A long winter in the north might mean nothing, in terms of discovering the truth. Or it might mean everything. Asindo had known of the possibility of murder, and no doubt Guildmaster Isidri did too, but many of the others who might have suspected foul play were likely dead now, cold corpses at the bottom of the sea.

For a sick instant Rasim wondered if the serpent could have been raised deliberately. Wondered if it was possible that the fleet had come under attack not just from sea monsters, but from some astounding magic that controlled them. For a horrible moment he distrusted even the Ilyaran fleet. But then he remembered the serpent's whistle-like blast. The beast had responded to the whistles sounding the shift change, nothing more. In most respects it was probably luck alone that had kept serpents from attacking Ilyaran ships in the past. Luck, and the fact that there were rarely as many as thirty whistles shrilling at once. The fleet didn't often sail together in such numbers.

Rasim would still mark the maps when he returned home, though: *here be serpents.* The terrible creatures must have a usual range they swam in, and it would be of use to have that noted.

A tap sounded at the door, polite knock that wouldn't waken a sleeping lad. Rasim got up to answer it, stiff from hunching in the window. Inga, looking as diffident as a woman of her height could, waited there with a jug of warm scented wine in her hands. Her face brightened when he opened the door. "Oh, good. I didn't wake you, did I?"

"No. Come on in." Rasim stood back, letting the princess past. His head didn't come up to her shoulder. He wondered how old she was, and whether he'd be as tall as she was when he'd reached his height.

"I brought wine. The rooms sometimes get chilly, and it's never as warm here as Ilyara." She spoke his language as if she'd been born to it. Rasim felt a flash of envy for that skill: he would like to know her tongue as well as his own. The common tongue was just that, useful but not personal to any particular people. Inga offered to pour him a cup of the wine, and he nodded.

"Not too much, please. I only drink it watered."

"Lorens could learn a thing or two from you." Inga poured two cups, hers with considerably less water than his own, then sat in the same chair as Lorens had, though with far more dignity. "I'm sorry for your loss, Rasim. My brother told me what had happened. Captain Donnin," she added with a lift of her eyebrows, "is astounded that you spoke on her behalf."

Rasim wrapped his hands around his wine cup and sat down, muttering, "So am I."

Inga flashed a smile. "We've sent a rider seek our mother's advice regarding Captain Donnin, but we probably won't help her."

"I know." Rasim drew a breath. "You might be able to help me, though. Not just to go home, but my fleet was coming here to ask about..." He couldn't think of a polite way to say it. "About spies. About spies you might have in Ilyara. About anybody who might help us to learn if the Great Fire was an accident or not. And—"

The princess's eyes darkened with interest, and she raised a hand to stop what he had to say next. "Do you have reason to believe it may not have been an accident?"

"There was another fire a few weeks ago. We put it out, but it didn't act naturally. It had to be quenched by sand, not water, and it stuck to the walls." Rasim felt he was fumbling the explanation, but hurried on regardless. "It happened in daylight so people could see it. The Great Fire was at night, and destroyed so much—I don't think there was anything left to show whether it stuck to the walls or wouldn't go out properly. But if this one wasn't an accident, then maybe the last one wasn't either, and..." He faltered. "If it wasn't an accident, then everyone who died was murdered, including..."

"Including Annaken." Inga was quiet a while, looking into her wine cup. "She was my aunt. My mother's youngest sister. I was fifteen when she went to marry your king. She was only nineteen herself. And now I'm thirty-two, and she has been dead for more than a dozen years. I still miss her very much. If there's a chance she died by murder and not accident, then we'll help you find the answers, Rasim." She finally looked up, blue eyes serious. "But you should know our people in Ilyara have never hinted at any such conspiracy. The chances are...slim."

Rasim nodded even though disappointment rushed through him. It would be nice to be a hero, someone who found the truth behind a disaster, instead of being the sole survivor of a fleet drowned by sea monsters. "Thank you. If I can go home and talk to them—" He made a little face. "Or have Guildmaster Isidri talk to them, more like. Then at least we'll have tried. And maybe your people will know something about the more recent fire. We're not good at sneaking secrets out," he confessed. "Not the Seamasters' Guild. The Sunmasters', maybe. They're diplomats and politicians. We just—"

"Fish and slay sea serpents?" Inga asked with a smile.

Rasim's ears burned crimson. "Mostly fish."

"Your fleet are soldiers, too," Inga reminded him. "They're renowned for keeping Ilyaran waters safe, up and down the sea."

"We're not really soldiers. We just have the magic to fight with. It gives us an advantage." A thought struck him. "You must have magic here too. The sewerage water was almost as clean as ours. Why doesn't anybody know you have magic?"

Inga shook her head. "Our magic is boiling water and reed beds, not true magic like your own. We have stories of when we had real power—you saw the murals in the council room?"

Rasim's gaze went to the ceiling as if he expected to see the paintings appear above him. Inga smiled. "Those deeds were done by our forefathers, who had magic bred in their blood. But it faded away over the centuries, until we were as ordinary as anyone but the Ilyarans. It's part of why Annaken agreed to marry your king. We wondered if the blood could be bred back in."

"But why have we kept the magic?" Rasim leaned forward, intense with curiosity. "If no one else has, why has Ilyara? The gods can't favor us that much, can they?"

Inga's smile came again, and turned into a laugh. "I think a properly pious boy wouldn't ask that. But no, I don't think they do favor you that much. The guilds are made up of Ilyara's orphans, aren't they?" At Rasim's nod, she went on. "I think that must be part of it. In most places it seems the stronger magic you had, the more likely you were to marry royalty.

After a time, only royalty had the magic, and after a longer time with no one from the outside to marry in and strengthen it, it faded away. But in Ilyara you teach orphans of ever-changing bloodlines to work witchery. Do the guilds even teach their own children magic?"

Rasim shook his head. "The guilds are for orphans, and you can't be an orphan if your birth parents are there in the guild with you. If people want kids, they leave the guilds and partner with traders or merchants."

"So the blood disperses back into the population, giving you all the potential. Ilyara's orphans are strong with it, and then taught to use it. No one else has a system like that, not that I know of."

"But our royal family has magic," Rasim countered. "They channel and guide the guilds in their great works."

"And yet your current king is weak," Inga argued. "How often do guild members marry into the royal bloodline?"

Rasim blinked. "Never. The nobility all marry each other."

"And how often do guild members marry nobility? Or even how often does the child of a guild member and a merchant marry so high?"

"Not very," Rasim admitted. "Sometimes."

"So the royals marrying nobility have thinned their magic blood too, perhaps."

Rasim sat back again and took a long drink of his watered wine, trying to hide astonishment. The world kept shifting beneath him, changeable as the sea. By the time he returned home, he would hardly know himself, not after fighting a serpent, teaching a stranger water witchery, and discussing magical heritages with a princess. "If the king has lost his witchery, then..." His head hurt with trying to understand what that might mean. "Then Ilyara is weak, and anybody who thinks they're strong might try for the crown. I thought of some people who might think they could get it, but most of them didn't have magic, so I thought they couldn't. But if even the king doesn't have magic anymore..."

Then Ilyara was in far more danger than Rasim had realized. More than even Asindo had realized, maybe, and more than Guildmaster Isidri knew. "I have to go home. I have to go home as soon as I can, and if you'll help me at all—" He broke off, remembering the question he'd meant to ask earlier. "Never mind helping me. Why are you even talking to me? I thought I would find Captain Asindo and he'd keep you from throwing me in a dungeon after I jumped off a ship full of pirates and broke into your palace. But you're treating me like a guest."

"Ah." The corner of Inga's mouth turned up. "That's because we need your help."

CHAPTER 17

"I can't do it." Rasim stood at the edge of a vast inland lake caught between mountaintops. It was half-frozen already, the water like slurry. He didn't need to touch it to know it was only half, and not fully, frozen, was its high salt content: he could feel the water's thickness, its sea-like consistency. "It's too much water," he said, mostly to the lake but a little to the two tall blondes standing next to him. "Why is it even salty? Shouldn't the snow run-off be fresh?"

"It used to be. It turned sour ten years ago or so. We think perhaps the lake bottom has worn through to a salt deposit. We've survived on run-off water and hauling it from longer distances, but it's getting harder as the city grows larger." Lorens waved toward the city they'd left below.

Rasim squatted at the water's edge, letting his eyes glaze as he looked out over slurry and ice. Inga had explained their need the night before, and he, dubiously, had agreed to come look. She'd left him shortly afterward and exhaustion had sent him back to bed. He'd slept until sunrise, which came as late as sunset came early, and had only been brought to the lake after noon. Not that it was easy to tell when noon was with the sun so low in the sky, but they'd taken a mid-day meal before setting out, so he trusted the Northern schedule. "If there's salt down there you'll need more than just a water witch. You'd need a stone witch, too, someone who can move earth. Otherwise it's just going to turn salty again."

"Not quickly," Lorens objected.

Rasim shook his head. "It's a lot of water, but unless it reaches the bottom of the salt lick, it'll turn salty faster than you think. You'd need a water witch — or a lot of them — to hold the water back while the salt was moved out, and then to purify it afterward. I can go in and find out if there *is* a salt deposit down there, but that's as much help as I can be."

Inga said, "You'll freeze to death."

Rasim smiled faintly. "I sailed in with a ship of pirates, broke into your palace, and asked for an army. I think the least I can do is try." More than that, he was afraid his presumption would be taken from his hide if he *didn't* try: the Northerners seemed reasonable enough, but he was too aware of being at their mercy. Less so than at Donnin's, maybe — Lorens and Inga probably wouldn't sell him to slavers — but he felt very far from home and far more alone than he had ever imagined being. Even if they had no intention of condemning him for failure, *trying* would at least make him feel useful. It would give him something to do besides being wrenched by loss, and that was important.

Crouched there at the side of a half-frozen lake, chilly winter air making his nose hairs stiff as he breathed, Rasim had a moment of bewilderment. A moment of wondering how he had come there, or at least at how strange the world around him had become. *His* world had expanded and shrunk at the same time, and he wondered if that was how survivors of the Great Fire had felt. He'd survived that, too, of course, but not in conscious memory. There were journeymen a few years older than he who were terrified of fire, but Rasim didn't even have that much recollection of the fire. Like Desimi, he had been an infant, much too young to remember anything at all about the fire. Like Desimi, like all the other orphans, his birthday had become the day of the fire.

And unlike Desimi, Rasim still lived. He straightened and kicked the boots and heavy coat he'd been given off. "I shouldn't freeze if I bring enough air down with me. It should help keep me warm. If it's too deep, though, I might not even be able to find the bottom. Light won't reach, and it'll get colder the deeper I go."

"Rasim." Inga put her hand on his shoulder, making him turn her way. She looked quite wise, her blue eyes sad. "Rasim, you have nothing to prove."

He shook her hand off and stepped into the water. It was shockingly cold, even colder than the harbor water, and rubbed his feet with thick salty swells. "That's where you're wrong, princess. I have everything to prove."

He dove, and ice water closed over his head.

It was saltier than most sea water, salty enough to resist his downward passage. Rasim pushed himself deeper with magic, conserving his physical energy and the bubble of air surrounding him. The air had been cold, above the lake. Within it, the icy pressure made the bubble feel warm and comforting. That was as dangerous as the sea serpent, in its own way.

He felt no life darting through the salt lake. It was too remote, he thought: too far above the sea, with no inlets to let fish discover it. Rasim had never swum in water so still. Only his own heartbeat and the lake's chill accompanied him, making him truly isolated for the first time in days. It should have worsened his sorrow, but he found it soothing. Nearly everyone he knew had gone to a watery grave, and he thought he felt their presence in the mountaintop lake, surrounding and encouraging him.

Desimi would mock him if he didn't reach the bottom. Kisia would tell him not to be stupid, but then, in the week she'd had to study water witchery, it had been clear that her natural talent was greater than

Rasim's. On one hand she would tell him not to be stupid; on the other, she would dive as deeply as she could, herself. For Hassin or Captain Asindo, finding the lake's bottom wouldn't even be a challenge. Rasim hadn't died with them, and so he would have to live for them. Determined, he pushed harder with his magic, feeling its power take him deeper into the lake. The indirect Northern light was almost gone, and his depth wasn't that great. It would be black before he reached the bottom. He wished he was a sun witch, able to conjure light from darkness.

As if his thoughts had awakened it, he saw a distant brightness. Not daylight: Rasim even glanced back, making certain the water *did* lighten above him. Making certain he hadn't somehow turned himself around, before he looked deep again and after a few moments watched the light re-appear. Not daylight and certainly not the crackling warm light of fire, like a sun witch might awaken. It was more like moonlight, silver on the water, a color that was both soft and hard at the same time. Rasim forgot to breathe as he went deeper, or at least forgot until his ears started squealing a protest. He popped his jaw, taking a breath and clearing his ears all at once, and the pain subsided.

The light brightened and the water came clearer under its brilliance. There was very little silt, no plant life, nothing but water and salt and the lake's distant rock floor, now visible in the light. Rasim squinted, turning his face away. Somehow it was easier to see the illuminated area when he wasn't looking straight at it.

There was a dark spot at its center, a shape both familiar and so incongruous Rasim couldn't place what it might be. The pressure increased as he dove toward it, clicking his tongue furiously to keep his ears clear. The water warmed as he got closer, which made no sense. If it had been a fiery light, like a volcano bursting through the sea bed, then warmth might be understandable. But it was a cool hard light, and the closer he got, the more difficult it was to swim toward it. Rasim was almost certain he'd gone deeper than this with the serpent, so it wasn't only the water's weight. It was as if the magic he used met resistance that was trying to push him away. There was something more at the bottom of the lake, something that perhaps had magic of its own.

The thought flared brightly in his own mind with a confidence strong enough to rival the silver glow below him. Rasim threw his legs into kicking downward too, no longer relying only on his magic, and moved through the water more easily.

A *fountain.* A massive fountain sat on the lake's floor. It poured light into the water, and with the light, salt. *Salt,* as if it sat upon an inexhaustible supply and could let it flow for eternity. The glow's brilliance was partly from reflecting off the salt, making a cloud of white that shimmered and spun at the lake's heart. Rasim stopped swimming and hung in the water, astonished and bewildered. Whomever had made the thing must have had a staggering amount of power.

It was the work of stone witches. It had to be. They alone would have the skill to shape the fountain itself. Some among them would be able to mine for the salt, even to set it flowing freely if they could find a vein of loose enough salt rock. But to make it run continuously for ten years—more than ten years, because the lake was too big to be poisoned overnight—to make it run that long spoke of inconceivable power.

Never mind how they had *gotten* it there: Rasim's best guess was they'd grown it on the lake floor, which meant either witches with deep-reaching skills, or they'd had water witch assistance, so they could come deep like he had, and grown their fountain from close by. Otherwise they would have needed to bring it secretly and drop it in, which seemed impossible. The fountain's size meant its weight would be too great for any but the largest ships, none of which could make it to the landlocked, mountain-top lake anyway. Even reaching for fanciful thoughts, Rasim couldn't imagine a sky witch with enough strength to *fly* the fountain out to the lake.

He'd receded from the fountain as he hung in the water thinking. The magic working within it simply pushed him away, palpable pressure even with water's weight to compete with. Rasim stayed there, drifting where the stoneworking magic pushed him, until he began to shiver with cold. Reluctant to leave because his curiosity was nearly bigger than his fear, he finally turned away and began to swim upward again.

There was no way a single water witch, even one far more powerful than he was, could destroy the fountain. Maybe if it was frozen and warmed repeatedly, quickly, until it cracked and shattered, but not even Guildmaster Isidri would be able to do that. Not alone, at least. A stone witch could break it apart, but he wasn't even sure if the salt spew would stop if the fountain itself was broken. Dumbfounded and out of ideas, Rasim surfaced only a short distance from where Inga and Lorens awaited him.

He tripped, leaving the lake. Now that his weight was his own to support, not the water's, he felt thick and heavy and moved clumsily. He was colder than he'd realized, his thoughts slow. Lorens and Inga stripped his clothes off — wet after all, because he'd let his magic go in the last few seconds — and buffed him dry with thirsty soft cloths. He couldn't even object as they dressed him in dry clothes, nor thank Inga when she pressed a mug of hot mead into his hands. They asked nothing of him, only guided him back down the mountain and into the palace, where a fire's heat began to thaw his bones.

It felt like a long time before he was able to lift his

head from over the mead, or to meet the royal siblings' eyes. Longer still before his tongue finally loosened and he was able to voice the conviction that had come to him as he'd swum back to the surface.

"You're under attack," he whispered, "and I think you have been for thirteen years."

CHAPTER 18

The council didn't convene until after sunset. By that time Rasim, well-fed and warm again, wanted nothing more than to sleep. Not that he thought he *could*, with dread excitement giving him heart palpitations, but he had used too much magic in too much cold that day, and his body was weary even if his mind wouldn't stay silent.

He hadn't expected to see the magnificent muraled room again, much less from a nervous stance just beside Inga's chair. There were far more people at the table than there had been the day before. All of them were in an uproar, shouting to make themselves heard. Only Lorens and Inga weren't bellowing. They were listening, heads tilted to catch key phrases. It was clear the council had been told about Rasim's suspicions, and equally obvious they wanted to hear it directly from him.

Assuming they ever stopped yelling so he could be heard. Rasim shifted nervously. Inga reached out but didn't touch him. It still soothed him, and he released a long slow breath, letting tension escape through it.

The two or three council members closest to them noticed Inga's motion. They turned their attention to her, falling silent for a moment, and like a cascade, so did everyone at the table. Within a handful of seconds the debate was nothing but a memory, and the princess had done nothing but move a few inches. Guildmaster Isidri, Rasim thought, would approve.

Inga, softly so that they would all have to pay attention to really hear her, said, "It appears we and Ilyara are under coordinated attack. I've spent the afternoon going through missives and letters from other heads of state. I remain uncertain if this attack has spread elsewhere, but the time line shared by Ilyaran incidents and our own difficulties seems clear.

"Ilyara suffered the greatest fire in its history almost immediately after their heir was born to their queen, my aunt Annaken. Our own water supply began manifesting signs of salt almost two years after that, and only became undrinkable some months later, but this young man is an Ilyaran water witch, and he assures me the sabotage began considerably before we realized its effects."

Voices rose again, a sudden thunder of sound. Rasim clenched his stomach muscles, holding himself still as Inga made another small motion. "This is Rasim al Ilialio," she said when the council had quieted again. "He was orphaned by the Ilyaran fire, and was an inadvertent guest of our friends in the eastern wing. It's he who discovered the reason for the saltiness of our drinking water. Rasim?"

He explained the fountain at the lake's bottom as clearly as he could, even stopping to answer questions about how he'd been able to dive so deeply. Someone asked how he'd been able to see in the depths, and he spread his hands helplessly. "The rocks glowed. I'm not a Stonemaster. I don't know what kind of rocks glow, but if someone went down to work under the lake, they'd need light. It looked to me like they just left it, when they were done."

The question he couldn't answer, though, was how the fountain had come to be there. "Witchery," was all he could say. "I can't see how else it would have gotten there. But I don't even know what kind."

"We have no witches," someone objected.

Rasim shrugged. "We have thousands. Someone hired or bribed them to do work like this. I didn't think any of the guild would be so..." He struggled for a word, finally saying, "mercenary," uncertainly.

Gales of laughter rose up, comments about Rasim's innocence and naïveté darting around the table. The man who'd spoken before said, "Everyone's got a price, boy," through a grin.

Rasim, hot-faced with embarrassment, stuck his jaw out and glared at the man, but couldn't argue. He could, though, say, "Do you?" and glower belligerently at the man. "Is there something you want badly enough to poison or burn a city to death?"

The man's laughter faded, as did everyone else's. "I might agree to it to save my childrens' lives," he answered softly, after thinking it through. "But that would be coercion, not deliberation, and this stinks of a plot, to me."

"We're bound by blood to the Ilyarans," a woman as old as Isidri said. "We've had no marriages into other kingdoms in decades, not since those terrible winters—"

Rasim glanced at Inga, who murmured, "During my great-grandmother's reign, there was a great deal of intermarriage between royal families across different kingdoms. It was thought to help keep peace. But then a dozen queens and princesses died in childbirth, and their children with them. For three years there was no summer. It seemed the gods had spoken against us, and we all retreated to our homelands, unwilling to risk our mothers and sisters." She nodded at the woman who'd spoken. "Rekka was a child then."

"Oh." Rasim nodded. He'd studied about those summers, though his teachings had said nothing of punishment by the gods. Instead, stone and sky witches, watching the clouds and winds, had concluded that somewhere very far away, a volcano of unprecedented size had erupted. For years the clouds had carried ash, and the wind's patterns had been nearly visible to ordinary men, never mind to the sky witches whose lives were dedicated to the study of wind and clouds. The ash had blocked the sun's heat and light from coming through. Three of the guilds called them the Cold Years. The fourth, the Sunmasters' Guild, called them the Dark Years.

Rekka was still speaking, emphasizing the marriage between Annaken and Laishn. "I'm not saying the marriage was a bad idea —"

An almost inaudible chuckle went around the table, suggesting Rekka had said many times that the marriage *had* been a bad idea. She ignored the laughter. "—but it could have frightened the other kingdoms. Some of us have long memories, but others might just see their countries sandwiched between Northern raiders and the Ilyaran fleet. I said this when the match was made," Rekka said heavily. "I said that we ran the risk of making others move against us. I wish I had not been right."

A fleeting thought darted through Rasim's mind: that Rekka, or someone like her, might be trying to make certain she *was* right. Trying to ensure that Ilyara and the North, that the islands and the continent, all remained isolated.

An isolated country would be easier to defeat than one with allies and friendly neighbors. *That* thought carried more weight, shocking Rasim so badly he startled. That was the sort of thing a strategist would consider, not a journeyman sea witch. Maybe Asindo had been right: maybe, when he got home, Rasim should ask for a tutor from the

Sunmasters' Guild. Or maybe he should bury himself in rebuilding the fleet, and never think again about things beyond his scope. The idea was appealing, but somehow Rasim didn't think he would really do it.

Lorens finally spoke. "Either our spies are very poor, or our enemy is very subtle. If there's movement against us, we should have some sense of it, not be left sitting here agape at the very idea."

"No." Rasim edged forward to put his fingertips on the long table. "I mean, yes, we should know about it, but I think we should be really careful now. We shouldn't let anyone outside of this room know we *do* think there might be a plot. That should make fishing it out easier."

A table's length of amused adult faces examined him. Rasim controlled the urge to stamp his foot. Someone else in the room *must* have thought of what he was saying. It wasn't his fault if he'd simply said it first, before someone older had the chance. "Nobody but the guildmaster in Ilyara knows where the fleet went. We set sail by the dozens all the time to fish, so there's nothing unusual in so many ships having left at once. And if they never made it here —"

His voice cracked and he had to swallow. "If they never made it here, then there's no one in the north to wonder why a third of the Ilyaran fleet landed on their doorstep. I didn't say anything to Donnin's crew about why we were sailing north. So it's just us who know there may be something going on, and that gives us the best chance to be — to be *sneaky*," Rasim finished a little desperately. He didn't know what being sneaky might entail, but he was only a journeyman, not a master or council member or queen.

Lorens, smiling, said, "I couldn't have said it better myself," and the man who'd spoken earlier snorted, apparently prepared to be unimpressed with the idea even if Lorens *had* said it.

Rasim, looking at the man, realized with crystal clarity that if the traitor was in this room, he might betray himself by acting on information only the council had. That would be priceless, if it could be made to happen. He would have to suggest it to the royal family and see if there was a way to tell different stories to different council members so their actions could be tracked back to them.

The man quirked an eyebrow at Rasim, looking as if he followed Rasim's thoughts. Guilty, Rasim jerked his gaze downward, then looked up again to see the man grinning. He was darker than most of the others, which meant he had brown hair instead of blonde or orange, as some of them did. Rasim, scowling, decided he didn't trust the man.

"Rasim's presence presents us with an opportunity to send ships south," Inga said. "His slaying of the serpent can be used as an excuse. We'll be a distraction: if we have enemies in Ilyara's heart, they'll be concerned at our presence and may make mistakes. If we have allies, they may make overtures. I'll need my mother's blessing to pursue this, but I think over the next few days we can assume her approval and prepare so that when word arrives we can leave on the next tide. Rekka, Derek, Lorens, Tersa, come with me, please. I'd like to discuss our options. Rasim, thank you. You're dismissed."

More surprised than he knew he should be, Rasim was jostled by the dark man passing him by along with the others who had been named. Within a minute or two, the chamber was clear, leaving an Ilyaran orphan alone under the murals.

CHAPTER 19

At home, Rasim would be part of the intensive preparation to sail. In the Northlands, he spent three days being ignored, shunted aside, and stepped on by tall Northerners who never quite noticed him. Twice he tried to find Donnin's crew. The first time he got lost in the massive Northern palace, and the second, found Gontur guarding an enormous double door. Their lack of a common language did nothing to hinder Rasim's understanding that the giant Northern guard would not allow Rasim through. It seemed likely the islanders were on the door's other side, but even if he'd had Desimi's water magic, there was no real way to move Gontur and visit Carley.

It was clear, though, that the pirates were prisoners and Rasim was not. He finally stopped trying to convince Gontur to let him in, and returned to the council chambers, where he'd spent long hours staying out from underfoot and studying the astonishing murals. There were accurate depictions of the sea serpents, which made him think the other monsters were as real as the serpents had been. One of the afternoons he'd spent in there, an artist had come in to draw him. Now there were charcoal sketches on one of the walls, Rasim's underwater slaying of the beast starting to become part of legend. The idea was equally horrifying and thrilling. Rasim snickered, staring at himself drawn as a warrior, and a woman's voice responded: "Do you think you don't belong?"

Rasim flinched so hard his feet left the ground, and came down clutching his chest as he wheezed with surprise. Inga was tucked into one of the council chairs that had its back to the door, rendering her invisible until she leaned forward. Her usual smile was faint, and she gestured for Rasim to take a seat across from her. Feeling slightly absurd, he climbed into one of the large chairs and tried to imagine himself a Northern councilman. It seemed no more likely — less likely — than being painted onto a wall of monster-slaying heroes. "I knew a boy who would think he belonged up there, if he'd killed a serpent. Desimi. He was a lot stronger of a witch than I am, and he..." Rasim swallowed. "It would've been important to him that it got painted. So everybody would know what he'd done."

"It's not to you?"

Rasim shrugged uncomfortably. "It's so big it doesn't seem like anybody would even believe me if I said I did it. I'm small and don't have much magic. I'm not a very impressive hero. I guess I like knowing I did it, that I can. That I could. But I wish I hadn't had to. I wish it had never attacked us and I wish none of my friends had died."

"Yes, of course." Inga sat quietly a moment, considering the rest of what he'd said. "Rasim, do you understand that you could — you could probably do nothing else the rest of your life, except be the boy who slew the serpent?"

Horror slipped down Rasim's spine, making him sit up straight. "Why would I want to do that? I would be bored all the time. I mean, I bet maybe Desimi would've liked that, but—" He made a face of dismay.

Inga laughed. "Some people prefer to live on their past glories. They find it easier. I'm glad you don't like the idea. I think you would miss a great deal of adventure."

Rasim slid back down in the chair. "I don't know if I need any more adventure. I've already had a lot."

"Mmm. Does that mean you'd prefer not to sail with the ship I send to the islands, to help Captain Donnin's people?"

Surprise so sharp it felt like his heart stopped beating coursed through Rasim. His face and hands went cold, then heated up again with hope and delight. "Really? You'll help them? I know they probably don't even really deserve it, but—"

"Pirates and brigands generally don't." Inga's mouth drew down with severity, then relaxed as she sighed. "But pirates and brigands don't often have a worthy goal in mind, or a loss so great it's driven them to their ends. Besides, I understand you've negotiated a war treaty with Donnin, and if I help her that treaty will extend to me. Don't look so surprised, Rasim. We have no way of knowing if our enemy is within our midst, within your people, or somewhere else entirely. Donnin's crew and by extension the army we mean to win for her are almost certainly the only innocent—and I use the word advisedly—outsiders I can bring into this."

"Does she know yet? Have you told her?"

"I thought you might want to. I've kept you apart from them deliberately, but I think they'd welcome you, especially bearing good news."

"That would be *great*." Rasim bounced in his chair. "One ship? How many soldiers? How many sailors? I wish I was a better witch, but a ship of Northmen will put them off for certain. Donnin must have some idea of how many men her enemy commands—"

"I've spoken to her about it," Inga agreed. "He maintains an army of good size, for a single landholder. Two hundred men. All I can spare for Donnin's cause is a single ship of fifty men, all able fighters. She has thirty or so on her crew, and you."

"I'm not worth a hundred men. I'm not worth ten. Desimi would've been." Rasim looked at his hands unhappily.

"Desimi was one of your shipmates," Inga asked quietly. Rasim nodded, and she said, "A friend?"

"Not really. I'd just known him my whole life."

Inga nodded, seeming to understand, then stood. "Gontur will let you past, now. Tell Donnin she and her people will be escorted to the harbor, and to prepare themselves. We set sail in the morning."

Confusion, then cautious hope, filtered over Captain Donnin's features when Rasim stepped into the pirates' quarters. They were nice, although not as nice as Rasim's, and large enough for most of the crew to linger in one room. Many of them came to their feet as he closed the door behind them, their expressions less tempered than Donnin's. Their anticipation weighed on the air as heavily as magic.

It was a fitting time for a speech, Rasim thought. Something about true hearts and good intentions and taking the right path through adversity. But he couldn't get the words right, so all he said was, "You have your ship, with fifty Northmen to fight for you. And me."

Cheers erupted from the crew. Donnin stood up abruptly, face tight with relief. Rather than thank Rasim, she turned away, stalking from the room. A wake of confused silence rippled after her, then was drowned by the crew's enthusiasm. Markus came forward to grip Rasim's hand, but Carley was there first, flinging herself at him for a hug. He caught her and staggered backward, thumping into the door as she said, "*Thank* you," fiercely.

She was surprisingly strong. Rasim didn't have enough breath to say, "You're welcome," until she released him and stepped back, her pale eyes shining. Rasim's heart thumped nervously. Girls looked at Hassin that way, not him.

Markus elbowed Carley aside, breaking the intensity of her gaze so he too could thank Rasim. The rest of the crew crowded around, enveloping Carley. Rasim smiled weakly, shook hands, and accepted their accolades with a degree of bewildered pride. He had gotten far less than he'd promised Donnin, but the pirates were still better off than they'd been. Maybe that was what most victories were like, rather than being as complete as slaying the serpent had been.

The serpent, though, had come at huge cost. Its death had been vengeance for a fleet, just as the Northern soldiers would help provide vengeance for Donnin's people.

Rasim, shaking hands and exchanging hugs, realized uncomfortably that nothing was simple, and that things would probably only get more complex as he grew up. He escaped the crew's delight, pushing through them to find Donnin.

She'd gone into another room, a sleeping room with views of the harbor. Her ship was just visible, its pirate flag no longer flying. Rasim stood beside her, waiting for her to speak. When she finally did, it was with clarity: "Fifty isn't enough. Not even with a water witch to help."

Irritation rose in Rasim, for all that he'd thought the same thing. "You could always go back to pirating. Then you wouldn't have a chance at all."

Donnin smirked. "You call it like you see it, don't you, Ilyaran? Well, you're the one who slays serpents and negotiates treaties. You tell me how to win this."

Rasim shrugged. "Be sneaky. You always have to be sneaky if you're small, like me, or someone will stick you in a pitch barrel. Don't go at them like you're an army, because you're not. Not a big enough one, anyway. Use the Northmen as a distraction. I've heard they raid seaside villages sometimes, so send them to raid the nearest town the earl's people would protect. Then sneak in and get your daughter. When she's safe, go after the earl. You don't kill a snake by hacking off its tail. You cut off its head. So don't waste time or people on his army. Kill him, and you're their new mistress."

The pirate captain got a peculiar expression as Rasim spoke. She looked amused, amazed, and annoyed all at once. When Rasim squinted at her curiously, she said, "I didn't expect you to actually *tell* me, Rasim."

"Oh." Irritation pulsed through Rasim again. If people didn't expect him to answer, they shouldn't ask him questions. Then he forgot irritation in surprise. "You know my name!"

"The Northern princess made it quite clear I should know the name of the boy who earned us amnesty. So will you sail with us, Rasim, or will you stay safe with the Northmen?"

Rasim did his best to look put-upon. "If I don't sail with you, you'll never keep up with the Northmen."

Donnin, chuckling, slapped him on the back, and together they went with the crew to the harbor.

CHAPTER 20

The islands were as different from the Northlands as the Northlands were from Rasim's desert home. Rocky beaches stretched to soft green lowlands that rolled back from the water toward unassuming hills. Farms turned the hills to patchwork, golden with the coming winter. It looked like gentle country, and approaching the shores, Rasim wasn't surprised that Donnin's people didn't know much about fighting or survival beyond their patch of land. The islands seemed to have none of the harshness of the north or the desert. People could live lightly here, so long as no one like Roscord demanded more than his fair share.

"It's pretty," Rasim said to the air.

Carley, bent over a knot someone had tied badly, stood up with her hands in the small of her back and looked toward the approaching shore. "You should see it when the mist comes off the water. It's ghostly then, and sunlight breaks through to make the mist glow gold instead of silver. You'd think you lived in the Otherworlds, then." She cleared her throat, pushing a tremble of sentiment away. "We were raided in the spring, before we'd even planted the crops for the year. It's been eight months since we've seen home."

"It's only been a month, for me." The longest month of Rasim's life, and the one in which he'd changed the most, but still only a month. It hardly seemed possible. "If the captain knows where we are now, we shouldn't sail any closer to shore. In fact, we should return to sea, and let the Northern ship come closer and be glimpsed while we head for Roscord's holdings. Let the gossip run ahead, so his people are on edge. That way they'll come faster when the Northmen raid, and we'll have more time to strike."

Carley eyed him. "You get other people in trouble a lot at home, don't you."

"What? No. I try to stay out of trouble!"

"Probably just as well. I wouldn't want to be on your bad side." She left him blinking after her and went to speak to Donnin, clearly relaying Rasim's suggestions. The captain gave him a look much like Carley had done, then sent an order around the deck. Within minutes the shore receded. On higher seas, they met the Northern ship, which came up broadside to Donnin's ship. She catapulted herself to their deck to talk to the dark-haired Derek, who captained the Northern ship. Jorgensson: he was Captain Jorgensson, not Captain Derek, though calling captains by their last names seemed strange to Rasim. Every Ilyaran captain would be *al Ilialio* if they did that.

Jorgensson spoke rapidly to Donnin, who laughed and pointed a thumb toward Rasim as she nodded. Jorgensson glanced his way with a barely-concealed sneer, then spoke with Donnin again. A minute or two later she returned to her ship and the Northmen sailed closer to land. "He had the same thought," she told Rasim. "I don't think he cared for sharing it with you."

"I told you," Rasim said, though he hadn't told anyone, only thought it to himself, "I hardly ever have ideas nobody else would think of. I just think of them fast and say them when I think them."

"In my country," Donnin said, "we say to think twice and speak once."

"In your country," Rasim retorted, "you're tall."

Donnin burst out laughing. Rasim slunk off feeling foolish. The argument had made sense in his head, though he had to admit it sounded silly spoken aloud. "I just meant I have to be quick with what I say," he muttered, "or no one will ever even notice me."

"You slew a serpent," Markus said from nearby. "You may be small, Ilyaran, but you're hard to miss."

Feeling a little better, Rasim scaled the mast to perch in the crow's nest. Clear skies meant they had to keep a greater distance from shore than they might have otherwise, but the air was fresh and invigorating, and there was the prospect of excitement ahead. Dreadful excitement: he had fought a serpent and barely won, and wasn't at all sure he *wanted* to fight other men, but it certainly changed the monotony of daily shipboard life.

From his vantage he could see the distant shadow of the island coasts on the northern horizon, and another faint shadow on the western. They'd sailed through straits to reach Donnin's homeland, and he supposed the western blur was the continental land mass. Rasim thought he would like to visit that part of the world sometime, too, though with the need to rebuild the fleet, it probably wouldn't happen until he was an adult. Still, it was something to look forward to, when a week earlier he hadn't thought of looking forward to much. The fleet's loss still caught him unawares and wrenched his breath away, but he was beginning to accept it. He would have to live for them, that was all. The idea left a pit of sadness in his stomach, but there was nothing else he could think to do.

The Northern ship wouldn't make landfall for at least a day, probably more. Rasim slipped down from the crow's nest to work and rest, and to try not to think about what was coming.

Donnin woke him at sunset the next day. Most of the crew had been too edgy to sleep, but Rasim, expecting he might need to use his witchery to its full extent, had fallen into his berth at mid-day and slept soundly. The captain's voice came as an unwelcome surprise. "Can you cloak us, Ilyaran? Can you hide us as we sail up the river to Roscord's lands? We're close enough to shore that I can hear Jorgenssen's men on their raid. I'll string him up myself if they kill any of my people."

"He swore they would only fight the soldiers," Rasim said blearily. "If you don't trust him, why are we even wasting our time trying this? Um." He pinched his eyes, trying to wake up enough to think. "A cloak. Like fog? I might be able to," he said dubiously. "But it's lifting water into air, and I've never been any good at that. If I manage it'll probably be the only thing I *can* do. Do you think you'll need me for anything else?"

"I don't know," Donnin said. "A man's blood is much like water, isn't it? Can you stop the very blood in Roscord's heart, just as you stop water from sloshing over the side of a bucket?"

Rasim dropped his hand to stare at the captain in horror. "*No!*"

Something unpleasant, like a smile but cruel, played at the corner of Donnin's mouth. "Does that mean you can't or you won't, lad? Never thought if that one, did you, clever boy?"

"Blood is *blood*," Rasim said fiercely. "Not water. It can't be stopped like that."

"Mmm." Donnin looked at him sideways, but let it drop, which only made Rasim feel worse. His vehemence was born from fear and he knew it. The idea of killing a man that way was shocking, and he was more than a little afraid it was possible.

Not by him. Never by him, not even if he could. "I'll try to bring up a fog," he said stiffly. Donnin nodded and got out of his way, letting him go up to the deck undisturbed.

The air was right for fog. Rasim could feel water in the air, waiting for the chill point. Guildmaster Isidri could have done it without a second thought, and Desimi with a little concentration. Rasim knotted his hands around the ship's rail, feeling a roughness of wood that wouldn't be there on an Ilyaran vessel. His life, and the lives of others, might well depend on him calling the fog. He had to do it. He closed his eyes, desperately encouraging his magic to change the water and air around him.

A soft gasp made him open his eyes a few moments later. Mist rose from the water, silver beads drifting higher as the crew watched. Fog rolled in from the sea to swallow the shore and snake along the river, a vanguard softening the land ahead of the ship's silent journey. Within a minute or two they were completely enveloped, mist reaching for the sky and hiding even their tall mast.

Rasim's mouth fell open as muted cheers and back-slaps congratulated him. Then the crew rushed to their duties, leaving him standing agape at the rail. Donnin murmured, "Our thanks," as she strode by.

Rasim nodded, but by the time she was past, also shook his head.

He had not done this. His witchery had never stirred, much less strained under the effort of a magic well beyond his talents. There was no weight in the air proclaiming magic had been done, either. The fog had risen naturally.

At just the moment they'd needed it. Rasim huffed a disbelieving breath, but the air had been nearly perfect for fog, and he had no other explanation. He shook himself, then ran to do his duties. For others, that was sailing the ship. For himself, today at least, it was leaning from the ship's prow, extending his witchery toward the water. Sailing an unfamiliar river wasn't difficult in daylight with a wise eye for tell-tale signs of danger reflecting what lay below the surface. But now it was night, and Donnin's crew lacked the experience to recognize the change of water flow that might warn about a sand bar or flotsam that might threaten the ship. Even Asindo would use witchery on a night like tonight, though most other times he would insist his sailors trust their eyes and instincts first. Rasim had never heard of anyone's magic disappearing, but the guild's laws meant they learned to sail without witchery as well as with.

Roscord's lands were settled off a small natural harbor in the river, distinct in its sensation in the water's flow. Other docks had small boats bobbing in the mist, but nowhere else had large ships displacing water. Only two, but even that was enough to make Rasim certain that he guided Donnin's crew to the right place. There was no sense of activity; Roscord's men weren't foolish enough to try coming at the raiding Northmen on ship. They would meet them over land, trusting their swords. Rasim felt faint, distant movement and again fought down frustration. A better witch might be able to carry information about numbers of men, the direction they went, and how quickly, from the disturbance in the fog. All Rasim could tell was that there were people out there somewhere, but any fool would know that. It didn't take magic.

They docked silently, Rasim at least able to quiet the splashes of a ship coming in to shore. The crew armed themselves and filed off the ship behind Rasim, who quested with his witchery to find the easiest path. Water always took that route, even when it rolled through the air instead of between river banks. Rasim felt its ease of passage inland, and found a hard-packed road with his feet. The fog was so thick it was almost impossible to see them, and he felt the warmth of the crew crowding close, all of them afraid to lose each other in the murk. Carley had been right about the island fogs, Rasim thought. He'd never seen anything like them.

The road was straight and well-kept. Even in the dimness, they traveled quickly. The sensation of moving bodies in the mist faded from Rasim's awareness, suggesting Roscord's soldiers had taken the bait and gone south toward the Northern raiders. Nervous triumph bloomed in Rasim's chest, though he said nothing to the pirates.

Ahead, fog swirled more freely, brushing against unmoving figures and stirred only by the slightest internal breezes. Maybe trees and small animals breaking up a clearing, though he wasn't certain what kinds of beasts filled a cool island night. He would ask Carley later.

A weight rolled through the air and firelight turned the fog to gold, dozens of torches coming to full life at once. There *was* a clearing, a broad crossroads directly in front of them. Armor-clad soldiers, swords glittering, became visible in the haze. Rasim's heart stopped, ice splashing through his body.

They were surrounded.

CHAPTER 21

A man's voice slipped through the fog, so soft and cultured that even Rasim, who didn't know his language, recognized it as well-bred. The speaker came after the voice, and disappointed: he was not tall, nor was he handsome or fit. But his voice made up for it. Rasim could understand how he came to power, with the smooth, convincing tones and the rich depth rolling in his words.

Donnin stepped forward, face dark with furious color. She spoke her own language, too. Markus, near Rasim, began to translate.

"Roscord wanted to know if we really thought we'd be able to sneak up on him. If a paltry band of pirates thought they could unseat one of the most powerful warlords in the islands. Donnin says warlords her —" Markus glanced at Rasim and obviously edited the rude phrase Donnin had used. "...her grandmother's teeth. She says he's a power-monger and a bully, nothing more, and demands he return her daughter and any of our people he's enslaved."

Roscord actually laughed at that, a sound as sweet as honey. Rasim, knowing the man was a kidnapper and murderer, still wanted to like him, just for the quality of that laugh. He spoke again, Markus's translation running quietly under the beautiful voice: "Perhaps I am, Lady Donnin. Or I should say Captain Donnin now, I suppose. Forgive me, but how far the mighty have fallen. Perhaps a warlord is precisely as you've said, Captain. A power-monger and bully." He smiled, startling and bright, but his eyes remained cold and deadly, like a snake's. "But whatever you wish to call me, I am the victor here, and you are fools. Bring me the water witch."

Markus nearly swallowed the last words, as shocked by the translation as Rasim was. Two soldiers shoved Rasim forward. He stumbled, but caught himself, unwilling to meet Roscord on his knees. His heart was hummingbird-fast in his throat, but he lifted his chin with as much bravery as he dared, and wondered how the islands lord had known he was with the pirates.

Roscord examined him coolly. Almost dismissively, though he wouldn't have called Rasim forward if he truly intended to dismiss him. Nor was Rasim surprised when the warlord addressed him in the common tongue. "You've chosen a bad lot to throw in with, Ilyaran. Rasim al Ilialio, if I'm correct?"

Rasim set his jaw. "Yes. How did you know?"

"I would be a poor warlord indeed if I had no sources hidden within foreign courts. Why have you thrown in with these reprobates?"

Rasim's heart hammered until he felt dizzy. Their plans were already in a ruin. They needed to do something new, something unexpected. He said, "It was better than being sold to slavers," without thinking. At least it had the advantage of being true.

Roscord let go his astonishing laugh again. "Slavers? Gods, Donnin, are you that short-sighted? Still," he said to Rasim, "you might have chosen to sail with the Northern raiders, rather than Donnin's crew. Perhaps they've swayed you with their sentiment. Perhaps you've made friends?" He gestured, and soldiers seized one of Donnin's crew, a man called Elex. Without warning, the soldiers cut Elex's throat and threw him to the ground, where blood shone red beneath the fog.

Donnin screamed and launched herself at Roscord, half the crew in her wake. Soldiers surged forward, stopping them without using killing force, though it took four of them to hold Markus, who bellowed like a bull. Rasim couldn't even blink, much less shout or move with horror. His thoughts were a cold hard jumble, panic slashing them to pieces and fastening them together again in ways that made no sense. He was going to die. They were *all* going to die, if he didn't do something desperately clever.

Feeling as though someone else controlled his actions, Rasim shrugged as casually as he could. "He wasn't a friend."

It was true. He'd barely spoken to Elex. That was the only thing keeping him from collapsing, from becoming as useless as water against the sticky fire. Had it been Carley at the edge of the soldier's blade, he would never have managed the mild disinterest he'd put in his voice. "I took their ship because it was more likely to come to your lands."

Donnin, still held by Roscord's men, made a furious sound deep in her throat. Rasim glanced at her and shrugged again. "I'm not a soldier. I didn't want to raid a village. Not when it's been made clear to me someone with real power might have use for my talents, and maybe even be willing to pay me for them."

"Someone with real power," Roscord echoed. "Someone like me."

Rasim nodded. Roscord gave his startling smile again. "You either think on your feet very quickly, Rasim al Ilialio, or you're telling the truth. But I've been given to understand that the Ilyaran guild members have...little interest in worldly advancement."

"Almost nobody leaves the guilds," Rasim agreed. "Almost nobody gets the chance. We're hardly ever out in the world alone. We're never told or shown how far we *could* advance, if we broke away."

"It's kept your magic strong," Roscord argued, but

Rasim shrugged again.

"Has it? Or has it just helped weaken everybody else's? I'm tired," he said bitterly, because it was true. "I'm tired of being small for my age and less adept at witchery than some of the others. I'm tired of being afraid of what other people might choose to do with me, or of what they might decide my fate should be. In the guilds, all I'm ever going to be is a minor witch. In the islands I might be a—"

A king, he'd been going to say, but a flash of warning in Roscord's eyes held the word in his throat. "A free man," Rasim said instead. "Able to choose my masters and name my price. Especially if I had a patron. Someone who would protect me in exchange for my skills."

He could almost feel the fury boiling off Donnin's crew. Their rage was as palpable as magic, and he knew if Carley's witchery was any more advanced he might be struck down by her anger. But he didn't dare look back at them, for fear Roscord might think he cared. If he cared, they were all doomed. And this was the only way he could think that he might at least get near Roscord's lands, and perhaps find Donnin's daughter. It was a terrible risk, but it was the only choice he could see.

Roscord's beautiful smile twitched his lips. "A patron like myself."

Rasim made himself smile, too. Made himself try to sound teasing, light-hearted, like he was confident enough Roscord would take him on that he could dare taunt him a little: "Unless you have a better idea?"

The warlord's eyebrows shot up. "You'd have to travel a long way yet to find a prince as strong as I am in the islands."

A prince. *That* was a word Rasim knew, unlike *earl* or *baron*. It was a much higher rank, and it said a lot about Roscord's opinion of himself, if nothing else. But there *was* something else in what it said, too: something that gave Rasim a way to flatter the man's ego. It was simple enough. Everybody knew to kneel before royalty, after all.

Swallowing bile, Rasim knelt, placed one arm across his knee, and looked up at Roscord with all the integrity he could muster. "Then I'll be your man, if you'll have me, my prince."

"And I'll have your head if you're lying to me. You're mine, Al Ilialio. Get up and do something about this fog."

Rasim's heart stuck in his throat, then hiccuped a relieved thump and settled again. Moving fog was much more like keeping water from slopping out of a bucket than raising fog was. He got to his feet, pressing droplets of water away with his magic. The air thickened, weight of witchery finding resistance, but then the mist swirled and billowed away from the roadway. Not from all of it, but certainly a broad enough stretch that Roscord could walk unhindered.

Or ride, Rasim realized. One of the soldiers led a

tall grey horse out of the fog. Roscord mounted it and set off at a good clip. Rasim, half afraid and half amused, watched him ride directly into the fog bank, far ahead of where Rasim could affect the water hanging in the air.

It took fewer than twenty heartbeats for him to return, snarling, "I thought you could witch the fog away."

"I can," Rasim said mildly, "but not very far ahead." He'd confessed to the pirates and even the Northmen that he wasn't much of a witch, but there was no reason to tell Roscord that.

The warlord glowered down at him. "I thought you water witches were powerful!"

Rasim, still mildly, asked, "Can *you* press the fog away so you can ride on a clear path?"

Roscord, lip curled, picked Rasim up and deposited him on the horse. Rasim lowered his eyes a moment, which was as much giving in to humor as he dared, then turned his attention to clearing the road. He could hear Donnin's crew being herded behind them, and refused to look back no matter how much he wanted to. They would hate him, but if he could find a way to get any of them out alive, their hatred would be worth it. In the meantime he had a guess, one that would tell him so much, if he could get Roscord to admit to it. Carefully, quietly, he asked, "Who is your Northern man, my lord?"

"Why would I tell a stripling water witch that?"

Confidence swirled through Rasim. Even if Roscord wouldn't tell him who, he'd just all but admitted he *had* at least one Northern spy, probably someone sailing on Jorgenssen's ship. Trying to hide his delight at confirming a spy existed, Rasim let his shoulders rise and fall, and let slip a little more information himself, hoping he might learn something else. "I thought he'd be at your estate, and that I'd meet him. But I guess he'd be more use to you sailing south to Ilyara and remaining your hidden spy. I shouldn't have asked."

Stiffness came into Roscord's smooth voice. "An Ilyaran spy would be of use, yes."

Rasim bit his cheek, fighting down triumph. He would bet Roscord's sourness was born of not knowing the Northerners planned to sail south next. His spy, whoever it was, had withheld information Roscord would consider important. If Rasim could drive a wedge between them, it might give him that much more chance to create an opportunity for Donnin's people to escape. He owed Elex that much, even if he'd barely known the man.

And he owed the Northern spy at least that much and more, for betraying them. Rasim wanted it to be Captain Jorgensson simply because he hadn't liked him. But it would be important not to be closed-minded, if Rasim wanted to discover who it was in truth. Inga and Lorens would no doubt be grateful to be told of a spy in their midst, and Rasim felt increasingly as if he could use whatever allies he found.

To his surprise, the fog didn't lift as they traveled inland. It weighed the air down, still resisting Rasim's work to thin it. Where wind captured it and swept some away, he caught glimpses of homes and farms unlike any in Ilyara: thick roofs of woven reeds over grey or white stone, not like the golden stone at home. Farms showed tilled earth that looked lush and black even with winter coming on. In Ilyara only the river banks were that rich, and private gardens were scrabbled from sandy soil. Then the fog closed again, making coiling demons with torchlight as their eyes. Rasim held off a shiver, not wanting to appear weak before Roscord, and looked hard at the road ahead.

A little while later they passed through iron gates on a tall stone wall. The road there was smooth and even, well-maintained. In almost no time, Roscord's manor rose from the mist. Rasim couldn't stop his quick inhalation: the house looked the size of the Seamasters' Guild house, and all for one man. Roscord said, "Well?" expectantly.

"Only a prince would have lands like these," Rasim said honestly. No individual in Ilyara could boast anything like Roscord's estate: the land was too harsh at home, and the people too interdependent. Even the royal palace barely outshone the dark building outlined by fog, and that was meant to hold hundreds.

Equally honestly, he added, "I'm surprised anyone dares to try standing against you."

Roscord chuffed pleased agreement, though his words were a threat: "They don't last."

Nor would Rasim, was the unspoken end of that comment. Nor would Rasim, if he did anything foolish. Grim, frightened, and trying not to show it, Rasim entered the home of his new master, hoping he would be able to leave.

CHAPTER 22

A guard was set on him. Not outside his room, but *in* it, showing just how far Roscord trusted him. Rasim couldn't blame him, but resented it anyway: it would be much harder to escape if he had to get through a guard first, and he couldn't go out the window if the guard was in the room. Which was, of course, the point, but knowing that didn't make it any less frustrating. Hoping he seemed calm, he ate and drank the small meal of bread, cheese and wine that he'd been left, then retreated into a bed so over-stuffed he slid toward the floor if he moved so much as an inch off its center.

Its height, though, allowed him to surreptitiously watch the guard. The man had a cold, snuffling dramatically every several seconds and wiping his nose repeatedly.

Nose drippings, Rasim thought, were mostly water.

Eyes half closed so he could just barely see his victim, Rasim concentrated on the idea of water in the man's head. A stuffy nose wasn't much different from a bucket of over-full water. It took concentration to keep either water or nose drippings inside, but a touch of magic could help it either way: in or out.

Within minutes, the guard's sniffling became a constant noise, until he let go a sound of dismay, looked at where Rasim was apparently sleeping quietly, and ran to find something to blow his nose with.

Rasim slipped out of bed as quickly and quietly as he could, shoving extra pillows into the space he'd been. There was no time to make certain he'd done a convincing job. He sprang for the window, searching for a lock or fissure that would let him open it, and found nothing. Nothing at all: the window didn't open. For a boy from a desert city where windows were covered in cloth if at all, the idea was incomprehensible. He searched again, and again found nothing.

Stomach twisting with panic, he ran for the door. There was no chance of escape that way, he was sure of it. The guard would be only a few feet beyond, or another guard would be outside. Still, he had to try, even if he could think of no excuse at all to offer Roscord should he be caught. Some hero he was: betraying Donnin's crew only to betray himself as one of them a handful of hours later. Maybe he could claim a nightmare, or bad bowels, though there was a chamber pot in his room.

The guard wasn't outside his door. Rasim froze with astonishment for the space of a breath, then closed the door behind him quietly before bolting to his left. To the left, because he'd been brought to the room from the right-hand hall, and knew that way led back to the common rooms and more people. Donnin's people might be somewhere back there, but he would do them no good if he got caught trying to learn where they were.

Voices sounded ahead of him. Rasim pressed against shadows, wondering if a sun witch might be able to deepen them and hide better. Not that he had a sun witch handy, but questions like that were forever popping into his head. There were doors along the hall, but he had no way of knowing what lay on their other side. In a house this size, possibly nothing—but he would be lost for good if he was wrong.

A sharp turn in the hall and a window that let him glimpse into a contained courtyard made him realize the house wasn't even a *house*, exactly. It was an enormous square surrounding a common area large enough to train three hundred men in. All of Roscord's people were probably housed here, differently from how the Ilyaran palace staff was kept, but similar enough that Rasim recognized the idea. He moved away from the window and squished himself against the wall, willing his heartbeat to slow as he tried to think.

Roscord clearly expected some resistance from his people, or from surrounding lords. Otherwise he wouldn't need his own home to be an army barracks. That meant Roscord himself probably slept in the safest place in his palace, and probably kept prized possessions — like Donnin's daughter, maybe — nearby.

Rasim risked glancing out the window again. The huge square below was largely empty, only a few sentries standing guard in faded mist. Yellow firelight splashed into the courtyard, brightest along the front-facing wall of the house, the one Rasim had just turned a corner from. Those were the common rooms, and if this was a stronghold, they were probably rooms mostly for soldiers. All around the square there were other single spots of torchlight marking entrances and exits. Soldiers would be on the ground floor, Rasim reasoned. Roscord would be up higher, safer. Not even on the first floor like Rasim currently was on, but one higher, even: Rasim could see the tapering roof of a second floor that didn't reach all the way around the building. Private quarters for a rich man, maybe. It seemed likely.

It was as good a bet as any. Rasim ran down the hall again, searching for a stairway. He finally had to risk peeking through doors, mostly finding dark, empty rooms on the other side. Roscord's army, impressive as it was, was obviously not at full strength yet, not if he had so many rooms waiting to be filled. The man seemed to have a terrifyingly large ambition, whatever it was.

One door finally opened on a stairway broad enough for seven men to come down it at once. Rasim darted up, pausing to peek around a corner where it turned, and ran lightly to the door at the top. He opened that as cautiously as the ones below, peeking through a sliver-wide crack at first.

A guard stood six feet away, across the hall and facing the door. Rasim didn't even dare let it close again, only stood there breathlessly trying to decide what to do. The runny nose had worked well with the other guard, but his nose had been dripping to begin with. This man's breathing was steady and deep, no hint of sickness in it.

Very steady and deep, Rasim realized after standing like a terrified rabbit for over a minute. Rasim had spent his entire life sharing space with others, and knew what breathing while asleep sounded like. The guard was upright, at attention, and totally asleep. Rasim would bet his life on it.

He *was* betting his life on it. He inched the door open, hoping it wouldn't squeak, and slipped through the moment there was room enough. He leaned on it to make it close slowly, afraid that even the breeze from displaced air would be enough to waken the guard even if the door didn't thump. The door eased back into place. Rasim scurried down the hall to squish himself into the depression of another door, giddy with relief.

The door behind him swung open silently and he fell inside with a muffled cry.

His first thought, after he'd hit the floor, was that the room was warm and faintly lit. Embers glowed in the fireplace, a promise that someone actually slept in this room.

That was a *disaster*.

Rasim rolled to his feet, trying to catch the door before it closed all the way. He missed, fingertips brushing the heavy wood as it slipped past. The door made a muffled thud as it closed. Rasim curled his fingers like they could capture the curse he wanted to speak aloud. He glanced over his shoulder, breath held, hoping that whoever slept in the room hadn't awakened with his arrival.

A light-haired girl who looked very like Captain Donnin sat in the middle of another overstuffed bed. She was about Rasim's age, stiff-spined, clutching a pillow in one hand and a knife in the other. A combination of triumph and alarm twisted Rasim's belly. He raised his hands slowly, carefully, showing himself to be unarmed, and turned toward the girl incrementally. Only when he was fully facing her and she hadn't yet moved did he whisper, "Adele?" tentatively.

She was pale already, but went paler still. Her fingers tightened around knife and pillow alike, as if she intended to use one as a weapon and the other as a shield. Her voice was a low hiss, but she spoke the common tongue: "How does an Ilyaran know my name?"

Rasim's shoulders collapsed in relief, though he didn't lower his hands. "I'm here with your mother. We're trying to rescue you."

Hope lit Adele's gaze, which snapped to the door, then back to Rasim. By the time she looked at him again, the hope had been driven out of her face, leaving dryness in its place. "Really. How's that working for you?"

She looked and sounded so much like her mother that Rasim grinned despite the litany of things that had gone wrong. "Not very well, honestly. Your mother's crew got captured and I've been lying through my teeth to keep on Roscord's good side, but at least I found out how we got caught. There's a spy with the Northerners who are supposed to be helping us. Do you know how to get *out* of here?"

Adele turned white. "He's captured my mother?" She got out of bed as she asked, bare feet slapping the floor. She went to a wardrobe, pulling clothes out, and gave Rasim a sharp look that expected an answer.

"A few hours ago. We'd meant to sneak in, but someone from our decoy betrayed us. Roscord seems like the kind of man who would make an example of people who stood up to him, so she's probably safe until morning." Not so the rest of the crew, but it was best not to mention that.

"He's the kind of man who would make an example of her for weeks." Adele found pants, a shirt, warm boots, and a heavier over-shirt, not quite a coat, that she dragged on with quick efficiency. A minute later she was dressed and pulling her hair into a twisty knot at her nape. Then she faced Rasim, her expression set. "We'll probably get killed if we get caught."

"Then we shouldn't get caught."

"Good plan." She sounded older than she looked, though she'd been captive for months, at least. That would make a lot of people grow up faster. "What's your name, Ilyaran?"

"Rasim."

"When we get out of here, Rasim, you'll have to tell me how an Ilyaran ended up in my bedchamber, a thousand miles away from his home. Come on."

She stepped into the wardrobe and disappeared.

CHAPTER 23

Rasim gaped before scrambling into the wardrobe himself. A small door — small enough that Rasim, who wasn't tall, had to duck to pass through it — was fitted tightly into its back. Astonished, he peered up at Adele through the gloom of a narrow passageway. "How'd you know this was here?"

Adele's face tightened. "I noticed the servants always kept this part of the wardrobe mostly clear. I wondered why, and found the door. I've gone through it a few times, seeing where it goes. To a lot of the other bedrooms, and the main passage leads to Roscord's. I think he uses it to visit his mistresses." Her voice was brittle, like she had spent so long being afraid that she couldn't quite let herself hope the need was ending.

After the past month, Rasim understood, but didn't know how to say so. He only nodded, then said, "Just a minute," and squeezed back into the room. He propped Adele's pillows as he'd done his own, then arranged the clothes back into the wardrobe as tidily as he could from the back side. "In case anyone looks in," he said. "Maybe it'll buy us another few seconds."

Donnin's daughter gave him a tense smile, then scurried deeper into the passage. It got taller after a few strides, making their quiet run more comfortable. "You never tried to escape before?" Rasim whispered to Adele's back.

"Not without some kind of allies waiting for me. He'd have caught me, and he might have stopped waiting for my sixteenth year, then."

Rasim blurted, "You're fifteen?" in surprise. Adele glared over her shoulder and he winced apologetically. He, of all people, should know better than to be surprised at someone looking younger than they were. At least Adele was tall enough, just childish of feature.

"Only for another month," she said when silence had chastised him. "I meant to try leaving in two weeks no matter what, because I don't want to be that horrible man's mistress, but if my mother is here, even captured, then right now is my—our—best chance. If you're lying to me, Ilyaran..."

"There's not much point in threatening me now," Rasim muttered. "You already decided to come with me." As if she'd had much choice, he wanted to add, but thought she would be angry. Instead he asked, "Where are we going?"

"There are servant's halls that these passages meet

up with. I haven't dared explore them, but I know where the kitchens are from my room, and if we can get there we can get to the stables. That's where he puts his prisoners."

"In with the horses?" Rasim asked, bewildered. "Wouldn't that upset them?"

"Upset the horses or the prisoners?" Adele breathed, but shook her head, dismissing her own whimsy. She was strange, Rasim thought. Strange and strong, if she could make even feeble jokes when they were running for their lives. "There's an entire barn that's not used for stables. Roscord's planning to bring more men here, but he hasn't yet. So right now when he has people he wants imprisoned, he puts them there. Shh, now. This is the entrance to the servants' halls."

She stopped at a panel that looked like all the others and pressed her ear against it. After a few breathless moments she nodded and put her weight against the panel. It gave slightly, then opened with an almost-inaudible click. Adele peeked out, then nodded again and slipped through the door as soon as it was open wide enough for her to do so. Rasim came out a half-step behind her, close as a shadow. They stayed where they were, breathing in tandem, waiting to see if their appearance had been noticed. Both decided they were safe in the same moment. Adele seized Rasim's wrist, keeping him at her side as they ran.

The passages were clear and quiet. Not even servants were awake at this hour, long after the master of the house needed duties done and still well before the kitchen staff began their work. Twice, Adele said, "This way," and tugged him down a hall he wouldn't have chosen. She didn't slow again until they'd reached the massive kitchens, as large as the guild's. She stopped in the doorway, pulse fast in her throat. "There'll be guards outside."

"If there's still fog I can keep us hidden." Rasim set his jaw as he made the promise. He *would* keep them hidden. He had to. He'd been terribly lucky to find Adele, and luck never lasted. His magic would have to be strong enough, just this once.

Adele gave him a sharp look, then nodded acceptance. They ran across the kitchen, staying on their toes to minimize sound. Rasim edged the door open this time, wisps of fog trailing through the crack. Rasim's stomach dropped. The mist had thinned, making less of a cover than he'd hoped. He couldn't just draw what there was around them: a single cloud of rapidly-moving fog would be just as noticeable as two people racing across the courtyard. He had to bring the fog up again, strengthen it everywhere so they could slip through unnoticed.

For a despairing moment he thought about how the mist had rolled in from the sea so easily. Too easily: it hadn't been his magic at all. There was no chance he would be equally fortunate this time.

At least there *was* fog. Maybe he could just encourage what there was to redouble. Rasim took a deep breath, reaching within himself for the magic. It quested out, discovering the droplets of water suspended in air: *that* was easy. It was splitting them, changing them, making more and more of them, that was difficult. He didn't even dare close his eyes in concentration, not with the possibility of discovery lurking. Adele kept an eye on the kitchen doors, and Rasim watched the courtyard. The fog thickened, just a little. Encouraged, Rasim clenched his hands and leaned forward, pouring magic into the cool air.

It happened so, so slowly. The courtyard became more difficult to see, mist making soft billows across the ground. No one came to disturb it, which was mostly good. Only mostly: if someone walked through it in the distance, Rasim might get a sense of how far his fog bank extended. A patch of fog wasn't unusual, as long as it wasn't only just large enough to hide two teenagers. It had to be of normal size.

Sweat rolled down Rasim's nose. His whole body trembled with effort, the magic within him already sputtering and weakening. He clenched his stomach, dredging for the power to keep them safe. It was all he had to do, make a little fog to hide them. Luck had brought him to Adele, and Adele had gotten them through Roscord's palace. *All* he had to do was get them across the open space to the barns. Even the very least water witch should be able to do that.

His magic faltered, and the fog began to fade. Exhaustion made Rasim's knees wobble. He slumped against the door frame, cold with misery. Any of the others, any of his friends — even his enemies — would have been able to do this one task. But they were gone, and he wasn't strong enough. He began to whisper, "I'm sorry," to Adele.

A scream cut the night.

Rasim and Adele both stiffened, terror locking Rasim's knees. Donnin's crew were the only ones who had reason to scream tonight. Adele seized his elbow and he grabbed the door frame, desperate resolution filling him.

Power he didn't know he had poured out of Rasim. The mist thickened, becoming almost solid. Unnaturally fast, maybe, but it didn't matter. Rasim caught Adele's hand — cold, even colder than his own — and ran.

The mist cleared in front of them, just enough to let them see the ground they ran across. Enough to make sure they kept their feet without ever losing the hiding power of the fog. Rasim felt people moving, the fog disturbed by their distant actions before they, and it, went still again.

Adele hissed, "I can't see! I don't know where to go!"

"I do." Toward the movement: at least a few men still bothered the fog, pushing it from the currents and eddies it wanted to follow. He wished there were horses in the barns. Their big warm bodies would be distinctive to the mist's cool touch, even if the fog was largely kept out of the barns. But by that logic, the whole of Donnin's crew, grouped together, should be as big and warm a lump as horses, and he couldn't feel them at all. Rasim bit his lip and pushed through weariness to run a little faster.

A fence came up out of nowhere, barely visible before they hit it. Hand in hand, they went over it together, landing on its far side with thumps loud enough to shake the earth. Adele gave a short cry, then silenced herself. Rasim rolled to his knees beside her.

She lay on her back, one hand clutching the opposite wrist. Her face was set with pain, lips pressed together and eyes crushed shut. Rasim had hurt himself often enough to know not to ask if she was all right, at least not for a minute. Instead he listened hard, wondering if their crash or cries had alerted anyone to their presence.

No one approached them. After waiting as long as he dared, Rasim looked down at Adele again. Her mouth was still thin, but her eyes were open. No tears stood in them, though there were tracks of water down her temple. "I landed hard. It's sprained or broken. At least it's my wrist and not my ankle." She kept her voice quiet, but Rasim could still hear the strain in it.

"Don't let it go," he suggested. "I'll help you up, and we'll run again."

Adele nodded once, sharply. Rasim put his hands under her arms and hefted her to her feet, trying not to jostle her too badly. She hissed again, clutching her injured arm more tightly against her stomach. Then she nodded a second time. "Let's go."

Strange but brave, Rasim thought again, and led her through the fog.

A knot of worry formed in his stomach before they'd gone much farther. Rasim breathed, "How far are the barns?" and felt Adele shake her head.

"Not very. And I don't remember the fence. It could be new." A different kind of strain came into her voice, less pain than bitterness: "I haven't been allowed to get out much."

Roscord's beautiful voice cut through the fog, shockingly loud after their murmurs: "And yet you've done a remarkable job of getting out now. What an enterprising pair of children you are. The Ilyaran obviously has to die, but I've gone to a lot of trouble for you, Adele. It would be a pity to put you to the blade now."

He came out of the fog, sword dancing with the mist. It was mesmerizing, as beautiful as it was deadly. "On the other hand, cutting your throat in front of your mother would be wonderfully dramatic. After she's tried so hard, and failed so badly? That would destroy her. I might even let her live after that, just so she had to live *with* it. And there have been so many deaths already. A shame about my men," he said to the shock of horror Rasim felt cross his own face, "but their deaths will certainly justify *yours.*"

Rasim's breath caught. Roscord's men were nowhere nearby, not even whispers in the fog. If they were to die, it would be at Roscord's hand, to make Donnin's crew look all the worse. He edged a step backward, wondering if he could escape notice long enough to warn Roscord's own men about him.

Instead he nudged something with his foot. He glanced down and went cold to the bone: a dead soldier, eyes still wide with surprise, lay hidden in the fog. Roscord had done the job already.

Which meant he expected to slaughter more than twenty men and women on his own. For an instant a twisted admiration rose in Rasim. He had never met anyone as insanely ambitious as the islands lord. He hoped he never would again. Shivering, Rasim looked up.

Roscord was gone. He had fallen silent after his threat, and now the thick fog swallowed him. Alarm spiked through Rasim. He reached out with his magic, searching for the disturbances that were human-made, not just wind moving water through the air, and found none.

None. Not even Donnin's crew, not even Adele, who stood so close Rasim could still see her. Rasim swallowed a sound of panic. He wasn't the strongest of sea witches, but even tired, he should certainly be able to find people in the fog. Maybe the reason witches stayed within Ilyara and the guilds was that the longer they were away from Ilyara, the weaker their magics became. A strong captain like Asindo could have remained away from the city for months before losing his power, but Rasim's small talents had bled away far more quickly than that. Why wouldn't they *warn* their journeymen about something like that? Or maybe it didn't matter, because normally witches with limited skills weren't assigned to sailing vessels.

Grimly, he shut his panic down. Wondering and fearing would do no good. If he couldn't use magic to find Roscord, he would manage some other way. They were close to Donnin's crew now; they had to be. Roscord wouldn't murder his own men at a distance, not if he wanted to hang it all on Donnin. Rasim stepped closer to Adele, guiding her into the mist. Roscord couldn't be everywhere at once, and they were better off moving than remaining where he knew their location.

He couldn't even move the mist to clear a path for their feet. Step after step they edged forward, Rasim with an arm around Adele, who still held her injured wrist close to her stomach. As long as they didn't lose each other, he promised himself, they would be all right.

Roscord appeared out of the fog again. Rasim and Adele both gasped and staggered back, but the warlord was staggering himself. He used his sword as a cane, and clutched his heart as he wheezed. Rasim took a bewildered step forward, uncertain of what was happening to the man.

"Witch," Roscord spat. The effort of speaking made him turn purple. "Squeezing… my heart!"

Too late Rasim realized if it was his heart, then the gods were doing Donnin's work for her. But he was too close to Roscord by then, and the dying warlord rallied the last of his strength. He swung his sword, leading with the hilt, not the blade, and bashed Rasim in the temple.

An impossible voice shouted Rasim's name, and the last thing he saw was his own blood dripping from the sword as it fell toward him a second time.

CHAPTER 24

Warmth surrounded Rasim, softness gentler than a down duvet. The air was warm too. Air. He was breathing, or dead. Darkness suggested dead, and then a familiar voice said, "Give us some brightness."

Dead, then. Dead without a doubt, and the goddess Siliaria had taken on a guise she knew he would find familiar. There was no other reason for her to ask for a light in Captain Asindo's voice.

The desired light flared. Rasim crushed his eyes shut against the sudden onslaught of brilliance, then pried them open again. A candle went into a glass box, softening its harshness, and from the gentle glow Rasim saw he was in Asindo's cabin. In the captain's bed, in fact, which was vastly more comfortable than the net hammock Rasim usually slept in. A pang seized his heart, as sure and as painful as what Roscord had suffered. He could never deserve accommodations as fine as these, not even in the goddess's eyes. "I'm sorry, Siliaria, but I'd feel better in a berth like my own. I'm no captain."

A little silence met his request. He expected

Asindo's cabin to fade into a less impressive berth, but it remained the same. After a moment or two, Siliaria spoke again, still sounding like Asindo: "He's addled."

That wasn't a very nice thing for his goddess to say. Offended, Rasim pushed up, onto his elbows. His head throbbed, dizziness sweeping him, but he got a look around before falling back into the pillows.

Asindo was there, and Hassin, and the ship's nurse, a water witch called Usia whose magic rarely met an injury it couldn't heal. Siliaria had made a mistake there, Rasim thought: his head shouldn't hurt if Usia was in the cabin. That seemed strange. Goddesses weren't generally acknowledged to make mistakes.

Slowly, slowly, it dawned on Rasim that perhaps Siliaria hadn't made a mistake at all, and that *he* had. "...Captain?"

A familiar chuckle rumbled. "Yes, lad?"

That was sheerly impossible. Rasim looked at the wood above the captain's bed. Polished wood, not rough or tarred like the stuff in his own berth. The diffused candlelight made it glow with warmth. They looked real, like they were part of the *Wafiya* he'd known. A goddess would get those details right, of course, but a goddess would also not make other mistakes if she got the details of a cabin room right.

The idea that he had been wrong, that the fleet hadn't been lost, that he had only somehow missed them in the North — that was too large to consider. He would drown in them if he let himself think too hard, so instead Rasim cleared his throat, still staring at the captain's cabin and not quite letting himself look at the captain himself. "I see you've promoted me. Thank you. I think I'll be very comfortable in this cabin."

Another little silence rolled through the cabin. Then Hassin laughed. "I told you he'd be all right. *Goddess*, Rasim, we thought you were dead! What happened?"

Rasim sat up again, very carefully this time. Usia muttered and came to examine his head, scowling when Rasim winced. He had a deep booming voice and surprisingly gentle hands, the former of which scolded Hassin and the latter of which brushed hair away from the pounding spot on Rasim's skull. After a moment the weight of Usia's magic rolled over Rasim, witchery calling to the water within a human body and speeding the healing process. The pain receded. Rasim slumped, and Usia finally spoke to him: "Sorry you woke up in pain. I couldn't finish the job until I was certain your brains hadn't been mashed by that idiot with the sword."

"Roscord." Rasim's hands turned icy. "Where is he? What happened? Is Adele all right? I thought I—"

He'd thought he'd heard a ghost. The voice of a drowned friend. Rasim clutched Asindo's blanket to himself and watched the older crew members exchange glances. Asindo nodded, and Hassin let out an explosive breath.

"Roscord escaped. The witchery being used on

him—well, no one expected to see you, Rasim. Everyone lost control for a moment, and he ran. We thought you were dead. Again. When you weren't, that girl—Adele? She thought we should keep it secret that you still lived, in case of spies among us. So we brought you back to the ship for a burial at sea, we said, and Adele went with her mother, that pirate woman. She said she'd explain to her mother about you later."

"Donnin," Rasim said hollowly.

Hassin nodded. "Right. Donnin. Except she's evidently not really a sailor, but landed gentry of some kind."

He paused and Rasim nodded, filling in the blank. "She's the lady of a holding on one of these islands. Roscord raided her lands and took her daughter. We were trying to...get her back." It seemed preposterous when said in such simple words. "Roscord escaped? How? Where?" Silly questions. Besides, Rasim knew the warlord had allies on one of the Northern ships. Rasim probably knew more of the how and why than his crewmates did. It didn't matter. What did matter was, "You're *alive*."

The others exchanged looks again. This time Asindo spoke. "We've been in no danger, lad. It's you we thought dead. What *happened?*"

"I killed the serpent." It seemed like a lifetime ago. Rasim stared at the foot of Asindo's bed, at a map pinned to the wall and at a braided piece of cloth from some distant land. He might someday have the same kinds of things in his own cabin, when an hour ago he'd thought he would spend a lifetime rebuilding the Ilyaran fleet. Small thoughts of that sort helped him say, "I did it in Kisia's memory," without tears sliding down his cheeks.

That was as much as he dared admit, though, so he changed the subject as harshly as he could: "The fleet, is it all right? Everyone's safe? Where have you *been*? I made Donnin sail north—!"

"We're four ships down," Asindo said after a moment. "We lost four score sailors, with that many more too hurt to work. It would have been worse, without your ideas. We fled," he said frankly. "We thanked you for your sacrifice and we sailed north at full speed. We spent two weeks in the Northeners' capital."

"But I was there," Rasim said dully. "Only a few days later. You weren't there."

"You undershot," Asindo said with odd gentleness. "You visited Hongrunn, lad. Their second city, not their first. It's a day's sail farther south. We left Ringenstand with the tide the day we learned you were there, but we missed you in Hongrunn. We've been on your rudder all the way south."

Dull surprise leaked through Rasim. He hadn't asked. Not once. He'd never thought to ask what city Donnin's ship had landed in. Not after they'd been met by royalty, not even when he'd been told Lorens and

Inga had to correspond with their mother in a different city. It simply hadn't occurred to him.

"You brought up the fog," he said after a while. "On the sea last night. I was trying to, but..."

"We called it up before we saw land," Asindo said. "We wanted to come in unseen."

Hassin, who had remained silent, suddenly couldn't anymore. Teasing delight shot through his voice: "You slew a sea serpent for a *girl*, Rasim?"

Heat burned from Rasim's jaw to his hairline. "She deserved better than dying shipboard on her first sail."

"Then she's lucky, for she got better than that." Asindo opened his cabin door to say, "He's awake," to someone in the hall.

Kisia crashed into the room and flung herself at Rasim. Her momentum slammed them both against the wall, making Usia grunt with irritation, but Rasim felt no pain as she hugged him. "*Keesha?*"

"Keesha," she said, "is well and truly dead. I'm Kisia through and through now. Rasim, you *scared* me!"

"I sca—you were dead! The ship, I saw you, I saw it —! How did—?!" Rasim cast a bewildered, grateful glance at Hassin, whose power had thrust Kisia from one ship to another. "I thought you'd lost her," he said. "When the serpent took down that ship, I thought you lost her."

"I did."

"You—what?" Rasim's gaze bounced back to Kisia. "I know you have talent—"

"A conundrum for the guilds in itself," Asindo said under his breath.

"—but you'd only been studying sea witchery a week. How did you—?"

"I didn't. I don't know what happened, Rasim. The serpent broke the ship and I was in the water so fast I didn't even see it happening before I was drowning. Then the sea rose and scooped me up, shoved me onto the next ship's deck, but they all said it wasn't them."

"A rogue wave, maybe. Siliaria knows that serpent reigned chaos on the seas," said Asindo.

"It felt like magic," Kisia said with a note that suggested they'd argued about it before.

Rasim took her hand, reassuring himself she was still alive, then looked around the crowded little cabin. They were *all* still alive. A smile unlike any he'd felt in the past month stretched his mouth. Suddenly anything seemed possible, if they had all survived serpents and Northmen and islanders alike. "What's— how did I get on the *Wafiya?* What happened to Donnin?"

"She's settling in as the lady of the manor," Asindo said a bit dryly. "She thanked us and set us on our way. Kisia and Desimi brought you back to the *Wafiya,* and we sailed with the Northerners at dawn."

"Dawn?" Rasim blinked, first at Asindo, then toward the blocked-off porthole window. "What bell is it?"

Asindo snorted. "It's tomorrow, lad. You've been asleep for over a day. In *my* bed, no less, so I'd thank you to get out of it and let me rest."

Rasim's feet hit the floor before Asindo was finished speaking, but the captain laughed. "I'm joking, lad. Don't hurry yourself. You need food, and," he added with a wry look toward the door, "and to tell your tale to the crew. There's no sense in trying to put you back to work until the morning at soonest, and that depends on your strength."

Offended, Rasim said, "There's nothing wrong with my strength."

"You've slept for more than a day. I'll be the judge of your seaworthiness, boy. Kisia, get him to the galley and feed him as much as he can take. He looks half-starved, and I won't have Northerners castigating me for mistreating my crew."

"You have Northerners too?" Rasim had heard Asindo say it before, but hadn't quite realized what it meant. "How many?"

"Just the one ship. If it comes to us needing more, then we've a full war on our hands, and that's —" Asindo broke off with a glance at Kisia and Usia. "It doesn't matter now. Go eat, lad. We'll talk more later."

CHAPTER 25

The galley crew cheered as Rasim staggered in with Kisia supporting his weight. He'd been wrong about his strength, though he couldn't understand his own exhaustion. The work on Donnin's ship hadn't been hard. He entertained the idea that he had actually called up the thickening fog after hearing screams the night before. That might have exhausted him, though it seemed more likely the fog had come in with Asindo's crew.

Two nights before, not last night. He'd slept a long time. Maybe that was why he was so weary. He just needed food.

He sagged all the more when applause and shouts of glee met his arrival. The head cook, a skinny sailor called Jisik, squeezed through his staff to clap Rasim's shoulder. "Don't look so confused, lad. You're the fleet's hero, through and through, and you're back from the gullet of a serpent besides. You're a hero, Rasim. I've saved you some oranges."

Befuddled but happy, Rasim left the galley several minutes later with enough food for three boys his size, hobbling up to deck to eat in the fresh air.

It happened again on deck, work stopping in the name of applauding him. Heat scalded his cheeks and he ducked his head, delighted and embarrassed at the same time. Kisia patted his back and slipped away to let him enjoy the accolades, though she caught a few elbows in the ribs and good-natured winks as she left him alone. "All for a girl, eh?" someone asked, and Rasim's blush grew even hotter.

"It wasn't like that. Besides, my stupid idea about drowning it in air wasn't working. I had to do something." He hunched over his meal, defensive and also grinning, then offered up chunks of bread and cheese to the crew nearest him. "I can't eat it all."

"Don't be sure." Cersia, the sailor who blew the morning whistle that had started everything, took a hunk of cheese anyway. "You'd be surprised how much you can eat after a day's sleep. You did well, Rasim. But Siliaria's fins, mate, what did you do with the whistle!?"

He blinked at her, dismayed. She laughed aloud, clapping him on the shoulder. "I found it in the crow's nest. For some reason the captain told me to rouse everyone with a shout for the rest of the journey, though."

A tiny smile crept over Rasim's face. "I wonder why."

She grinned again, smacked his arm, and left him to take ribbing and congratulations until he could hardly stand it. Being a hero was less comfortable than he'd imagined it would be. He mumbled, "Anybody could've done it," once, only to have the sailor next to him bark disbelief.

"Anybody bloody well could not have. Who'd think of it?"

"Someone not too smart," Rasim said wryly, and everyone laughed. They didn't disagree, though, and that took some of the puff from Rasim's chest.

Finally Asindo came on deck, his presence clearing away Rasim's flood of admirers and sending them back to work. Equally relieved and disappointed, Rasim made his way to the prow, where he could watch and feel the ship's motion without being too much in the way. The water was turning blue again as they sailed south, and the wind was warm. With food in his belly and the ship's hull protecting him from the breeze, he was cozy enough—and still tired enough, it seemed—to drowse.

"You must think you're pretty smart." Desimi's voice was as hard as a foot in the ribs.

Rasim came awake with a startle. Desimi stood above him, arms folded over his chest, short black hair standing in the wind and a scowl pulling the corners of his mouth down. If they weren't actually on board, Rasim was certain he'd have been wakened by a kick, not angry words. He sighed and turned his face against the ship's curved prow. "Actually I think I'm pretty stupid, and really lucky. I should be dead."

"So should half the fleet, but no, you went and saved us all." Rage washed off Desimi with the weight of magic.

Rasim looked up at him in astonishment. "You didn't want everybody to die, did you?" Half a breath later he understood: Desimi had wanted to be the hero. Again, like he'd been when he'd listened to Rasim's command at the docks and begun lifting the waves that would save Ilyara. A laugh choked Rasim's throat. "If I'd thought of throwing you in instead of me I would've done it. Your magic's a lot stronger than mine. You wouldn't have almost died."

His voice hardened, a bitterness he tried to keep buried finally rising to the surface: "You would've killed the serpent and come up out of the sea on a whirlpool, looking like Siliaria's own son, instead of being dragged unconscious from a pool of blood by pirates and getting yourself almost sold to slavers. *Goddess*, Desimi, what does it take? You're bigger than I am, stronger than I am, and my magic is *never* going to match yours. *Captain Asindo* followed your lead at the docks. I saw it, Desimi, I felt it. He didn't take control of the magic until the water had to be lifted free of the harbor entirely. That was *your* witchery that saved the city."

"It was your idea."

"Ideas are cheap," Rasim snapped. "They don't mean anything without the talent to see them through, and I'm never going to have that on my own."

"I'm never going to have the ideas," Desimi snarled back, then spun on his heel and stalked away, leaving Rasim staring after him in bewilderment.

"He hates that he jumped when you said hop, at the docks." Hassin joined Rasim as Desimi, fierce and lithe as a big cat, leaped to the sails and swarmed up to correct an already perfect knot. Rasim transferred his confused gaze to the third mate, who watched Desimi, not Rasim, as he went on. "It's not your northern blood he hates, though he doesn't realize that. It's your wits. I've watched you grow up together. You're the natural leader, not just with Desimi, but with others. It wasn't just he who jumped when you said to, after all. We all did."

"It was a good idea," Rasim whispered, a little defensive and mostly uncertain.

Hassin chuckled. "Yes, it was. But you're thirteen, and you gave an order that witches four times your age responded to without thinking. Desimi's smart enough to see that, and smart enough to recognize people don't react to him that way."

"They might if he didn't try to push them around so much."

Hassin's mouth twitched again. "Maybe. He wants a fight, Rasim. He wants to be able to defeat you so he knows where he stands."

"I'm not *going* to fight!" Rasim burst out, then lowered his voice into frustrated intensity. "First, he'd

kill me, so what's the point? We both know he'd kill
me. But all I want is to sail, Hassin. I just want to be
on the sea. Fighting would get me kicked off the
Wafiya." His hands made fists and loosened again,
over and over. "I wish I *could*. I wish I could fight him
and show him who's stronger, but I wouldn't just lose
the fight. I'd lose everything."

Hassin pursed his lips, looking at Rasim. "Not
many boys your age see that clearly. Including
Desimi."

"It'd be more fun if I didn't," Rasim muttered. "But
we're already orphans, Hassin. We already lost
everything once. Losing it again is just...stupid. I wish
Desimi could see that."

"Maybe he will someday. In the meantime, not
fighting is smart."

"Sometimes smart isn't as great as everybody
thinks." Rasim slumped against the ship's wall. "I'm
just glad he's alive. I'm glad you're *all* alive, even if he
hates *me* for being alive. And I didn't even get to say
goodbye to Donnin. Why did we leave so fast?"

"Mmm." Hassin sat beside Rasim. "Lady Donnin's
daughter said there was a Northern spy aboard the
ship that had sailed with Donnin, someone who had
betrayed you to Roscord. She said you'd told her about
the spy." He lifted an eyebrow, asking for verification
of Adele's story. After a moment of struggling to
remember when he could have possibly told her—the
moment he met her, maybe!—Rasim's face cleared and

he nodded. Hassin, satisfied, nodded as well. "We thought if there were spies among them, we'd best sail for home on the first tide, in case there's any trouble brewing there. They've a half-night's head start on us."

"A ship of Northerners is going to get looked at funny if they just sail in," Rasim objected. "They haven't been welcome since the fire."

"They're still our trading partners, and they still come, once or twice a year. They won't be turned away."

"And when we show up with another ship full of them?"

"Someone," Hassin said toothily, "will notice. Rasim, are you ready to talk to the captain? I think you have a lot to tell us."

"I think you have a lot to tell *me*." Only when Hassin looked at him oddly did Rasim think perhaps it had been an arrogant thing to say. He drew breath to defend himself, then let it go. He hadn't intended to end up at the center of a whirlpool, with events speeding around him uncontrollably. But he was there, watching pieces of flotsam flash by. The Great Fire and the smaller one just a month ago, and how they linked to Queen Annaken's death; the sabotaged water supply in Hongrunn; even Donnin's plight with Roscord, which was unrelated but still whipped around Rasim. But maybe it wasn't unrelated after all, because Donnin had promised Rasim an army if he needed one, so she might yet be drawn into the Ilyaran war.

His stomach clenched at that last thought. *War*. It wasn't a word he'd used, not even in the silence of his mind, but now that it lay there in his thoughts, stark and harsh, Rasim knew it was the only word *to* use. Cold with the realization, he followed Hassin to Asindo's cabin.

Night fell before he finished telling them about his adventures over the past weeks. They, like he, had confided their suspicions about the Great Fire to the Northern queen, Jaana. They too had garnered support, and Jaana's conviction had increased when she'd learned about Hongrunn's poisoned water supply from Inga.

"I still haven't figured out how to get that salt fountain out of there," Hassin had said then, and all three of them had fallen silent a little while, considering the problem. Then Rasim had begun his story again, remembering to mention Inga's theory about the weakened magic outside of Ilyara, and possibly even within its royal family.

That, he saw, was no surprise to Asindo or Hassin. Rasim felt young and foolish for a moment, wishing he had access to the same information that his older crewmates did. But then, there were many things he knew that most of the others didn't know. Things that not even Kisia, whose observations had set Rasim on this path, didn't know. That was considerably more unfair than Rasim not being privy to observations that had no doubt been made long before he'd been drawn into this intrigue.

Growing up, he thought grumpily, was much more complicated than it seemed from the outside. "What will we do when we get home? Who can we trust?"

"Ourselves," Asindo replied, and it was a long moment before Rasim realized there would be no further answer.

CHAPTER 26

Ilyara hadn't changed in the weeks Rasim had been gone.

Standing at the ship's prow, watching the golden sandstone city rise up from the river banks, Rasim realized he'd expected it to. He'd never been gone from his home so long before, or experienced so much or changed so much himself while gone. It seemed reasonable to expect that the city would have changed, too.

But it was the same, from the gold-and-white splashed banners that flew from the highest points all the way down through the sweeping broad streets and the crystal blue water fronting the city. From this distance there were no visible scars from any fire, not the great one and not the smaller one only a few weeks earlier. People weren't visible as individuals, only as a moving stream in the streets, their clothing bright between yellow walls. The Seamasters' Guild's distinct shape rose up near the water, sending a pang of homesickness through Rasim. It seemed silly to be homesick now, less than an hour from the Ilyaran docks, but he'd hardly had time before.

Footsteps sounded on the deck behind him. He glanced back to see Kisia, and at a slightly greater distance, Desimi as well. Kisia smiled and came forward. Desimi stayed back, but they were both watching Ilyara, and looked the way Rasim felt: surprised the city hadn't changed, homesick, relieved, and somehow sad.

There were duties they should be attending, but no one came to scold them as Rasim turned back to look at the city, too. Maybe the older sailors understood. Maybe it was like this for everyone, the first time they came home for a long sail. Maybe they all stood at the prow, wondering how the city could be so much the same when they felt they had changed so much.

It remained the same until they came around the long spit of earth that protected the city's harbor from the river and sea. Rasim had seen tall masts peeking over the spit, but not until they entered the harbor did he see that they were on Northern ships.

Ships, not ship. There were five Northern ships just within the harbor's mouth, blockading it. *Blockading* it, their ships linked by booms and chains and casually dangerous warriors who kept watch from the decks, obviously prepared for a fight.

A bark of incredulity ran through the *Wafiya's* crew. Asindo came forward, raising a hand for silence. Rasim and Kisia fell back from the prow, getting out of the captain's way. They ended up next to Desimi, who muttered what Rasim was thinking: "Nobody can hold the Guild back with a handful of ships. Why don't we just sink them?"

"There must be a reason," Kisia breathed. "Maybe Isidri wants them to feel as if they're doing well."

Rasim and Desimi both looked at her, nonplussed. Kisia shrugged and flashed a smile. "Don't tell me it doesn't seem like something she'd do so that when they started getting confident she could just—" She opened her hand, then crushed it into a fist, indicating the Northern ships' inevitable fate.

Rasim exchanged a glance of alarm with Desimi, for once in agreement. Not that Kisia was wrong, but the fact that she thought like Guildmaster Isidri—well, it was probably better to stay on Kisia's good side.

Still, Desimi said, "I don't think so," and Rasim agreed with that, too. Maybe not for reasons Desimi understood, because he didn't know about the threat Ilyara faced, but Rasim thought he was right anyway. He said so aloud, earning a startled, suspicious look from the bigger boy.

"No," Rasim said, "I really do think you're right. The Guildmaster might privately think of that, and even think it was funny, but I don't think she'd risk the city to amuse herself. Something else is going on."

"More than half the fleet is in there," Desimi

whispered furiously. "Five ships shouldn't be enough to hold the harbor. Not against witches."

Rasim nodded. He'd had the same thought when they'd sailed north, only in reverse. The Ilyaran fleet could hold any harbor, because of its magic. And no one could stand against them, because no one else *had* magic.

Unless they did.

A stone dropped through Rasim's belly, cold and sickening. He caught Kisia's arm and backed further away from Asindo, who had called Hassin and the other mates forward. Desimi looked between the captain and Rasim, then, with obvious anger, chose to stomp after Rasim, elbowing in as Rasim said, in a low, tense, voice, "You started learning magic late, Kisia. It made me try to teach one of the pirates some witchery, too, and she learned it, even though she was even older than you."

"You did *what?*" Fury sharpened Desimi's voice, even though he kept it low.

Rasim snapped, "They were going to kill me otherwise," though he knew Desimi wouldn't care. The fact he'd taught Carley magic would come back to haunt him. "It doesn't matter. The point is, what if someone else has been teaching the Northerners magic? What if they can learn late, just like you did, Kisia? And what if their magic is—is *different?* What if ours doesn't work against it?"

"How can it be different if we taught it to them?"

Kisia looked over Rasim's shoulder toward the Northern ships. "If that's what's going on, Rasim, then what do they *want*?"

"I don't know." Rasim turned to look at the Northern ships, too, then edged a few steps back toward Asindo and the higher-ranking crew surrounding him. They were working magic, their witchery reaching into the sea and trying to waken it. Rasim felt the power's weight in the air, but the blue water around them remained calm. More than calm: almost frozen, like they'd brought the Northern chill into Ilyaran waters. Rasim looked over the railing, seeing hints of glacier blue in the still sea.

Guildmaster Isidri was one of the few water witches who could manipulate water's temperature. It was part of why she was Guildmaster: she had skill beyond everyone else's, even Asindo's. He was a storm master, like Desimi would be, but he couldn't create a storm in frozen waters. Isidri might be able to. She could bring water to a boil or freeze it with a touch. And judging from the stillness of the harbor, the Northmen had a witch who could do the same.

No. The thought hit Rasim with the clarity of fresh water. Not one, but *many*. *One* would never be able to chill a body of water as large as the harbor, or even just the mouth of it. Besides, Guildmaster Isidri was unquestionably a match for any individual witch. Only numbers could defeat her.

The weight of Asindo's magic changed, growing

deeper. The upper crew were standing together now, shoulder to shoulder, working as one. Even Rasim, whose magic was limited, could tell the depths they were reaching to. The harbor wasn't enough: they were reaching out to sea, reaching for the power and warmth and strength of the ocean itself. A surge shifted far below them, a tidal wave preparing to rise. There was no way the handful of Northern ships could stand against them. The Northerners had to know that.

Rasim whispered, "Stop."

Kisia gave him a sharp look, then without asking, darted forward to grab Asindo's arm. Her hiss was audible across the whole ship: "Captain, *stop.*"

Asindo shook her off and she cast a despairing glance at Rasim. He stepped forward, not quite sure what drove his certainty. "Captain, stop. But — falter. Let the witchery stutter. Like they're defeating us. *Do* it, Captain Asindo!"

The captain scowled over his shoulder, his expression a demand for explanation

Rasim crushed his eyes shut, barely able to trust himself to think. He was afraid that if he tried too hard he would lose the idea burgeoning in his mind, like it wasn't strong enough yet to be put into words. But words were all he had, so he began to whisper again, trying not to hear himself as he spoke. "They *have* to know we're stronger than they are. Either that or they're unbelievably confident. If they're confident maybe they have reason to be, in which case we should *let them win.*"

"Are you *crazy?*" Desimi's voice shot up, outrage lending it depth. Half the crew moved closer to him, supporting his anger and confusion. Kisia, seeing that, deliberately returned to Rasim's side. Asindo did nothing, only held the forming magic and waited on Rasim's answers.

"I don't think so. If they're confident it means one of two things." Rasim lifted two fingers, touching their tips to enumerate his points. "Either their magic is much stronger than we think, in which case we're better off not challenging it until we know more about it. Or their magic isn't that strong and they *want* us to sink them because it'll give someone in the city an excuse to do something terrible. We *don't know* what's happening in Ilyara, Captain. Anything we do might make it worse."

"Anything we do might make it better!" This time even Asindo nodded at Desimi's protest. But the captain's grip on the witchery loosened a little, too. The sea shivered way down deep, relaxing as the power wakening it faded.

Rasim's shoulders slumped. He whispered, "Thank you," then made himself straighten, trying to sound brave even though his heart slammed in his chest like a fish on the beach. "Put up a fight, Captain. Just...don't win it. Not yet. We need to know more, first."

"You have a strange way of waging war, boy," Asindo growled, but gave the nod to the crew standing with him. "We'll break down one at a time. Make a show of it. Somebody signal the rest of the fleet to follow our lead."

Desimi snarled and stalked off the deck, his rage as palpable as magic. Rasim went after him, catching his arm a step or two into the hold. "Desimi—"

The bigger boy came around with a fist that caught Rasim by the jaw and knocked him back up the stairs he'd just come down. Stunned, he slid down again, thumping until his butt hit the floor. He looked up in pained amazement, then had the wits to cover his head with his arms to ward off another blow. Desimi snarled again, but to Rasim's astonishment, didn't even try to hit him a second time. He only stomped away, leaving Rasim a glazed lump at the bottom of the steps.

Kisia came down the stairs at speed and nearly tumbled over Rasim. She gave a wordless shout after Desimi, then sprang over Rasim and crouched before him. "Are you all right?"

Rasim waggled his jaw, feeling pain shoot toward his ear. "I think so. Desi! *Desimi,* for Siliaria's sake—!" He got up, staggered, and put his hand to his jaw. "Goddess, but he hits hard. *Desimi!*" Still a little bleary, he followed Desimi with Kisia chattering concern as they went.

Desimi wasn't hard to find. The ship wasn't that

big, and with the exception of the upper crew's quarters, there was no privacy aboard. Desimi was at his berth, though not in it: he stood facing the ship's hull and working his fists like he wanted to hit something again.

Rasim stopped a prudent distance away. There was no point in *asking* to get hit again, after all. "Desimi, you didn't give me a chance to finish talking, up there."

"*Talking.*" Desimi spun, fury sparking in his dark eyes. "That's all you ever want to do. Why don't you go talk to the Northerners? They're your kin anyway. Go talk to them and don't come back."

Rasim rolled his jaw again. He knew he should be angry, but the not-quite-graspable thoughts that had prompted him to stop Asindo were still racing through his mind. He felt like they were running through the top of his head, where he had to stand up extra straight to reach them. Standing up so straight, struggling to catch the ideas, took all his attention and left none for anger. "I talk because I'd never win a fight. You hit like a yardarm. Listen, Desimi, I bet you anything the Northerners will try to board us."Desimi snorted. "The captain will never let them."

"He should. He needs to find out what they know, what they're doing. And *we* need the distraction."

Desimi eyed Rasim warily. "We?"

"You and me."

"Don't you even think I'm not part of whatever you've got in mind, Rasim," Kisia warned.

Rasim grinned, surprising himself. "I would never dare. You got me into this whole mess, after all."

Kisia, sounding self-satisfied, said, "Yes. Yes I did."

Desimi scowled at them both. "What do you want me for? I'm not your friend."

"No, but you're another new journeyman, and we're the least likely to be missed if the *Wafiya* gets boarded. And you're the only one strong enough to get us off the ship and into Ilyara without anybody noticing."

"Why would I do that?"

"Because." Rasim smiled. "Because once you have, you're going to get to hit something."

CHAPTER 27

Ships were not made for sneaking away from. There could be no secret doors in the hull for fear of sinking the whole thing, and the windows were far too small even for someone Rasim's size. Slipping back up onto deck so they could then silently climb down the rigging at the ship's stern lacked subtlety, but it was better than just diving off the side in full view of the Northerners.

The water was cold. Nearly as cold as the Northern harbor had been, which spoke to the strength of the witches whose magic chilled it. Desimi gave Rasim a dirty look as they sank in, and Kisia whispered, "This can't be good for the fish."

"It's not good for us, either," Desimi snapped, but then his magic pushed them deep into the harbor. An air bubble larger and steadier than any Rasim could imagine creating enveloped them as they sank, and a minute or two later they were clearing their ears on the harbor floor. Desimi muttered, "The water's sluggish. It's not as easy to move through as it should be. We need to get beyond the Northern ships as fast as we can. Maybe the water will warm up then, but mostly then at least they won't see us if they look down."

Rasim, alarmed, looked *up*. The harbor's legendarily clear waters were less clear than usual, thick crystals of ice suspended in them. Blue light still penetrated to the depth they were at, and it was definitely possible that a Northerner glancing down might notice a journeyman-filled bubble of air hurrying across the harbor bottom.

"Their magic is pushing at mine," Desimi said. "I'm trying to keep it from noticing me, but we'd better get through before the captain gives up fighting. We have to run."

Without discussing it, they each took one of Kisia's hands. She looked between them, obviously amused, but said nothing. All three broke into a run, Rasim fighting to keep pace with Desimi, whose legs were longer. Once Desimi looked at him with an expression that made it clear he was running that fast just to make Rasim work for it. Exasperation rose in Rasim's chest. Even at the bottom of the ocean, some things would never change.

The shadows from above changed, though, as they passed beneath the Northern ships and then ran through relatively clear harbor water toward the shore. Rasim's own magic might have gotten them half the distance, he judged, but there was still plenty of air when they arrived at the deep-reaching sea wall. Desimi slowed, judging their location, then turned left and let the bubble begin to rise. After a moment, Rasim laughed. "Masira will kill you."

Desimi actually gave him a tight grin in return. "This was all your idea."

Rasim laughed again. Kisia looked between them, then stomped a foot on the rising bubble. "What are you talking about?"

"There's a private door in the sea wall," Rasim said cheerfully. "It's a secret passage to our bath houses. The captains usually slip away half an hour before they dock after long journeys. Especially during festivals. They go in just like we're doing, get cleaned, change into clothes too fine to bring on board, have their queues rebraided, and come back out to their ships so when they come in to port they're at their best. Only the captains are supposed to know about it."

"So how do *you* know?"

"Everybody knows," Desimi said, almost as pleasantly as Rasim. "You can't slip off a ship without somebody noticing. It's one of the things apprentices do, figure out where the captain's gone. I don't know anybody who hasn't gotten the life scared out of them by Masira standing there at the door when they finally make it into the captains' bath chambers."

Kisia squinted at Rasim. "How did you do it? Is your magic strong enough?"

"It's strong enough for one. I just couldn't bring all three of us the way Desimi's doing. There, that's the door. Can you — oh."

Desimi brought them to the sea door — and it *was* a sea door, built well under the surface even at low tide — and pressed the air bubble against the wall, flattening it on one side. Then he opened the door, air meeting air, with no flood of water from the harbor.

"Oh," Rasim said again. His ears burned, partly with embarrassment and partly because he was impressed and embarrassed by that, too. "I made a lot more mess than that. It took me three hours to slop out the water I let in."

An air of smug superiority settled around Desimi, enough so that he let Rasim go up the steps first. Of course, that meant Rasim would be the one who faced Masira's wrath, but Rasim didn't quite begrudge Desimi that. It *had* been Rasim's idea, more or less.

He still pushed the bath house door at the top of the stairs open with more caution than absolutely necessary, hoping maybe Masira wasn't lurking there that day. He peeked out, recalling Adele doing the same in Roscord's mansion only ten days before. That had ended badly. This, he promised himself, would not.

Masira *was* there, but not lurking. She sat at the

far side of the room, her back pressed against a wall and her feet drawn up on one of the ledges that ran around two sides of the room. Her arms were looped over her knees, her forehead resting against them. Despite her broad shoulders and the steel grey in her black hair, she looked like an unhappy child.

She lifted her head as the door scraped open, hope lighting her face. She'd crossed the room before Rasim stepped out, her voice hardly more than a whisper: "Oh, thank the goddess—oh, *no.*" All the hope fled from her expression. "Rasim? *Desimi?* And who's this? Ah, gods and goddesses of the sun and sea, where's Asindo? Where's Narisa or Lansik? We need master witches, not apprentices and tag-alongs!"

Rasim and Desimi, as one, muttered, "Journeymen," while Kisia sniffed. "I'm a Seamasters' apprentice myself, so you don't have to be rude."

Masira gave Kisia a hard look, then a sharper one. "You're that baker's daughter that Isidri took in. Keesha al Balian."

"Kisia al Ilialio," Kisia said firmly, then elbowed Rasim.

He jolted. "The captain and mates are at the harbor's mouth. Northerners are blockading it. What's going on? Why hasn't Guildmaster Isidri stopped them?" Slowly, things that were wrong in the bathing room filtered between his burst of questions. The baths were low on water and no steam rose from them. The air was chilly, the floors cold, and he could hear no voices from other rooms. This one should have one or two masters lounging, even if a third of the fleet had sailed a month ago. There were still plenty of Seamasters left in Ilyara.

Or there had been, a month ago. Dread rose in Rasim's chest, making him as chilly as the room. "Masira, what's going on?"

Masira's mouth set in a thin, grim line. "Guildmaster Isidri's been arrested as a traitor, and the Guild disassembled."

Ocean sounds rushed through Rasim's ears: a roar of water, of waves beating endlessly against the shore. The sea seemed to wipe away his vision, too, whitecaps and storm grey smashing the world to white. He even felt like he floated, suspended in disbelief as surely as he might drift in salt water.

Masira's words knocked him about, buffeting him like the open ocean. "It's her own fault, too, sending the whole fleet away. Nobody liked it, and when the Northmen came a week ago, claiming Asindo had come searching for an army, what were the people to believe? And you know how Isidri is. She won't take guff from anybody, and people like her or loathe her for it. I don't know where the rumor started, but all at once the whole city was talking about how the Seamasters' Guild had had enough of a weak king and how Isidri was planning to make a power play once she had the Northmen on her side. Can you imagine it? Queen Isidri?"

"I can," Kisia said faintly, and Rasim agreed. Not that he imagined her wanting to be queen—he thought the guild was quite enough for her—but it was easy to imagine someone with her presence and power *being* queen. And it was easy to imagine that other people might think her power might mean she did want it. Some guildmasters would be terrified. Worse, some might be inspired. But even those who were inspired would want Isidri out of the way first, so they could make their move without fighting through her.

Masira's outrage flattened into a sigh. "Yes. So can we all. So could others, obviously. They came to the guildhall by the hundreds, ready to tear it apart to get to her. She left without a fight, to save the hall, but the king proclaimed the Seamasters disbanded."

"Where has everyone gone?" Desimi wondered. "The hall is all we've got to live in."

"Scattered here and there throughout the city. Enough are staying at the hall, rotating through, to keep it safe from vandals. The Sunmasters came to burn us." Ferocity lit Masira's strong features. "We fought them with the sea, for all that it's half frozen. We would rather die than see our hall burn again. And we've enough friends in the city, even still, that the Sunmasters finally went away again. The people are getting hungry," she said more softly. "This frozen water is bad for the fish."

"I knew it!" Kisia shrank in on herself at Masira's sharp look. "Well, I did," she muttered. "I didn't think about people getting hungry, but I knew the cold water had to be bad for fishing."

"Even if we could get beyond the harbor," Masira agreed.

That finally shook Rasim from his ocean-shock stupor. "Why can't we? Even if the whole of the fleet was out there, that would still be only half the guild. What kind of magic are the Northmen using?"

"Cold and hot and wood and metal," Masira said without hesitation. "It's not magic like ours. I've never seen anyone draw cold into a sword so the metal itself shatters, or anyone but the strongest Sunmaster turn a blade molten. Their magic is different, up there in the north. I didn't even think they had any."

Rasim, thinking of the murals and of Inga's theories, said, "They used to," then pushed the memories away. "Who warned the king about Isidri?"

"An Islander," Masira replied. "A man called Roscord."

CHAPTER 28

For the second time in a handful of minutes, Rasim's head swam. This time he sat down, dragging in deep breaths of air. Kisia squatted by him and put a hand on his shoulder. "It can't be," she said quietly. "It can't be the same man. How could he have gotten here a week ago? We left the islands on the next morning's tide, and the Ilyaran fleet is the fastest there is."

Desimi snorted. "Northern magic. Or island magic, since Rasim was *teaching it to them.*"

"I taught one girl to purify water," Rasim said to his knees. "No one could use that to sail from the islands to here in three days. That's...if every wind was with them, if the seas were calm, if everything was perfect, maybe then." He thought again of the Northern city of Hongrunn, and the salt fountain at the bottom of its lake. He lifted his head, examining the far wall as if he could see the Northern witches if he studied hard enough. "Maybe it *was* perfect. Maybe their witches did it. We can, if we have to."

"We control the water," Masira said.

Rasim shrugged. "And we bring sky witches along with us to control the winds. Maybe they've got something similar, and Roscord knew he needed to get here fast enough to sow dissent against us. We didn't know we would need to defend our names, so we didn't hurry."

"Wait. You *know* this man?"

"Rasim does," Kisia answered.

Rasim, almost absently, said, "He tried to kill me," then blinked in surprise as Masira wheezed with shock. He began to explain, then gave up immediately, only saying, "It's been a strange month. Do you know if Roscord is a witch? He cursed me when he thought I was using magic to squeeze his heart..."

Kisia looked suddenly uncomfortable. Rasim was reminded abruptly of the impossible, familiar voice he'd heard shout his name in the moment before Roscord had struck him the second time. He got to his feet, staring at Kisia. "That *was* you. I thought it couldn't possibly be. I thought you were dead. You saved me? You saved me!" Then his stomach twisted, another realization following hard on the first. "Goddess, Kisia. Was that *you?*"

"It's my fault he got away," Kisia mumbled. "I had him with my witchery—"

"She has magic?" Masira demanded. "That's impossible."

"It gets better," Desimi muttered. "I told you, he's

been teaching Northerners magic too."

Kisia ignored them both, her brown eyes fixed on Rasim. "—squeezing his heart like squeezing water out of cheese. But then I saw you and I was so surprised I shouted, and let him go. He could breathe all of a sudden. I think that's why he didn't hit you hard enough to kill you. He took a big breath and it pulled him back from you some. And then he ran and I—I let him go." Her shoulders caved with guilt even as her gaze remained defiant. "I couldn't just let him *kill* you! Not when I thought you were already dead!"

Desimi breathed, "Like that makes sense," but Rasim understood perfectly. It was hard, thinking a friend was dead. He would let anyone go, even the one who'd started the Great Fire, if his choice was stopping that person or saving Kisia. He nodded foolishly, and Kisia's smile burst through her defiance.

For some reason, Masira was grinning when Rasim looked away from Kisia. "Nothing," she said to his questioning gaze. "Nothing. We have to get you to the king, Rasim. He needs to hear what you know about this Roscord."

"Will he listen? I'm a journeyman from the disbanded Seamasters' Guild. I'm not even a good witch."

"I think you are," Kisia said, but Rasim ignored her as she'd ignored the others, earlier.

"We have to make Roscord betray himself. How can we—"

"Just show up where he is," Desimi said. "Trust me, he'll try to kill you."

All three of them looked at him. He folded his arms over his chest and glared at them in return.

A smile twitched at the corner of Rasim's mouth. The longer Desimi glared, the more that smile wanted to turn to a laugh. Just before it did, he said, "Sure of that, are you?"

Desimi's glare turned to a glower. "Yeah. I am."

Somehow that made Rasim's humor fade. He glanced down, then met Desimi's eyes again. "I guess that means the question is whether you'll stick your neck out to help keep me alive if Roscord feels the same way you do."

Desimi stared at him a long moment, then cursed and stomped away. Not far: just to the door leading to the rest of the bath house. He stopped there, fists working, and finally turned his head toward the others. "Are you just going to stand there, or what?"

It was a good enough answer. Rasim caught Kisia's hand. They ran after Desimi, only to be snagged firmly on each shoulder by Masira. "Are you mad?" she asked, almost pleasantly. "You're barely journeymen. What do you think you're going to do against an island witch? You can't go without a master. Or several."

Rasim shook her hand off. "We can't go *with* one. You

said yourself the guild's been disbanded. Everyone will recognize masters and probably even high-ranking journeymen. But you're right. We *are* barely journeymen. Nobody will know us, Masira. We're the only ones who *can* do anything to an island witch. Desimi's as strong as any sixth-year journeyman, you know that, and Kisia — "

He broke off with quick shiver. Kisia, it seemed, was ruthless, if she'd been able and willing to use her witchery to squeeze Roscord's heart to a pulp. But she picked up where he left off, describing herself very differently: "I'm from the traders, and my father's bakery is popular. Lots of people know me. They won't think anything of me being out, even if it's somewhere they wouldn't usually see me. I can get us into the temples and maybe even the palace, if I have to."

Masira's eyes narrowed at Rasim. "And what about you? You're not much of a witch, Rasim."

He sighed, making mockery of himself as he said, "No, but I'm clever. I'll think of something."

"You'd better," Desimi muttered.

"I don't like it." Masira scowled.

Rasim shrugged. "You don't have to. Come on, the faster we find Roscord the less time he'll have to plot and plan. He's got to know the fleet is out there already."

This time Masira let them go, though the weight of her disapproval followed them like magic. Once out of her sight, Kisia gave Rasim a funny look. "You're a lot like Guildmaster Isidri."

Desimi snorted. "Right. Except he's thirteen, a boy, and can barely keep water out of his nose when he washes."

Kisia scowled at Desimi. "No, I mean, he can talk people into doing what they don't want to do. You should have seen the Guildmaster convincing my parents to let me join her. They didn't want to, but she just kept being sensible at them until they couldn't think of any more reasons to say no."

"Your parents," Rasim said thoughtfully as they left the bathhouses. The docks were unusually quiet for daytime. There were no ships in, no fish to haul to shore, and too much chill came off the water for it to be pleasant walking, even though the sun was shining.

Rasim was aware that all of those things made them stand out, but none of the few people nearby paid attention to them. They were obviously children, so young their hair hadn't grown out enough to even pretend to tie back in a queue. Children went places they weren't supposed to all the time. Sneaking in and out of the Seamasters' bathhouses when the guild had been disbanded was hardly less than might be expected, and within a minute or two the three of them were away from the docks and hurrying toward the city center.

Only then did Rasim speak again, guessing the general sounds of business and gossip would drown out his quiet voice. "You're right, Kisia. You can get us in to the temples or maybe the palace, especially if we're bringing gifts. It's been a month since you left. It'd be a good time for your parents to send an offering to the gods for your safe return, wouldn't it? And I bet your parents know exactly which pastries and treats the Sunmasters' apprentices at the palace like best."

"What good's that going to do? It's not like this Roscord is going to be bunking with them." Belligerent or not, Desimi followed when Rasim turned toward the bakery, and made an irritated face of agreement when Rasim said, "No, but I bet they'll know rumors about where he's staying, or maybe about what's happened to Guildmaster Isidri, and they'll trade rumors for treats. We would."

"And once we're inside the palace gates we at least have a chance of finding Roscord." Kisia's features set with determination. "I won't let him get away a second time."

"It'd be better if we can get him to betray himself, than killing him," Rasim said uncomfortably. He didn't like the idea of killing anyone, especially not so cold-bloodedly they were discussing it ahead of time. "If we just kill him, it'll make the Seamasters look all the more guilty. We don't want that." He took a deep breath and smiled a bit. "I can smell the bakery now. It's the best-smelling bakery in Ilyara."

"It is." Kisia flashed an immodest grin, then broke

into a run, clearly eager to see her family again. Rasim and Desimi chased her, the scent of fresh bread making Rasim's stomach grumble with hunger. People stepped out of their way, some smiling and some scowling, as the three raced through the streets. Kisia kept the lead, and began shouting her family's names as they got closer.

Her older brother Nereek came to the door as they ran the last block to the bakery. Broad-shouldered and big-bellied, he was usually good-natured, liking to throw the youngest apprentices into the air and make them yell before he would hand out cinnamon breads. But he filled the door with tension now, and his face was pale with fear and anger as the three guild orphans skidded to a stop.

"Keesha. Keesha, goddess, thank the stars you're alive." Nereek didn't move, didn't try to offer his younger sister a hug or any further greeting. He only took another half step out of the door and dropped his voice: "You have to run. You have to run *now*. They've taken our parents."

Shock flooded Rasim almost as sharply as it hit Kisia. Her knees buckled, though, and his didn't. He caught her elbow, and Desimi caught the other one. They began backing away, following Nereek's order, but Kisia threw them off and ran forward. "What? Why? *Why?* Nereek, what's going on?!"

Nereek advanced another few steps, keeping just close enough to be heard. His gestures were sharp, like he was casting Kisia out. She stopped short, then backed up too, injury crushing her features even though Nereek's words were as soft and kind as they could be. "Because you joined the Seamasters. They took our parents so they could get to you—"

"*Of course they'll get to me!* Where are they? What do I have to do—?!"

Nereek shook his head once, hard and angry. "Don't do it, Keesha. Don't go to them. It won't get Mother and Father back, it'll only put you in their hands."

"Who?" Rasim asked. "Who are they?"

Nereek's focus snapped to Rasim, then went back to Kisia, though he answered Rasim. "It was Yalonta herself who came."

The name hit Rasim like a wall of water. Commander Yalonta was one of those he'd imagined might have the support to succeed with a coup. It seemed like forever ago that he'd even thought about such things.

"But *why*," Kisia wailed. "What's wrong with joining a guild?"

"It's not how things are done." Nereek looked heartbroken, his greater understanding of how the city worked giving him no joy. "If you challenge the way things are done, people get upset. And then with the guildmaster being a traitor—"

"She's *not,*" Desimi said with a ferocity that surprised Rasim.

Nereek opened flour-covered hands in a gesture of apology and helplessness. "With her being accused as one, anyway, having a baker's daughter joining her guild makes the people in power afraid of sedition. What if thousands of ordinary Ilyarans began studying magic? It's bad enough for the king with the fire's orphans numbering in the hundreds, and his own witchery weak. He's only ever a step away from losing his throne, and then the Seamasters made an alliance with a faction of the Northmen—"

"We have *not,*" Desimi protested, but Rasim gave him a despairing look that both enraged and silenced him. Desimi wasn't dumb, Rasim thought. Not by a long measure. That might make Rasim's wit and ability to be listened to by adults sting even more. Rasim put the thought away for later, even though it pained him to do so.

"It doesn't matter," Nereek said. "You have to *run.*"

A woman's calm and casual voice said, "I'm afraid it's much too late for that now."

CHAPTER 29

Rasim had seen Commander Yalonta before, though never from up close, and never when she spoke in a casual voice instead of a shout. Her voice was lighter than he expected, though the rest of her fit his memory: surprisingly small, for someone holding the highest ranking position in the king's guard, and surprisingly light of hair. Not as yellow-haired as the Northerners, but gold, like she'd been left in the sun too long. She wasn't pretty, not like Captain Donnin or even Kisia, but Rasim could see wanting to look at her for a long time. Her strong, confident features were interesting.

Or at least they were if she was arresting someone else, and not him. The guard appeared from everywhere, out of nearby buildings and from down alleys and streets. They'd been waiting, Rasim realized. They'd guessed Kisia might return home, and Yalonta had laid a trap. Judging from Nereek's expression, he'd had no idea. He looked tortured, his face anguished. Rasim suddenly *hoped* that was because he'd had no idea, and not because he'd sold Kisia to Yalonta for his own safety.

"Take them away," Yalonta said, still casually. "Put them with the others. Watch the big one. He's probably the ringleader."

"They're only children," a guard protested.

Yalonta's eyebrows shot up, adding a depth of mockery and strength to her features. "They're witches, and that one, at least," she said, pointing a thumb at Kisia, "has sailed with Isidri's right-hand man, Asindo. They may be in the heart of this conspiracy against the king."

"We are *not!* It's Rasim's stupid fault, he—"

Kisia whirled around and slammed her fist into Desimi's belly. The big boy wheezed and collapsed in on himself, utterly shocked. Kisia, face flushed with rage, snarled, "Shut up about what you don't know, Desimi. Just because Rasim doesn't have much magic doesn't mean he's stupid, or that I'm uninformed."

Rasim saw Yalonta reassess all of them, and with a sick twist in his stomach, understood what Kisia was doing. She was making herself the leader, making herself seem like the threat. She was the one who'd joined the guild late, making her a point of interest to the guard already. Now she'd established a hierarchy, putting Desimi below her by physical means and making it clear Rasim's magic was lacking.

It was a terrible, risky calculation, and it could get her in as much trouble as it might save Rasim and Desimi from. Yalonta jerked her chin at all three of them. The guards separated Kisia from Rasim and Desimi. Kisia gave Rasim one wild-eyed look. He offered a tiny nod, trying to say he understood what she was doing. For an instant she slumped in the guards' grasps, relief briefly visible in her eyes.

Then she became a struggling, squirming snake of girl, shouting absurdities toward the sky: "The sea will rise! The magic lives in all of us! *Don't be afraid!* I am Kisia al Ilialio, chosen daughter of the river, and *I will never give up!*"

Desimi, hauled upright by a pair of guards, was so long-faced with astonishment it was clear he'd forgiven, or forgotten, that Kisia had hit him. The guards threw him together with Rasim and made a wall of armored, bristling men around them, giving them an unexpected chance to talk under the rattle and clank of weapons. Desimi's bewilderment was so profound it sounded impressed. "What's she *doing?* Has she gone mad?"

"She's drawing attention away from us," Rasim breathed. "If we're lucky they'll think she's the troublemaker, the dangerous one."

Desimi gave him a look. "If we're lucky?" And then another look, more disgusted. "Neither of you have mag—"

"Tssst!" Rasim hushed him as harshly as he could without making too much noise. They crashed together again as the guards set off down the street, leaving a commotion at the bakery behind. Rasim, still whispering, said, "Let them think you're big and dumb and have no magic worth mentioning. That's going to be our only chance of getting out of this."

"Me," Desimi said in a tone Rasim didn't recognize. "I'm your only chance."

One of the guards barked, "Stop talking," and pulled Rasim away from Desimi. Rasim looked back, but Desimi's eyes were fixed forward, his jaw a firm-set line.

Rasim closed his eyes and stumbled along with his captors, wondering how he would get out of this one alive.

One way to look at it, he thought an hour later, was that they had successfully gotten inside the palace gates.

Yalonta hadn't spoken with Rasim or Desimi. She'd only made a throw-away gesture, and they'd been hauled into the Sunmasters' temple on the palace grounds. It was magnificent, enormous windows cut through golden sandstone so sunlight poured in and made it an astonishing place of worship. Rasim caught glimpses of mosaics that told the story of Ilyara's rise.

And then he was dragged down a set of stairs, losing sight of Desimi.

The air below the temple was shockingly hot, as if huge kitchen fires roared everywhere. Rasim reeled in his captors' grips, but they lifted him and carted him along, unconcerned with his reaction to the heat. They went deeper, finally entering a narrow hall marked with three doors only half Rasim's height. A sun witch old enough to be a master stood outside the middle door, and looked uninterestedly at Rasim. He pointed at the door to his left, and the guards threw Rasim in.

For an instant it seemed like a strange prison. A gutter ran around the walls, making a hand's-width break between the floor and the door. Other than that, there was no barrier at all between Rasim and escape. On hands and knees, he rushed for the tiny door.

Fire erupted in the gutter, chasing Rasim back. Flame sheeted up the walls, swallowed by another gutter up above. There was no scent of wood or coal, just pure flame, living through the will of a sun witch. Rasim crept forward again, wondering if he could somehow brave the flames long enough to fling himself through, but they intensified, driving him back again.

The heat was appalling, worse than sitting under the desert sun. Then, at least, it only came from above, even when the air wobbled with it. Here, in the Sun temple prison, fire roared on all four sides of him, baking every drop of water away. Even sweat dried before it could be of any use, not that Rasim's magic was strong enough for sweat to help him. He lay down, trying to conserve energy, but the heat baked it out of him.

After what seemed like a terribly long time, the sun witch brought a cup of water. Rasim was too parched to do anything but drink it, even though he thought—he *knew*—he should hoard it somehow. If he could only save enough up, he might be able to make a path through the fire just briefly. Long enough to break free.

Somewhere in this same building, Guildmaster Isidri was probably having the same thought, but Rasim couldn't imagine how even *she* could protect such a tiny cup of water from evaporation in the unrelenting heat.

His head hurt. Rasim edged his way to the very middle of the room, as far from every wall of fire as he could get, and sat in a defeated lump. He had no sense of how long he'd been in the room: the fire cooked it out of him. He didn't know why he hadn't baked alive, for that matter. Certainly the water they offered wasn't enough to keep him from roasting. He stripped his clothes off and sat up straight, trying to at least keep the heat even on all sides, to make it a little more bearable. It didn't help, but at least he was trying. The sun witch brought more water, several times. Rasim thought it was probably at regular intervals, and probably not all that long apart, but it seemed like forever between each desperate gulp of water.

His head wouldn't stop hurting, but after a while he began to find a kind of serenity in the pain: it let him know he wasn't quite cooked yet. Heat rolled against his skin the same way water did, almost soothing in its constancy. Rasim thought he would be as brown as any full-blooded Ilyaran if he ever got out of the fire room.

It *did* feel like water, in a way. He could feel the magic that gave the fire life. It didn't have weight, not the way water did. Instead it lifted up, light as air, ephemeral. Fire left lasting scars, but the flame itself didn't last. Rasim thought, idly, that sky magic, controlling the wind, might well have weight in the same way water magic did. Wind and air were constant too, after all. And sand magic, stone magic, that would probably be heavy too. Only sun magic felt like this, like something so light it leaped toward the heavens and disappeared. It was barely there. It should be easy to make go away, he thought dizzily. Something that was hardly there shouldn't be hard to make go away.

He was so *tired.* The heat drained him, made his muscles lax and loose until it was all he could do to keep from falling over. There were so many problems to solve on the other side of that wall of fire, if only he could get through it. If only he could care enough to try. But it was too hot to think, and the top of his head felt like it was floating. Distant, quiet, unattached, entirely separate from Rasim himself.

Way up at the top of his head, where it didn't quite belong to him any more, Rasim felt a tremendous surge of magic.

The wall of fire came down.

CHAPTER 30

The room instantly cooled, as if even the heat had been magical in nature and had no way of staying once the fire was out. Rasim gaped at the door, then gathered strength into melted muscles, hauled his pants on, and scrambled out as quickly as he could.

Desimi and Isidri stood ten steps down the corridor, the sun witch a collapsed heap at their feet.

All three of them gawked at each other. Isidri looked terrible, her face gaunt and drawn, like all the water had been sucked from her body. Desimi looked better, just tired, like Rasim felt. Water rolled between their feet, thin trickles with no evident source. Rasim staggered against a wall, exhausted and shocked. He snapped his own mouth shut only to feel it dropped open again. At once they all blurted, "How did you— you're free—what happened?!" and all at once fell silent again.

Desimi finally broke the silence, his head lifted high with pride. "They threw me in with the Guildmaster."

Isidri's astonishment turned to a sharp, wicked smile that was all the more unnerving because her face was thin with dehydration. "The sun fools should have known better than to put anyone else in a cell with a master witch, but especially they shouldn't have put a burgeoning storm master like Desimi in with the Guildmaster. What I couldn't do on my own I could certainly do with a gift like Desimi's to help me."

A sting of regret pierced Rasim's chest even as he felt a rise of pleasure for the bigger boy. Desimi was puffed up, as confident as Rasim had ever seen him. Lavish praise from any master would do that, but coming from the Guildmaster herself it was the highest compliment possible. "I told you," Rasim said with a cracked smile. "I told you it would be your magic that got us out of here, Desi."

"Yeah." Desimi's smile turned to a slow frown, though he lost none of his pride. "How'd you get free?"

Rasim looked back at the room he'd escaped from, then shook his head wearily. "I don't know. I felt a lot of magic push the fire down. Maybe it was what you two were doing. Or maybe when you knocked the sun witch out."

"We didn't," Isidri said. "He was unconscious when we came out."

Rasim stared at the fallen man, then shook his head, pushing the concern out of his mind. "How long were we in there? Where's Kisia?"

"Desimi tells me it's been five days I was in there," Isidri said grimly. "I lost track. The heat was..." She shook her head, explanations unnecessary. "They brought water four times an hour. I could tell that, at least, from how much was left in me with every cup."

Desimi and Rasim both blinked at her. It was Desimi who said, "You can *do* that?" in a low, impressed voice, but the Guildmaster waved the question off.

"What matters is you boys haven't been in here more than six hours, and Kisia's not here." Isidri ducked into the third room, then cursed. She backed out again and said, "Nothing," sharply to Rasim and Desimi. "You don't want to see. It isn't Kisia, that's all you need to know."

"Someone cooked to death, didn't they," Rasim whispered. "Another master."

"I barely survived, and I'm the strongest Guild-master the Seamasters have seen in three generations. I should know," Isidri said shortly. "I've lived through that many." Her eyes glowed with rage, like a moonlit storm was rising in them. Power crackled from her, the temple's heat fading in the face of her wrath. Every breath Rasim drew was cooler, more humid. It restored him as much as it invigorated Isidri. "They've had me caged away from water, but they should have put me to the sword outright. I'll take this palace apart block by block—" She was moving by then, long strides that ate distance. The water she and Desimi had called from the deep stones ran after her, darkening the floors and bouncing up the stairs as she took them two at a time.

Rasim and Desimi hurried behind her, Rasim breathless with questions: "What do you know, Guildmaster? Is Roscord a witch? Is the king under his influence? What are the ships in the harbor doing, what do they expect us to do? I stopped Captain Asindo from fighting them, he was supposed to guide the fleet into failure, just in case they were waiting in the city for him to win, so they could do something — " He gasped in sudden comprehension. "Something awful," he finished in a whisper. "They would have executed you, wouldn't they? They were waiting for an excuse."

Isidri gave him a sharp, approving look that turned into another of her vicious smiles. "Now I'll give them one."

"No!" Rasim grabbed her elbow, trying to haul her around to look at him. She stopped, at least, and looked at the hand on her arm as if it was a parasite. Rasim swallowed and let go.

"Do *not*," Isidri said with wonderful precision, "do not *ever* do that again, young man, or I'll hang you by your fingers and let you watch while every drop of water in your body drips out of your nose."

It should have been a funny threat. It wasn't. Rasim swallowed again., "Sorry, Guildmaster."

Isidri nodded once. "Now," she said with the same fierce precision, "why should I not have my vengeance?"

"Because that's what Roscord *wants*. He went to all the trouble of getting here as fast as he could, he had a Northern spy that maybe even the king would listen to —maybe Derek, he's on Inga's council—and the Seamasters' Guild, the fleet, we're the only people who can prove that he's lying. But we have to stay alive to do it, and we can't just start killing people!"

"He keeps saying that," Desimi muttered. Water was up to their knees now, flooding toward the magnificent upper hall. Someone would notice soon. Rasim stared at the rising wetness, then jolted suddenly.

"You know what you need to do, Guildmaster?"

Her eyebrows rose, silent and sarcastic questions. Rasim ignored the sarcasm and pointed upward. Outward. "You need to go down to the harbor, thaw the water *quietly*, so the Northmen hardly notice, and then bring fish straight to the docks. People are starting to get hungry out there, Masira said so. They need to be fed, and the Seamasters need to look like heroes. What would be better than the Guildmaster feeding the city?"

"And what," Isidri wondered, still rife with sarcasm, "what do you intend to do?"

"Desimi and I are going to find Kisia and surprise Roscord into doing something stupid."

"Like trying to kill Rasim," Desimi said with a note of dour pleasure.

"Why would he do that?"

"Because I'm the one who caught him murdering his own men to make someone else look bad," Rasim said grimly. "He has to kill me before I get near the king, but really, killing a journeyman who's still practically an apprentice is going to make him look silly. Especially since everybody seems to know I'm not much of a witch or a threat to begin with."

Isidri gave them both hard looks, then exhaled. The water began to recede. "Letting you go in there alone is against my better judgment. I should go with you and deal with the harbor later."

"No." Rasim shook his head to emphasize the word. "You need to have escaped and be nowhere near here when we make things messy. People have to *see* you somewhere else, so you can't possibly be considered part of this."

Isidri frowned at him a moment, then exhaled again, even more noisily. "Find that baker's daughter. I don't want to tell her parents I got her killed."

"Yes, Guildmaster!" Rasim ran past her, splashing in the remaining water, before she could change her mind. Desimi cursed, then followed him. Isidri came a little more slowly, weaving a shield of water as she went. She wouldn't be caught by sun witches again, Rasim thought. That was good. They would need her, and her heroics.

All three of them burst into the temple's upper floor almost at once, water spraying over sunwashed stone.

Startled priests and witches shouted and fire splashed up much like the water did.

Isidri, a few steps behind Rasim and Desimi, extended her hands.

Water roared up, forking so it didn't knock her from her feet. It went where she guided it, cascading showers defeating fire before it gained purchase anywhere. A master sun witch stalked forward, conjuring fire as easily as Isidri did water. They threw their elements at one another, and where they met, steam hissed and billowed.

Desimi grabbed Rasim's upper arm and dragged him out of the temple while the master witches battled. Rasim kept looking back, desperate to watch the fight, until Desimi grabbed both his shoulders and rattled him. Rasim's teeth rattled and Desimi stuck his face in Rasim's. "This is your idea, you idiot. If you get us killed because you're just dying to watch a couple masters fight, I'll kill you myself!"

Rasim twitched a smile. He was dead at least three times in that sentence, all by different methods. He started to comment, but steam exploded from the temple behind them, sending both of them running again.

Guards, palace staff, and nobility poured out of nearby doorways, shouting with curiosity and confusion. Rasim ran for the largest set of doors, Desimi slow on his heels. Rasim looked back once to see steam shaping itself into sea serpents and sand monsters, and wished he could stop to applaud Desimi's craftsmanship. There were masters who couldn't shape water, much less steam.

And there were no doubt Sunmasters who could see through Desimi's water works and burn them out of existence, but those masters were not among the screaming, running throng. Running *away* from Desimi's creations, which meant the crowd that had been running toward Rasim and Desimi was now running the same way they were: back toward the safety of the palace. Rasim was swept along, almost losing sight of Desimi, but the bigger boy made use of his size and shouldered his way to Rasim's side. They shared a wild, excited grin—the first real smile they'd exchanged in years—and then in a fit of inspiration Rasim bellowed, "The king! To Taishm's side! We must protect him!"

To his astonished delight, the crowd around him swerved, his cry picked up and carried by others. He and Desimi ran with them, letting the masses guide them through wide marble-floored halls and under silken banners that hung from high arched ceilings. Uniformed guards tried to stop them and instead leaped out of the way, their swords and spears no match for a mob shouting, "Save the king!"

They burst into the throne room by their hundreds, and only then did the front-runners begin to realize what they were doing. They slowed, stumbled from the weight of people crowding behind them, then stopped. Stillness ran back from them like a wave, like the sea suddenly growing calm after a storm. Rasim and Desimi surged forward, edging through small spaces until they broke through to the front of the now-whispering crowd.

They were nearly halfway into the throne room, which was far longer than it was wide. Taishm, the king, sat at the far end in a throne set three steps up onto a platform. The throne dwarfed him, even though he was bolt upright, hands fisted on the arms of the throne. Alarm pulsed from him like magic, not that Rasim could blame him: hundreds of commoners had just smashed into his throne room, and he'd spent the last week being told the Seamasters, at least, were in revolt against him.

Roscord stood to Taishm's left, at the foot of the platform. Rasim's heart gave a little shock to see Lorens, the Northern prince, standing opposite Roscord, on Taishm's right.

And Kisia, in chains but with her head lifted in defiance, knelt between them.

CHAPTER 31

"*Kisia!*" There were a hundred things Rasim should say. Calling Kisia's name wasn't one of them, but it seemed to be the only thing he *could* do. Her head snapped around, eyes round with first surprise and then dismay. He wondered what she'd told them, or what they thought of him, that she didn't want him there, but it was too late. He was already running down the hall, Desimi in step with him.

Beyond Kisia, Rasim half saw furious shock flit across Roscord's face. He snarled, "You're *dead*—!" loudly enough to carry, realized his mistake, and shot a quick look toward Taishm.

The king came to his feet, paying no mind to Roscord. His attention was for Rasim, who skidded on his knees as he reached Kisia's side. "Are you all right?"

"Me? What about you? Where's your shirt? You look awful!"

Rasim had forgotten he was only half-dressed, and blinked at himself, surprised. "It's in the prison cell. *I* look awful, you're the one in chains—!"

Magic poured from the throne dais, a weight that felt nothing like the witchery Rasim knew. It seized his breath like a sky witch might, and squeezed his heart the way he'd learned a water witch could. Pressure flattened him against the floor with the heaviness of a sandstorm, and his blood boiled with heat as raw as the sun witch prison.

Lying flat on his belly, gasping for air, Rasim couldn't even lift his head as Taishm stood and stalked down the hall toward him. Roscord and Lorens fell in behind him like dolphins riding a ship's wake. Roscord's expression was vicious, mouth pulled back from his teeth. Rasim would run from that look, if he could move. Kisia lay flattened on the floor beside him, and though he couldn't see Desimi, Rasim suspected the other boy was subject to the same treatment.

Taishm, unwillingly crowned after his cousin had died of grief, was known to be not much of a witch. Rasim could hardly imagine what kind of power a *strong* Ilyaran royal could command, if this slight man could flatten them with his magics. And he *was* slight, narrow-shouldered and thin-faced, but there was nothing small about his voice. He stopped ten feet from Rasim and demanded, thunderously, "Who *are* you?"

Rasim weighed so much—like stones were pressing down on him—that he thought he wouldn't be able to inhale enough to speak. He dragged in as deep a breath as he could, then coughed until tears came to his eyes: breathing wasn't hard after all.

"Water witches," Roscord snarled. "Part of that woman's conspiracies."

Rasim's heart lurched in panic. He blurted, "No!" but Taishm had already looked away from him, his expression mild.

"How do you know that, my friend?"

Roscord pointed an accusing finger at the crowd. Rasim couldn't move to see them, but even under the weight of Taishm's magic, he could sense the answer with his own witchery. Dozens, perhaps hundreds, of the crowd were soaked from the steam and water battle, and Ilyara was a desert city. There was never that much water to spare, not unless a water witch had a hand in it. "Who else could they be?" Roscord demanded. "They know this girl, their ringleader—!"

Rasim heard Desimi mumble, "Ras is the ringleader," into the floor, and almost laughed. Trust Desimi to make certain the blame lay squarely on Rasim's shoulders. He deserved it, but still, it felt so normal that for a moment even being squashed by a king's magic wasn't too worrying.

That carelessness faded instantly, though. Rasim wriggled his fingers to his sides, pressing his palms against the floor. He wanted to stand, to face Roscord on his feet. That seemed important somehow. Maybe because he'd fallen, last time he'd faced Roscord. Because he'd been hit, and knocked to the ground.

That would *not* happen again.

Anger surged through Rasim, taking some of the weight away. He pushed upward with the emotion, just like it was magic itself, and felt more of the stone witchery break apart. Teeth gritted, he pushed upward just a few inches.

Taishm's attention broke from Roscord, coming back to Rasim in astonishment. Rasim didn't care. Didn't care that a king was gaping at him, didn't care that his limited magic would do him no good, didn't care if guards came to strike him down with swords and spears, just so long as he *got to his feet.*

With a roar, he shoved himself all the way to his feet, feeling Taishm's magic shatter around him. They both staggered, Rasim with utter exhaustion and Taishm with equal amazement. Lorens and Roscord came to support Taishm, who threw them off vehemently. Kisia, although chained, came to support Rasim, and to his surprise, so did Desimi. Rasim sagged against them gratefully.

"Roscord's right," he whispered. "We're Seamasters' Guild journeymen, your majesty. I'm Rasim al Ilialio. This is Desimi and I guess you've met Kisia."

"Yes." Taishm sounded dry. "How did you do that? Throw off my magic?"

Rasim shuddered. Thinking about it made him even more tired than he already was. First the fire prison, then the weight of stone. There was nothing left inside him to fight with.

Nothing except stubborn determination. He stuck his jaw out and fastened his gaze on Roscord, refusing to show weakness to the island warlord. "I wanted to be on my feet to face him again, your majesty. He struck me down last time."

"Last time," Taishm said neutrally, studying Rasim as though he was something unexpected and interesting.

Rasim didn't want to be interesting. He wanted to prove Roscord a danger, and he wanted to sleep. It wasn't very heroic, but he thought he'd had enough of heroics for a while.

The longer Taishm looked at him, though, the more determined he felt, and that lent him strength. He straightened up, no longer leaning on Kisia and Desimi, and squared his shoulders. He was a journeyman in the Seamasters' Guild, he had slain a sea serpent and discovered a threat at the heart of the Northlands. He could, by Siliaria's seas, stand up straight and face his enemy. Holding on to that thought, he met Taishm's eyes, and thought he saw the faintest smile cross the king's mouth.

"Tell me about last time," Taishm said.

"I met him in the islands, your majesty. I was trying to help a girl he'd kidnapped escape, and he almost killed me."

Roscord spat a derisive sound. "I've never seen this boy before in my life."

Taishm looked at Roscord. They were nearly of a height, Rasim realized, though Taishm seemed taller because he was so slender. The king made the most of that perceived height just then, looking ever so slightly down his nose at Roscord. "Is that so," he asked. "Then why did you think he was dead?"

Relief slammed through Rasim as hard as horror seemed to take Roscord: the warlord turned white, while Rasim's feet felt like they'd left the floor. Taishm *had* heard Roscord's unwise comment, and had only waited until the right moment to reveal it. Rage flew across Roscord's face, then sheeted toward panic as he failed to have an instant, acceptable answer for the king. "They should all be dead," he finally spluttered. "All of them, dangerous mad witches that they are! Your own city rises against you, Taishm!"

Taishm's eyebrows lifted in a show of polite disbelief. Roscord went from white to red, realizing his second mistake: he should never have used the king's first name. His beautiful voice turning hoarse, he croaked, "Your majesty," but it was too late. He had, for a moment at least, lost the king's faith.

Taishm, without so much as looking at Rasim, said, "Speak."

"I caught him murdering his own soldiers, your majesty, so their deaths could be blamed on the kidnapped girl's mother, so *she* could be put to death. He tried to kill me then."

"Someday," Taishm said, "someday I think I'd like to hear how a Seamaster journeyman ended up in a position to discover an islander's murderous tendencies, but today I'll forgo that. William, is this true?"

Rage worked across Roscord's face, answer enough. Taishm closed his eyes a moment, shoulders loosening in defeat. "We've been friends since childhood, William. Since those wretched letters my mother used to make me write. Practice at diplomacy, she told me. You can never know when you might need allies from afar. I had thought, when you came here, that she had finally been proven right. That my people had tired of a weak king, and only my distant friend cared enough to come so far and warn me of what he'd learned. But that isn't it, is it. You saw a weak king, just like everyone else, and now I think you've come to try to take my throne away from me."

Every word hit Rasim in the chest like a hammer. He hadn't realized Taishm and Roscord had known each other. Neither, from the murmurs of astonishment racing through the throne hall, had most others. No wonder. No wonder Taishm had listened to Roscord's warnings about the Seamasters' Guild. Sympathy crashed through Rasim. Taishm had almost nothing, only a crown he'd never wanted, and now not even the long-time friendship he'd believed in.

Roscord inhaled deeply, obviously reaching for control over his lovely voice. He achieved it, speaking softly. Convincingly, Rasim thought: even *he* was almost convinced as Roscord murmured, "I'm not your enemy, your majesty. The Seamasters have allied themselves with the Northmen—"

Taishm gave Rasim a sharp, questioning look. Rasim swallowed, but nodded. "Not to displace you, your majesty. We came across an idea that was too awful to be true, and thought we'd better get some proof before we tried to tell you. We thought the Northmen could help us, maybe, and—" He faltered, because the last part was painfully accurate: "And because we thought they'd be a distraction while we did our investigating."

Taishm barked a laugh. "They are that, at least."

Rasim blurted, "Yes, but the ones you've got here are working for Roscord, not the Seamasters. They're distracting you by making you distrust your own people, not distracting the people while you find out the truth."

"And what is the truth, young man?"

Rasim didn't want to answer. Not in front of hundreds of witnesses, any of whom might know something about the Great Fire and the Northern queen's death. But there was no choice. Even a hesitation would make him look like a liar, and he couldn't afford that. Afraid but determined, he opened his mouth to speak.

Roscord snatched his sword from its sheath and leaped at Rasim.

CHAPTER 32

More magic than Rasim had ever felt a single person use surged through Desimi, and a wall of water slammed upward through the marble floor.

Chunks of stone broke and slid on it like a wet avalanche. Smaller shards flew high and rained back down, making the water deadly. The throne room audience screamed and scattered, running for the doors. Roscord flew backward, slammed across the width of the room by a forceful bolt that Desimi channeled with immense confidence. A second, narrower bolt of water crashed into Taishm's chest and shoved him halfway back to his throne, putting him well out of danger.

Desimi collapsed. Rasim caught some of his weight, and Kisia slid around them to help get Desimi to the floor gently. She put her fingers at his throat, then snapped her gaze to Rasim. "He's alive. *Go!*"

For a bewildering instant Rasim still didn't know what had happened, much less where he should go.

Then he followed the trail of wet destruction to the room's far side. Roscord was gone already, not defeated, just running through a door nearby. Lorens, the Northern prince, was already after him, his own sword drawn and long legs eating the distance. Taishm, abandoned by both his counselors, stood where he was, purely astonished.

Rasim was running before he was fully upright, fingertips scrabbling for purchase on the wet floor. The marble was cold, wet, slippery under his bare feet: dangerous. Rasim reached for magic, shoving water away to make a clear path and drying his feet with witchery as well. He slipped once, but then had his feet under him. He was half a room's length behind Lorens when the Northern prince reached the door. Rasim raced into the next room, then, following wet footsteps, into the room beyond, and came to a shocked stop.

Roscord lay in a pool of his own blood with Lorens kneeling over him.

Lorens looked up, icy calculation in his blue eyes. That slid away in an instant, leaving regret and horror so profound Rasim doubted what he'd seen in the first place. "I had to," Lorens said grimly. "We'll get no answers from him now, but he was a master swordsman. I had no choice."

Rasim nodded frantically, a tiny scared action that had no thought behind it. He wanted to believe Lorens. He had loathed and feared Roscord, and he liked the yellow-haired Northern prince very much. But cold trickled through his chest, then lodged in his belly, growing larger by the moment.

Roscord had no weapon in hand. His sword wasn't even within sight, and Rasim had the faintest recollection of seeing it against the throne room wall, probably dropped when Desimi smashed him. And one of Roscord's hands was sliced open like he'd thrust out his hands to stop a knife and had failed. His expression, too, was one of wide-eyed shock, as if he'd never anticipated the blow that took his life.

Lorens took in Rasim's expression, and, without speaking, crawled beneath a nearby table. He emerged with a long knife in his free hand. It was unbloodied, but clearly deadly. "I kicked it away," he said quietly. "You don't trust me anymore, do you?"

Sick exhaustion rose in Rasim's stomach. "I'm sorry. It's been a bad day. Are you all right? What are you *doing* here? Why are the Northern ships barricading the harbor if you're here? What have you told the king?"

"I stowed away on Derek's ship," Lorens said cheerfully, though his humor faded quickly. "When I realized he was working with Roscord I thought I should go along with the story. I hoped if I seemed to be one of them, some of the other conspirators might betray themselves to me."

"You almost let Guildmaster Isidri *die* for that!"

The Northman's blue eyes became icy. "This may

be war, Rasim. There are casualties in war. One guildmaster is nothing to the safety of a city."

Rasim's stomach lurched with sickness again. He could see Lorens's point, though he didn't like it at all. Lorens waited a moment, then got to his feet and offered a cautious hand of friendship. "I'm glad to see you, Rasim. I thought you were dead, in that moment."

Still uncertain, Rasim took Lorens's hand. "I thought so too. Desimi saved me. I can't believe he saved me. The whole idea was to get Roscord to do something stupid, but..."

But Rasim hadn't really thought about what it would be like for the island warlord to actually attack him in cold blood. He hadn't thought about how to *survive* that, and he knew that without Desimi's help, he wouldn't have. "I have to go see if he's all right. He used way too much magic."

"He'll recover." Taishm spoke from the doorway, startling Rasim. He came in, dry and tidy despite Desimi's deluge. Water witchery, Rasim thought: any water witch could at least dry himself, and the king seemed to have more power than he was generally believed to. He went to Roscord's body, crouching beside him in silence before finally asking, "What did you suspect him of, Rasim? Why did he strike rather than let you speak?"

There was no one else in the room. Only a king, a prince, and a journeyman, and the prince already knew Rasim's suspicions. Rasim slumped against the same table Roscord's knife had been under, and spoke mostly to his own feet. "I didn't have any kind of proof it was Roscord, your majesty. It's just that the fire last month didn't look like an accident. We were afraid if it wasn't, then neither was the Great Fire. And if *it* wasn't, then maybe Queen Annaken had had been murdered, not died accidentally, and...Guildmaster Isidri thought we needed support from outside if we were going to find out. The Northmen seemed like good allies. She was their princess too, after all."

Taishm's eyebrows quirked upward a little. "And you now think Roscord may have been the mastermind?"

Rasim shook his head. "I don't know, your majesty, except why else would he have tried to kill me? He fought hard to gain power in the islands. Maybe he was even more ambitious than that. The Northmen have been under attack, too. Their water supplies are being poisoned by witchery. If Roscord has been behind all of this, he's..."

"Thorough," Lorens supplied dryly. Both Rasim and Taishm made sounds in their throats. Not quite laughter, but a sort of raw humor regardless. Lorens half smiled, then stepped forward. "Your majesty, I haven't been entirely forthcoming with you. It became clear to me on my journey here that my captain was in league with Roscord. I allowed them

to continue their charade, even to the point of
encouraging you to dismantle the Seamasters' Guild,
in hopes of exposing more of their brethren. We *have*
offered an alliance to the Seamasters, but it's not
represented by those ships out there. They're a
faction we're eager to rid ourselves of."

Taishm's expression grew increasingly grim as
Lorens spoke. "You ought to have included me in
your plotting, Prince Lorens. Arson and murder
aren't new thoughts to any of us. Your guildmaster
should have come to me."

"Your majesty," Rasim said in a small, painful
voice, "I'm sorry, your majesty, but you stood to gain
from arson and murder."

Taishm went very still. His voice was strange when
he spoke. "Is that what my people think of me? That I
would murder my cousin's wife and child, and hope
grief poisoned him to his grave, so that I could have
the throne?"

"*No!*" Embarrassment brought scalding tears to
Rasim's eyes. "*No*, your majesty, it's just that once I
started thinking about who could gain from murder,
there were so many possibilities, and you were one
of them. That's why we thought we needed to go to
the north. We thought they would have spies here
who might be able to tell us something. Only it all
went...wrong." He gestured at Roscord's body, then
rubbed his hand over his eyes. "And the Northern

ships out there in the harbor have magic, and—oh, goddess, the ships! Isidri! We have to—!"

He was running before he'd finished the thought, much less the sentence. Running back the way he'd come, only this time with a king and a prince in his wake. They tore back through the throne room, stragglers from the crowd gaping and clearing the way.

Kisia, unchained now, still knelt beside Desimi, who was half-conscious. She watched Rasim race by, and over the pounding of his own footsteps he heard her say, "Get up, Desimi. We don't want to miss this."

It was astonishing how much easier it was to run *out* of the palace with a king in tow than it had been to run into it. A dozen steps outside the doors, Rasim knew already that his half-considered fears were right: the air was freezing, as cold as it had been in the north, and the harbor's blue was all wrong, icy and cold.

A vast weight of magic rolled in from the Northern ships. Rasim remembered Masira's belief that they controlled cold and heat the same way Ilyaran witches might control air or water, and was convinced. The Northerners were freezing the harbor, icing the air, killing crops and fish with their magic. There would be nothing to feed the city, and it would be weakened for years to come. Roscord's ambitions had known no end.

Rasim stumbled, looking back over his shoulder as he ran. *There*, and *there*, within the palace windows: light glinting brilliantly, but away from the setting sun. More than one person in Roscord's pay was signaling to the Northern ships, ordering them to act. Rasim had known it in his gut from the moment he had seen the Northern ships: they had only waited on a signal to tear the city apart. The Ilyaran fleet had backed down, not providing the excuse, but the chaos within the palace had been more than enough.

The king, Rasim thought with cold certainty, had been meant to end up dead. Desimi had saved not only Rasim, but also Taishm. That should be heroics enough for a lifetime.

A flare of magic dragged Rasim's attention back to the harbor. He staggered to a stop, astonished at the view. He could see the entire slope of the city from the palace grounds, all of it lit red and gold as evening came on. The whole curve of the docks and harbor lay below them, easily visible.

A single woman stood on the docks, a point of warmth against the cold. Guildmaster Isidri, her hands uplifted and magic stronger than even Desimi had used pouring out of her.

In front of her, the sea melted. Crystal blue came back into the water, its white sheen fading. It crept forward inches at a time, one woman fighting against the strength of five ships.

Someone else joined her, someone broad-shouldered but female. Masira, Rasim guessed, and with

Masira came others. All the disgraced guild members, from apprentices to shipwrights and seamasters, all of them who had been left in the city and who had hidden near the guildhalls to protect their home. They all came to join Isidri, and the weight of their magic grew greater yet. Now the ice melted feet and yards at a time, crackling and snapping as it ran back toward the Northern ships.

"Come on," someone whispered, and Rasim discovered Kisia and Desimi at his side. "Come on," Kisia whispered again. "The harbor life will *die* if they don't win, and fast. Ilyara will be destroyed. *Come on!*" she cried aloud, tears running down her face. "*Come on, Isidri!*"

Taishm stepped up to Rasim's other side, glancing beyond Rasim at Kisia. He nodded once, seeming to accept or understand something, and then his voice cracked and rumbled, louder than thunder. Rasim staggered with its weight, at the domination of sky magic allowing a single man's words to be heard across the breadth of Ilyara: "Seamasters, *fight!*"

CHAPTER 33

For the rest of his life, Rasim would remember the explosion of ice and water that erupted at Taishm's command. He had felt the fleet fight together before, struggling to save themselves against the sea serpent. That was nothing compared to the fury of witchery unleashed against an enemy of Ilyara.

Cracks shattered in the ice, water forcing its way up through the gaps Isidri's water-warming magic offered. The rest, Asindo and the guild could do: dragging the ice down into the water over and over until it shrank away to nothing. Whirlpools leaped up and slammed into the Northern ships, breaking holes in the holds and snatching sailors away. Storm surges rocked the harbor, shaking the Northern hold until it collapsed.

Within minutes, Ilyara's harbor was its own again.

As the water witchery faded, cheers began to rise from the city's people. Desimi muttered "Hypocrites," but Kisia elbowed him sharply in the ribs. "Be quiet," she whispered. "We're a lot better off with them changing their minds and thinking we're heroes than staying constant and thinking we're traitors."

Desimi muttered again, but didn't argue. He looked too tired to argue, really: his eyes were sunken and the hollows looked bruised, and he was leaning heavily on Kisia without even trying to hide it. Rasim said, "Thank you," to him, and after a moment of looking like he was searching for something to say, Desimi nodded.

Rasim nodded too, then caught his breath as he glanced at the sea. Guildmaster Isidri had fallen to her knees, no longer a strong white-haired beacon. Rasim jolted forward a step, then looked at Taishm.

The king inclined his head. "Go. See to her. And expect a summons, children of the river, because this is not yet over."

Rasim moved to Desimi's other side, and all three of them ran for the docks.

The streets were madness, people thronging toward the docks. Everyone wanted to have been there for the battle, and would later all claim they had been. Rasim, Kisia and Desimi, who knew they *hadn't* been, only wanted to get to their friends. It took forever to reach the guild halls. By the time they did, the light had failed entirely, darkness come on full, though by the shadows on the water, Rasim knew that the *Wafiya* and other fleet ships had docked.

Asindo met them just inside the guildhall gates. "Usia is with her," he said without preamble. "She needs rest and water, but he thinks she'll be all right." Concern flickered in his face, though. Rasim thought there was something he wasn't telling them, but the captain frowned at all three of them, his concern deepening.

"Desimi, you look as bad as Isidri, and you're nearly as bad as the both of them, Rasim." He examined Kisia's collar—she had never been released from the iron band around her throat, though the chains had been removed—and began to ask. Then he lifted his hand and shook his head. "Never mind. Go to the shipwrights and get that thing taken off, apprentice. Journeymen, with me. Usia needs to see to you, too."

"But the king said he'd summon us," Rasim blurted.

Asindo stared at him. "The king." A silence followed the two words before he said, very steadily, "Then the king can wait for morning. You two need healing, food, and rest, in that order." He eyed Kisia, added, "And you need food, healing, and probably rest too, once that thing is off you. Come to see Usia when you're free of it."

Kisia murmured, "Yes, Captain," and scampered off with more energy than Rasim felt or Desimi exhibited.

Desimi snorted, noticing the same thing. "She's only been in chains all day, not half-baked."

"And not digging into the city's bedrock for water weapons," Rasim retorted.

Asindo looked between them both, then wordlessly put his hands on their shoulders and steered them toward the healing hall. There, Usia gave them water fortified with wine and looked between them a long moment, obviously trying to decide which of them required his help more. "You both feel like the Guildmaster," he said accusingly. "Like the water's been drained out of you. More than the water. The very magic in your bones."

"We did get roasted for most of the afternoon," Rasim said weakly. "And Desimi used more magic than anybody I'd ever seen."

"What's your excuse?"

Rasim shook his head. The watered wine tasted wonderful, and he drank most of it in gulps, but watered or not, it went to his head, too. Sleepiness had him in its grip already, and he could hardly think of an answer for Usia. He'd used very little magic today, and had no reason for it to be drained out of him. "Maybe being around so much being used tired me out..."

He heard Desimi disagree, but he toppled into sleep before the words made sense.

#

"Wake up. Wake up, Rasim. We let you sleep as long as we could, but the king is calling for us. Rasim, wake up."

"I'll wake him up," Desimi growled.

Rasim sat bolt upright, wary even half-asleep, and Kisia giggled as Desimi said, "Knew that would work."

"Come on," Kisia said. "The king wants us. You have to get dressed."

Rasim swung his feet over the edge of the bed, still not really awake. His head hurt, and as if knowing it, Desimi pressed a cup of water into Rasim's hand. He drank it, handed it back for more, and drained that too before he started to feel well enough to say, "Thanks."

"Put these on." Kisia shoved soft clothes at him. They were of much finer weave than anything Rasim owned, but he was too bleary to argue, and got dressed. The linen lay smooth and richly blue over his chest. He patted it in confusion and looked up.

Kisia and Desimi were dressed similarly. Desimi's shirt had the loop of a journeyman at one shoulder, while Kisia's had the apprentice's mark. Rasim put a hand to his own shoulder, finding the journeyman's braid there, too. "Guildmaster Asindo said we weren't going to embarrass the guild by showing up at the palace in our normal clothes," Kisia explained.

"Oh." Rasim got up, then stumbled. "Wait. Guildmaster *Asindo?*"

Desimi and Kisia exchanged glances. "There was a vote last night," Kisia said carefully. "Asindo was made Guildmaster until Isidri is..."

"She'll be *fine*," Desimi said ferociously. "Come on. We don't have a lot of time."

"What's wrong with her? What time is it?" Rasim dragged his feet until Desimi got behind him and gave him a shove.

"She's exhausted, that's what, and she's old and she used too much magic. And it's nearly noon and we're supposed to be there at noon, so *move*."

"We can't get to the palace by noo—" Rasim swallowed his own protest as Desimi got him out of the guild hall.

A carriage waited for them, with four prancing horses at its front and an infinitely patient-looking coachman holding the door. Desimi all but lifted Rasim into the carriage, then climbed in after and turned to offer Kisia a hand up. All three of them sprawled across padded leather seats, Desimi and Kisia gleeful with excitement and Rasim still waking up, but with growing astonishment.

They flew through the streets more quickly than he'd ever thought possible, arriving at the palace within minutes, when it had taken hours to get home the evening before. And unlike the day before, guards came to escort them politely through the palace halls, rather than chasing them as if they were criminals. They were let into the throne room, where dozens of people already stood.

Some were familiar: Yalonta, the commander of the guard; Lorens, the Northern prince, and several Seamasters guild members, including Asindo. Far more were strangers, and some of them gave Rasim and his friends curious glances as they stepped inside.

The room had been partially repaired from Desimi's dramatic witchery the day before. The floor, though still cracked and pitted, was smooth again, and there was no sign of water damage. Taishm once more sat in his throne at the far end of the room, but this time the person kneeling halfway down the hall was Captain Jorgensson, rather than Kisia.

As they came in, Jorgensson cast a guarded look at Prince Lorens, then slumped and responded to something Taishm had obviously just asked: "We followed Roscord's orders, your majesty. He paid us well, and there was a promise of..." He glanced at Lorens again, then sighed. "Of noble titles and land. Things we would never see in the north. It seemed worth the risk."

"I'm sure," Taishm murmured. "What's a little regicide, after all?"

Jorgensson lifted his gaze, mouth a thin tight line, and gave a sharp, telling shrug. "You're not *my* king, your majesty."

Taishm, still softly, said, "Nor are you my subject. I think I would be within my rights to judge you, but

I'll leave that to Jaana. I'm sure condemnation from your own queen will be much more damaging."

He flicked his hand and guards took Derek away. Only then did Taishm seem to notice Rasim and the others, gesturing them forward. "Kisia al Ilialio. Desimi al Ilialio. Come here."

The two of them exchanged nervous glances and Kisia looked apologetically at Rasim before doing as the king commanded. Rasim hung back, his heart beating fast enough to make him dizzy, as Taishm looked Desimi and Kisia over.

"You have an astonishing loyalty to a guild you've only just joined," he said to Kisia. "You could have gotten yourself killed yesterday, with those antics of yours."

"I had to do something, sire. You have my parents."

"Had," Taishm said. "Yalonta overstepped her bounds. They have been returned home and recompense made. I apologize for the indignities they suffered."

"Don't apologize," Kisia said tartly. "Make their bakery your favorite. That'll do the trick."

Taishm's eyebrows rose. "You're not afraid of your king?"

"Your majesty," Kisia said with great restraint, "I almost got eaten by a sea serpent. Not much scares me anymore."

The king's mouth curled up at one corner. "Fair enough. I'll ask for a basket of breads from your bake—"

"My parents' bakery," Kisia stressed. "I'm Seamasters' Guild now."

"Brave and brash," Taishm muttered. "Very well. From your parents' bakery, and I'll let it be known I favor them. Now. Desimi. I believe, young man, that you acted to save my life yesterday."

Desimi shrugged slightly. "Seemed likely that if Roscord was going to start killing people, you'd be high on the list. Sir."

Taishm cast a bemused glance at Asindo. "They're a bold lot, your apprentices."

Asindo, straight-faced, said, "Journeymen, sire," and Taishm laughed aloud.

"At least they come by it honestly. Journeyman Desimi al Ilialio, come here." Taishm stood and pointed to a spot directly in front of him. Desimi swallowed hard and walked forward, then knelt, which surprised Rasim but seemed to please the king, who gestured to one of the retainers near the throne. The uniformed man stepped forward and offered Taishm a heavy silver necklace from which a gleaming blue pearl dangled.

Taishm settled the necklace over Desimi's head, then drew him upward and lifted the jewel in his fingertips, turning it over. "This is the mark of the king's guard," Taishm said quietly. "Normally it would be stamped in silver on the hilt of your sword, but I thought for a seamaster it was more appropriately set into pearl. Anywhere in this city, anywhere in my kingdom, this mark will be recognized and your needs will be answered. Thank you, Desimi al Ilialio, for my life."

For the first time in years, the anger that had shaped Desimi's face disappeared completely. Color swept his ears and he gave a jerky nod, then backed away from Taishm with the pearl clasped carefully in one hand. When he reached Kisia's side, they backed up together, until they reached Rasim again. Kisia's eyes were enormous, and a flush of pride made Desimi stand even taller than he usually did. Rasim offered them a tentative smile, but then Taishm sat back in his throne, expression thunderous over steepled fingers. "*You.*"

Rasim flinched and looked forward guiltily to whisper, "Yes, your majesty?"

"What are we to do with you, journeyman? You seem to be at the heart of a great deal of trouble."

"I didn't mean to be," Rasim said miserably. "All I wanted to do was sail with the fleet, your majesty, I swear it."

"I have no doubt." The corner of Taishm's mouth twitched upward. "But it seems Siliaria had greater things in store for you. I understand you were poorly treated by the Sunmasters."

Rasim gritted his teeth. "They did think we were traitors, your majesty. I can understand what they did."

"But can you forgive it?" Taishm sounded enormously serious.

Rasim frowned. "Do I have to?"

"It would be best," Taishm said. "It would make studying under them easier."

"What? But—what? No! No, I meant it, your majesty! I just want to sail with the fleet. I don't want to be a Sunmaster!"

"I don't believe you can be," Taishm said. "The magic to command more than one element belongs only to the royal family. But you have a knack for being in the heart of trouble, and I may as well use that. I want you to study with them to learn diplomacy, not sun witchery."

Rasim clapped his mouth shut and looked for Asindo. The *Wafiya*'s captain's expression was perfectly neutral, except for a sparkle in his brown eyes. He had threatened exactly that fate for Rasim, and Rasim had no doubt Asindo had put the idea in the king's ear. Jaw thrust out, he looked back at Taishm and folded his arms over his chest. "Fine, but I'm not leaving the Seamasters' guild hall. You can send your sun witch to me, if you want me to learn."

Taishm's eyebrows shot up. "I can, can I? This is the demand you make of your king?"

"This is your idea," Rasim retorted. "I'm not leaving my family. If you want me to study with the Sunmasters, they can come to me."

"I begin to see how you end up in trouble. A compromise?" Taishm suggested, poorly-hidden amusement. "You spend the morning hours studying with the Sunmasters, and in the afternoon return to your journeyman's duties with the Seamasters?"

It sounded like a lot of work. Rasim sighed dramatically and nodded. "All right, fine. But if the *Wafiya* sails, I'm going with her, Sunmasters or no."

"You drive a hard bargain," Taishm said dryly. "Very well, Seamaster journeyman and Sunmaster apprentice, so it shall be. Beginning tomorrow you study with the Sunmasters."

Rasim's stomach dropped nervously. "What about today?"

"Today?" Taishm leaned forward with a sudden grin. "Let me think. In the past month you've slain a sea serpent, befriended pirates, discovered treachery in the Northlands, rescued a kidnapped girl, been imprisoned, and saved the city of Ilyara.

"Today, Rasim al Ilialio, I believe you can have the day *off.*"

to be continued in

STONEMASTER

Acknowledgments

Seamaster is, first and foremost, for my nephew Breic, who asked me (a distressingly long time ago now) whether I was going to write any books for little boys. This book and this series are for him, for my nephew Seirid, for my son Henry, for all of my not-actually-niblings (all those first cousins once removed), and for my friends' children who are all readers like we once were. This is for them.

It's for my mom, Rosie Murphy, too. Mom taught me the song that inspired the series, a lullaby that I sang roughly fifty thousand times to my son when he was an infant: *there's a big ship sailing on the Illy-ally-oh, the Illy-ally-oh, there's a big ship sailing on the Illy-ally-oh, hi, ho, the Illy-ally-oh.*

That song has a lot of variants and spellings, but that's how I heard it, and rendered it to the Ilialio in my mind. One night, as I was singing it for the 93rd time, I thought: *well, if there's a big ship sailing on the Ilialio, then there must be a crew. And if there's a crew, there must be a cabin boy. And if there's a cabin boy, there must be pirates…*and thus the Guildmaster Saga was born.

All my thanks are due to Aleksandar Sotirovski for his wonderful cover art, and all my love goes to Henry and Ted, and to my dad, Tom.

About the Author

There are those who say CE Murphy began her writing career when she ran away from home at age five to write copy for the circus that had come to town. Her own recollection is that she wrote her first serious work for a school magazine at age six, which is almost as good. She has since gone on to write in science fiction & fantasy, romance, graphic novels, and, with *Seamaster*, debuts in middle grade and young adult books.

She was born and raised in Alaska, and now lives with her family in her ancestral homeland of Ireland, which is a magical place where it rains a lot but nothing one could seriously regard as winter ever actually arrives.

CE Murphy can be found online at:

mizkit.com

@ce_murphy

fb.com/cemurphywriter &

her newsletter at tinyletter.com/ce_murphy, which is by far the best place to get up-to-date info on what's out next.

CPSIA information can be obtained
at www.ICGtesting.com
Printed in the USA
FSHW011254130421
80443FS